£5   16/23   FIC
           MATT

Fiction Gift Aid

Mer de Glace

Mer de Glace

Alison Fell

Methuen

The poem referred to on page 68 is 'Phantasia for Elvira Shatayeva'
from *The Dream of a Common Language* by Adrienne Rich.

'As Time Goes By', words and music by Herman Hupfield.
Reproduced by kind permission of Redwood Music Ltd,
Iron Bridge House, 3 Bridge Approach, Chalk Farm, London NW1.

'When I Fall In Love', (Heyman/Young).
Reproduced by permission of Warner Chappell Music Ltd.

Excerpt from *Letters from Colette* translated by Robert Phelps.
Translation copyright © 1980 by Farrar, Straus and Giroux, Inc.
Reprinted by permission of Farrar, Straus and Giroux, Inc.

Dr Faustus, copyright 1947 by Thomas Mann.
Excerpt reproduced by kind permission of
Martin Secker and Warburg Limited.

First published in Great Britain in 1991
by Methuen London, Michelin House, 81 Fulham Road, London sw3 6RB

A CIP catalogue record for this book
is available from the British Library
ISBN 0 413 18210 X

Typeset by Hewer Text Composition Services, Edinburgh
Printed and bound in Great Britain
by St Edmundsbury Press, Bury St Edmunds, Suffolk

'Passion is too much taken up with itself
to be able to conceive that anyone
would be seriously against it. At least,
it is so in matters of love, where feeling
claims for itself every right in the world
and, however forbidden or scandalous,
quite involuntarily reckons on understanding.'

Dr Faustus, by Thomas Mann

Part One

The Ice Mirror

– But then helicopters always make me want to cry, always. Even when I was . . . The noise of the blades, the emergency. Right under your heart, you hear it. You look up, even the sky freezes; you feel sick with unshed tears. You know there's danger, someone could be dead. Also they're so beautiful somehow.

'The chop', that's what they called it. 'So-and-so got the chop.' (*Laughs.*) The boys in the Bar Nash. Ever so cool. Although I suppose you'd have to be, with the possibility there all the time . . .

– The heroic means withholding? The man who withholds emotion?

– Then there's this woman in sunglasses, a navy blue intense sky gathered, a snow like nothing you have ever seen – white as a whip, blank, edible, maddening.

– And what's Will doing?

– He's surrounding her. She's frightened but he's containing her . . . Snow on his eyelashes.

– I'm aware that you've often expressed a wish to be contained here, by me . . . and a fear also that you might destroy the container with your rage.

– The chop and the chopper.

– I'm trying to remember: was it winter? When your father died?

3

– (*Inaudible.*)

– *Mm?*

– No. Summer. Hot. Hot as it ever was in Belfast.

–

– In the dream Will came back all stitched up like Franken-
stein, stitches like bicycle treads across his forehead, a terrible
sort of Resurrection. I said I'd still love him, but he said,
very bitter and punitive, 'We've got to give up on the sex
stuff.'

– *Both damaged and withholding . . .*

– I felt my fists screw up like a baby's.

– *The baby he denied?*

–

The helicopter hovers, winching the body off the Mer de Glace.
No stretcher – it wouldn't have been necessary. The body
seems swaddled though, somehow. Once I read an account of
what happened to babies in the seventeenth century when they
got farmed out to wet nurses, often for years at a stretch.
Mother love isn't what you think, you know – natural,
universal. Not a bit of it. Wet nursing was a sort of disguised
infanticide. The wet nurses were poor, sick, they had smallpox,
scrofula. They had to work in the fields, leaving the baby to
itself, drowning in its own excrement, bound like a criminal,
eaten alive by mosquitoes. The child wore a little shirt of rough
linen that fell in folds and creases, with a swaddling cloth over
it; then the baby's arms were pressed against his chest and a
large strip of cloth was pulled around the arms and wrapped

4

around the legs. Then the linen was refolded and the strips wound between the thighs. A circular cloth pulled as tight as possible, from the legs to the neck, fastened everything together. The results of this packaging were horrendous. The tightening pressed the folds against the baby's skin and, when the linens were removed, the little body was creased, red and bruised. Packs of linen folded between the baby's thighs created the same problem and kept urine and excrement next to the body, which caused inflammation and rashes. The tightened cloth had, in the eyes of the nurses, two advantages: it prevented the dislocation of the spine and pushed fat up under the baby's chin to make him look plump. But the cloth band also created pressure on the ribs and reduced the lungs' normal functioning. This induced laboured breathing, coughing and vomiting, because digestion was also impeded. The child, trussed up like a turkey, cried his head off and often went into convulsions. Specially since the nurses also hung them by their swaddling bands from nails for hours at a time, to prevent them from attack by farm animals . . .

Anyway, as I was saying: the body seems swaddled. This is how I see it, all whitish-blue and swaddled and stiff somehow against the snow, and when they winch him up it's like some terrible statue or demolition, like the seedy Hollywood sets in *The Last Tycoon*, vulgar and tacky, this rigid angel being hoisted up into the sun. Meanwhile, 8,ooo feet below in the shadow of the mountain, the lights of the town are coming on. Yellow in the windows, white in the streets, blue above the entrance of the Préfecture de Police where Joanna is. Waiting. Where Jean-Yves stands, hand on Joanna's shoulder, trying not to translate the messages which crackle from the radio receiver, head bent, white-faced, torn trainers on his feet.

   – To go back to the swaddled child image, what comes to mind is the

impossibility of changing sex, of transforming yourself into the boy your father wanted . . .

–

– *The little hero, even.*

– But listen, in the early hours of the morning there'll be a police car, blue light flashing, by a wooded strip of waste ground on the outskirts of Chamonix. Inside the car Joanna will be waiting, while Jean-Yves and the *agent* search Will's tent by torchlight. Underneath the foam carry-mat Jean-Yves finds a Walkman, tapes, a plastic folder which contains a passport and two airmail envelopes. One of the envelopes is addressed to Joanna, and this Jean-Yves will hand out of the tent to the *agent*; the other, which is bulkier, he'll conceal in the deep front pocket of his anorak.

Later, at dawn, when the wagon comes to spray the empty streets, and the pigeons in the Place Balmat flutter up in fright from the thick jets of water, Jean-Yves will pause in front of the granite PTT building. Then he'll drop the envelope into the slot marked *Étranger*. The bulky envelope, the envelope which is addressed to Kathleen.

The Notebooks
(The first notebook is red-covered, spiral bound, and small enough to slip into a pocket.)

Autobiography: for K's class.

Evan was the older, taller, faster twin, but in Billy's honest opinion he was also a tease and a snot-nose. On the path up the low shaly cliff to the house Evan would run way ahead, leaving Billy a mile back, crying out crossly what Mommy said: Mommy said we got to stick together, Mommy says stay back from the edge; but up above on the higher zigzag Evan would be a bird or a helicopter and too bored to wait for Billy, far behind. One time Evan got so far ahead that Billy couldn't see even the top of his fishing rod. Billy cried from fright, seeing Evan fallen to the beach and limp as a broken gull down there, and he ran puffing and sniffling to the top, to find Evan flat on his belly, staring idle-eyed at the surf, his mouth slack and easy and stained with blueberries, and smiling – hiding something you couldn't see but wanted to push him face down in the dirt for, he'd made you so scared. But Evan opened up his hand on the blueberries he'd saved for you, silly Billy, I'm OK, sorry Billy. Later there was the wolf-chest by the bedroom door, sometimes Billy had night-mares and didn't go to the john in the night because of what Evan made him see in the mirror. It was a black lacquer chest Dad sent back from Indo-China

7

where he mostly was and it had Mom's sewing and things, some clothes too from when they were babies, she took out the gowns sometimes and Evan put his hands on his hips – Mom, these are girls' things – but Mom laughed and said all babies wear dresses at first, look at the embroidery your Mom did all by herself. It was real pretty but Billy didn't like to say with Evan there. The chest had a mirror with black claws and Evan said if you pass it and don't see yourself you're dead, that's how you know, you've got no reflection, or else maybe you'll see somebody you never even knew in it, which is bad luck too. Then there was Christmas when Evan got sick and hot, it was meningitis and he said a wolf came through the mirror at him no kidding, Billy, and Billy truly did see it too but next night Evan was dead making no reflection in a coffin and next day Mom sat in the big window seat waiting for Dad to come from Indo-China in a silk dress. She had a Martini and Billy got to drink a Coke real early, just past breakfast, she put her cold arm round Billy in his best jacket and it was so quiet apart from gulls and the grandfather clock and some planes going over.

The notebook continues with equipment lists: spare head-torch batteries, glacier cream, harnesses, prusik cords, extra descendeur, étrier slings from Ellis Brigham.

A detailed schedule of a week's introductory Alpine course follows, including alternative suggestions for the less fit members of the party. On the Monday of arrival, for instance, the morning was devoted to rock-climbing and abseil practice on some limestone slabs upriver from Les Lanches, and the afternoon to a training climb through the forest to the glaciated Lac d'Étroit: 1,300 metres at an ascent pace of 300 metres an hour, the pace of descent to be no slower than 600 metres an hour.

Tuesday am was given over to crampon-fitting and crevasse rescue techniques using an overhang on the rock slabs. 'Obligatory,' Will has written.

'ie, anyone who thinks of venturing above the snow line without having mastered the technique of prusiking up a rope is a lemming, will hereafter be designated "walker", and will have to stay below 2,000 metres and catch butterflies.'

The week continues with more altitude acclimatisation, this time on the 9,000 foot Aiguille du Grive. By Thursday, the stronger members are noted as having acquitted themselves well at ice-axe self-arrest and rope techniques at 10,000 feet on the Col de Pichère, later continuing to the summit in uncertain weather but without incident. Will notes that the ascent of the 12,500 Mont Pourri, which was to be the climax of the trip, was delayed by adverse weather conditions.

'A day of festering for all, enlivened by foot-doctoring and hourly calls to an increasingly disconsolate answering machine at Bourg Météo. Andy treated us to his own version of Queen's "Bohemian Rhapsody", complete with instrumentals and falsetto – he's quickly becoming a star of rock-slab and campsite, tho' his technique of descent on snow is more marmot than Messner. This guy would rather ski down on his nose than ram his heels in like the rest of us. Well, anything for a laugh, I guess, at least on the Col, where it isn't crucial. Gregor, predictably, wasn't amused and tore Andy off a strip.'

The Mont Pourri ascent itself was noted briefly:

'A real snatch between *orages*. All to summit except Dave, out of action with an infected toenail. Andy a liability again on descent, slipping and sliding and later pooped out with exhaustion on the moraine. Tracey tired, but kept on keeping on. She was really digging deep, a credit to herself.'

9

The notebook continues as a diary with dated entries:

Train to Victoria, 14 May

OK, so how many times and to how many people have I
said that England – more particularly London – is the one
place I feel at home in? Hard to credit it now on this small
shabby train with its dirty windows and geriatric tremble
after the sleek class of SNCF, *plafond bleu* for *non fumeurs*,
courtesy of Gregor and Outdoor Exp. Inc., and it sure
made a nice change from the bumpy old Chamonix bus.
Easy money, Gregor said, nursemaiding mainly, and easy
money it was, just what's necessary with the summer
season coming along and new climbing gear to invest in. As
for the nursemaiding, *tant pis*, since I know the mountains
and their moods could sustain me through a far more
yawn-inducing trip than this one. A good group, though.
(Andy now spaced-out as always, champagne cork replac-
ing the lost rubber on the point of his ice-axe, crooning to
himself: 'There'll be white birds over, the blue cliffs of
Dover . . .' Going back to the tedium of British Telecom,
but at least he's got his mountain bike and a few triathlons
to bag. How will the others get on though? Derek and
Kung-Fu Chris going back to the City, and Lee to
Liverpool and seven days a week on the lump, living with
his nan, saving money, dreaming Mercedes dreams . . .)

Yes, it's the familiar depression and confusion of slotting
back into life at sea-level on this cloudy little island. *Retour à
la normale*, maybe, but what price desire? Back of my retina
says blue is desire, still bears the imprint of that bat's wing
of snow, delirious white, swooping up from Pourri's
shoulder, every step I ever took pitted in the snow behind,
and all the answers as always tempting me from up ahead
. . . Or else it's the karabiner glinting against sun-dry
granite as you climb out of the chimney, strenuous, sustained, protection weak so you're looking at forty foot falls;

but if the runner holds, you think of each one as a hook and you the fish slithering up with all your strength and instincts and chthonic determination.

Flat, flummoxed feeling as the intensity drains away and the train idles through Dreadful Dorking or some such ugly Tory suburb. Thoughts trickle not unpleasantly to what's doing with home and Joanna. Maybe the cat kittened at last. Maybe my tax rebate even came through. Wondering if K got my note explaining my absence from the workshop.

With luck and application the writing course will bridge the gap between experience – which is fine and good and no complaints – and the communications of it, which promises a new expansion and direction. K's doctrine is that first you have to learn to perceive with the heart and senses as an antidote to the thin years of just mind and received ideas, and I guess I'm learning. (Already I notice, say, the drab, nose-tickling smell of English soot and English air, the angle of the rain which streaks the window, the pinpricks of mascara on the eyelashes of two very red-headed twins who are twenty or so but still dressed identically and smiling in unison, rather freaky in my opinion.)

Affection swings my memory back to that first class when K emptied a bag of what looked like garden refuse onto the middle of the floor. We all hung back, but she forced us to choose something, and then forced us to know it, whether it was a scrap of moss or a damp crumbling mushroom or a dead leaf. Mine was a sycamore seed, although she had to name it for me at the time. See it fly, she said, standing over me, and then she threw it up in the air and it came down spinning like the blades of a helicopter, falling and falling, and I laughed at her laugh, at the mouldering spreading garbage on the clean classroom floor, at just the whole idea of being there. At the relief, maybe, of sensing even back then that K is one of the relatively few people I've met in my life so far who know things that I actually want and need to know, things that somehow feel barred to me, although I recognise, however dimly, that they're the stuff of life beyond money and categories and the rational reserve of day to day intercourse.

15 May, Sunday

Joanna is still sleeping off the excesses of Brian and Felicity's party, and will get up in a couple of hours swearing not to drink spirits any more, or under no circumstances to have more than four pints, or mix beer and wine, or some similar resolve designed to identify the problem in enough detail to seem sincere, but in fact too much detail to be of help in practice.

Must do character study to show willing then; Andy is of course the obvious person.

'Keep a tight rope till we're past the crevassed area,' Will called out. They were descending the Col fast and in line. Tracey, just ahead of him, was moving well, flicking her heels in deep, feet angled at the regulation ten to two. Further down the steep snow slope Lee plodded carefully, uncertain. The rope sagged between them, trailing on the surface of the snow. 'Slow down, Trace, let Lee take up the slack.'

'Falling!' Lee yelled. Will thrust his axe in hard and threw his weight across the curved pick. Tracey and Lee were on their knees too, braced against their axes. It was Andy, first on the rope, who had slipped and fallen. He was giggling, flat on his back in the snow, his blond hair spread out like straw strewn for animals in a winter field. Through Will's glasses the colours were intense: the acid blue T-shirt, searing red of his tracksuit pants, the sun flashing off his mirrored goggles. Andy staggered to his feet and resumed the descent, sidestepping, slithering, still laughing. 'Get a grip, Andy,'

Will cried. 'Side-step and you'll fall on your face. Face out and dig your heels in.' An inaudible reply came back up the slope, and he saw that Andy was floundering once more, his arms pumping helplessly. Splintered snow flew up around him.

'I can't do it, for Christ's sake!' The Hereford accent echoed up the slope. Lee was laughing too, calling Andy a wanker, demonstrating: 'Look, you arsehole.' Will stood back and let him get on with it, pleased that there was so little rivalry in the group. Share and share alike seemed to be the motto. Andy tried to copy Lee's technique, and failed, and tried again, spreading his feet wider than wide, his ice-axe flailing like Chaplin's walking stick.

'Better,' Will called, as Andy found his balance, and the rope party moved forward at last. 'Keep your weight forward, else you'll be on your ass again.' He checked his watch. They'd been on the move for eleven hours, and there were still three hours of descent ahead. At the bottom of the Col, where the snow dribbled away to a few isolated patches, they stopped to unrope and remove crampons. Standing on one foot, Andy overbalanced and swore sweetly. A speed freak, Will had decided, when he'd seen Andy on the platform at Victoria: amphetamines, definitely. Andy's skin was acned to hell, his foot tapped, his head moved with grim jerks on his neck. He had been silent and glum all the way to Calais; and then, when Tracey, shy as she was – and gay too, or so Will suspected – introduced herself and asked his name, he'd leapt back. 'Andy,' he had said, in a bark of pure anguish, baring his teeth more in defence than greeting, as if daring the rest of them to laugh at his farm-boy accent. Later, with attention and appreciation, or perhaps simply because he was forced by circumstances into communality, he had thawed, and the thaw had released a gamut of personalities – jester, rock star, Neanderthal man, anarchist – all of which delighted the others, no less because they had drawn these riches out of him; had even, in a sense, created them.

Will packed away the coiled rope and strapped on his rucksack for the descent. The Lac des Lanches lay below them, a mile of black water which stretched to the end of the hanging valley and crashed out in a white torrent to the valley 500 metres below. To the east the Grande Motte was a pink wedge against the evening sky. When they moved off again, he slipped into place behind Andy. The path was steep and rough, and it wouldn't hurt to keep an eye on him. Andy's ice-axe swung loosely from the back of his rucksack and his arms hung sleepy and apish. Will closed up, so that Andy was within easy reach. If he stumbled, he might not save himself. Andy's Walkman dangled from his neck, silent. The bugger's got his eyes shut, Will thought suddenly. Then he heard Andy singing, a sudden sweet private sound, no performance this time: 'You must remember this, a kiss is just a kiss, a sigh is just a sigh. The fundamental things apply, as time goes by.' Maudlin Hollywood lament on that bare hillside by a man asleep on his feet, and although Will wanted to reach out and shake him, make him take care, at the same time he was unwilling, somehow, to break the spell: 'It's still the same old story, a fight for love and glory, a case of do or die . . .'

Well this is crap and then some, says the familiar voice. No, I haven't caught Andy at all, not the flavour of personality or language, let alone what tenderness I have felt sometimes for men on the mountain and have been unable or unwilling to express except through the petty practical attentions permitted in that kind of partnership – in its own way like marriage, since when you are roped by love you must be extra respectful of boundaries and separateness and walk carefully.

Go deeper, K would say. Just write and write, write rubbish, get well acquainted with mess or you'll never get past it. Yet her work, that I've read, is a million light-years from mess, giving powerful expression to feelings we can hardly articulate even to ourselves. That really is the problem with writing fiction. It's so exposing to be honest even with oneself, let alone writing to be read by one's friends and enemies or even a class of similarly repressed, artistically immature people to oneself. How to acquire that honesty, how to overcome that repression is what I want to know. Sure, just write and write until something clicks, but for me that's such agony, when each sentence slaps me in the face with its lack of fluency. It's as if something in me feels guilty about the ease with which I've gotten on with other aspects of life, other things I've wanted to do, and now some chilly voice says, forget it, this is one ability I'm not giving up to you, so you'll just have to get along without it as best you can. And if that makes things a bit difficult or a lot difficult, that's tough. You don't deserve any better. Then I have to ask myself what I've done to make someone, even myself, treat me like this. Maybe it does come back to the question of honesty, but surely I've been as honest as most people and certainly realise that using any talent I may have to manipulate people or cover up the truth about myself not only does nothing for other people but hurts me as well. . . .

16 May
Letter in the mail from Jean-Yves, pressing me for my summer dates already – old Calvinist that he is, regular as clockwork in his fervour for organisation (not to mention

that intense burn-scarred face of his across the camp-fire
every night, he sure is no barrel of laughs but there's always
the Europa Disco, I guess). Come on, Ryan, I tell myself;
good climbing partners are hard enough to come by even in
Chamonix, where there's no shortage of rock-jocks but with
most of them I get this certain feeling that they lack the sort
of real survivor's stamina which is crucial for the higher,
mixed Alpine routes that I desire. Also, their sheer competitive anxiety can turn them into quite a liability since
they either refuse to admit or perhaps simply don't know
when they're over-reaching themselves, and thus have
definite headbanging tendencies which you can really do
without at the crux of a route. Strikes me oftentimes that
the Alps have always attracted more than their fair share
of crazies, from the artistically sublime, like Nietzsche or
Goethe or Nijinsky, to the merely ridiculously dangerous.

At the reception Felicity closed in on Joanna, badgering about marriage. Blue silk ruffles rose and fell on her breast. Her dress had a wasp waist, a huge belling skirt. Like the cake with its clever icing, like the repartee in the registry office, like the wedding car with its bright red ribbons, the dress both celebrated romanticism and laughed at it. 'Seven years!' Felicity cried. 'Come on, you two, give us a few hints.'

Joanna shrugged. 'We had to do it for my visa,' she replied, and would have left it at that – she had never liked that sort of brash talk, party talk for public consumption – but Will was high and wide and expansive.

'Miss Lila Freebody, that was her name. A Seventh Day Adventist or something. We told her we didn't go much for weddings or ceremonies, although we loved each other, of course. In the end she must have figured that was good enough for God.'

Brian's smile made allowances for children and Americans. 'It's legal, though?'

Will laughed. 'Signed and sealed in Chattanooga. Joanna ground her teeth the whole way through.'

Just then the crowd parted, as crowds will when you least want them to, and Bob Martinson stood there with champagne and self-conscious bonhomie and a fat cigar for Brian. 'I name this ship the My God This Is Mumm Cordon Rouge etc, etc . . .'

Joanna saw Ann-Marie by the window, fiddling with the flash on her camera, and headed towards her. 'Everyone looks as pissed as I feel,' Ann-Marie said. 'Give me black and white any day – at least you get a rest from all the red eyeballs.' She looked pityingly at

Joanna. *'I see his lordship's here. I hope you're not going to go all wobbly on me.'*

Joanna grimaced. *Once upon a time Martinson slid his hand over hers at the crux of an argument. My dear . . . Leaning back in the ghostly light of the college bar; My dear, why don't we just stop the mind-fucking and do the other? It had been winter, a long wait for a taxi with the wind gusting and unkind; when they linked hands, his wedding ring dug into her finger. 'Nadia's in New York', he said casually, facing her over a cold untidy bed. A digital alarm winked greenly from the stereo as he plied above her. He had bright black eyes. He had a small red mouth. You could tell that he thought he was good at it. The lust would have come later, of course – if she'd let it. With the real mind-fucking.*

On the other side of the kitchen table Will and Martinson were talking. *'I'd say Freud's emphasis on sexuality as a dark immutable force does us no favours at all,'* Martinson was saying. *'It makes sex too autonomous at the expense of recognising it not only as part of a relationship, but as a social act influenced by culture and history.'*

'Quite frankly,' Felicity broke in, *'quite frankly, I'll be glad to see the back of it. The Sexual Revolution, I mean.'* The two men smiled at her vaguely. She was wheezing, her asthma aggravated by the smoke and stress. *'God, wasn't it exhausting?'*

'But surely it pre-dates Freud?' Will persisted. Fully engaged, he looked so fervent, so unabashedly the student, that Joanna wanted to tear him away, protect him. *'I mean, separating sex out as an activity? Doesn't it occur with the rise of capitalism and commodity fetishism?'*

Martinson gave an efficient little smile. *'Absolutely, if you look at the history of pornography you'll see it clearly . . . around the beginning of the eighteenth century, when images of disembodied pricks and headless torsos became popular . . .'*

Ann-Marie focussed the camera on the group. *'Sounds a lot like Foucault to me,'* Joanna muttered.

'Well, it looks a lot like a disembodied prick to me,' Ann-Marie retorted, clicking the shutter viciously.

*

Joanna eased herself into a sitting position and reached for the glass of water on the chair beside the bed. At the thought of Will and Martinson, her headache thundered. She shut her eyes and momentarily saw headless torsos; under her nightdress her stomach was a painful drum.

Will backed through the bedroom door with breakfast: tea with toast balanced on top of the cup, a bowl of muesli. He wore faded shorts and was barefoot for, England or not, as soon as May came he insisted it was summer and dressed accordingly. He looked down at her and laughed. 'Christ, the disaster looking for somewhere to happen!' He drew back the curtains on a day luridly blue, a sky drifting with white spores. 'Is it existential, or just nausea?'

Once again she saw Martinson's thumb go up to stroke his cheek, the very picture of considered debate. His other hand lodged in his trouser pocket, thrusting it forward, turning change over and over. The sub-text, she thought bitterly: I ought to tell him one day, he'd probably enjoy the irony. That counting of secrets, that measuring of power – his against Will's. Knowing that from her hiding place by the window she was watching; yes, it was a violation of both of them.

'Les rang, so it looks like we're playing.' Will rummaged in the black lacquer chest at the end of the bed and produced a set of cricket stumps, 'He says are you coming? He says Jessie is.'

'Essay,' Joanna mumbled. 'It's due in on Tuesday.' She fought a crazy urge to confess, to wipe out Martinson's unfair advantage. Equalise. Reconstructured according to an ideal they still aspired to, the scene at the party came out cleaner. She and Will, the independent but loving couple, concealing nothing from each other. While Martinson, punctured by her honesty, has nothing left to gloat over, and slinks away, disinherited. Disinheriting her, too; taking with him all the hidden machinations of rage, betrayal, desire, leaving her with the glare of the morning bedroom, the toast which stuck in her throat, and the claustrophobia of living with

19

a man – or so it seems right at this moment – who's too bloody good
for her.

'I'll leave you to it, then.' Will's hair was damp from the shower
and he looked keen and scrubbed and restless. Scooping keys
from the dressing table, he hurried out.

'Look, don't take the car keys, will you?' she shouted after him.
'What if I have to collect the Ward papers?' Suddenly and un-
reasonably angry, for it was her fling, after all, and it was well and
truly over. As for Martinson, what had he ever been but a once-a-
fortnight collision in an afternoon bed, hardly worth confessing. For
a moment, thinking about it, she wondered which would be worse:
a magnanimous, accepting Will, or a Will hurt and human and
holding it in.

Half a mile away, in the flat which faced Kathleen's across a
courtyard, the young Turkish couple were quarrelling.

People live close in council flats. See each other's visitors come
and go. When they'd moved in that summer they had no curtains
and she saw everything. They owned two chairs, a television, and a
painting. Some days later uncles and brothers and bell-bottomed
cousins arrived en masse for a house-warming party. In dark
suits, spreadeagled against the wall, they took turns with the
painting: ordering, pointing, twitching the frame this way and that,
and when the nail was finally hammered in, they all stood back
to admire, circled, raised their glasses to this greenish girl who
was smooth and shiny with tubular flesh and bold breasts metallic
enough to ring. The young wife, meanwhile, was missing the
exhibition. Kathleen saw her at the kitchen window, pregnant,
filling glasses and chopping some foodstuff finely with a long blue
knife.

In the colposcopy clinic the nurse had held Kathleen's hand tight,
as if to tell her in advance that it would hurt awfully, and of course
she tensed, and of course it did. Her chewing gum, discarded

before she stepped up on to the couch, lay incongruous and unremarked in a bin full of tampons and swabs. Her knees had disappeared under a tented sheet inside which nothing happened except pain, except imagination: a mirror, a microscope, a speculum stretching her vagina. Turned inside out, she was magnified into a moon: nothing else existed.

She smelled the vinegar which was being used to swab her cervix and stain the errant cells. 'Relax a bit for me,' said the freckled Australian registrar. 'That's the girl.' There was a sharper pain, and he passed a pair of silver tongs to the nurse. In the pincers was a piece of flesh the size of a rice grain. She jerked her head round, panicky, some notion of a perfect self outraged. The nurse patted her hand patiently. 'Don't you worry yourself, dear.' Her black stockings looked too hot, her legs bowed from so much standing.

'CIN cells,' said the registrar, when she climbed down from the couch.

'Sin cells?' she repeated, aghast.

The registrar smiled carefully, squinting up through reddish eyelashes. He was drawing a diagram: a doughnut-shaped cervix with biro dots speckling the area round the os. He spelled it out. CIN cells: cells which may at some stage undergo a cancerous shift. In this case there was a thirty per cent chance, so they'd better nip them in the bud, hadn't they?

Wide-eyed, on automatic, she nodded. Then she started to cry. The nurse fetched tissues, scolding a little. 'Think yourself lucky they can catch it so soon, dear.'

Holding up his thumb, the registrar pinched the tip of it. 'A piece of flesh no bigger than that.' Yes, it had to be a cone biopsy, the cells were located too high in the os for a laser excision. Did she intend having children, he asked, leafing through her file: age, marital status, occupation. Sweat slicked the hairs on the back of her neck. 'No, no,' he said hurriedly. 'It won't be a problem. We just need to know for the op.' Already he was on his feet, hand politely extended. 'Righty-ho.' She remembered that obligatory smile. 'You *look very fresh and bonny for a lady of forty, if you don't mind my saying.'*

She sat quite still at her desk and pushed the memory away. Outside the window it was May – a good time, you'd think, for beginnings. Impossibly pink blossoms crowded the trees in the Square. The desk top was cleared of papers and tiger lilies flared beside the typewriter, but that hadn't solved the problem of how to begin. That itch you must scratch. She felt the familiar scurry of fright, the longing for a structure to cling to. As if there were any way you could avoid that journey into chaos, as if you could take a wide step across time to the place where the loose strands were already sewn up. Closure. Finale. The happy end. She looked on with a kind of appalled amusement as her mind darted this way and that. She was at her desk, she was frightened to death, and she was trying to tell a love story. When the truth was, of course, that you just had to get used to invasions. Her dreams, knowing this better than she did, had already been preparing her. Last night an unruly twin sister had filled her flat with foreign students who played her records, left tapes scattered about, kept parrots, notated the books on her shelves in scrupulous italics for research purposes. Bloody bedlam, that's what it was. That place where the unwritten book lived inside her. While she raged for it to be outside, complete. Tidy, totemic – yes, phallic even, like the awful woman in the painting.

'Don't block it out,' Louise had urged on the phone. 'Ring Helen, I've got her number for you.' In quick succession she'd talked to Helen, Sam, a friend of Sam's called Sybil. It was a network of illness, easily plugged into. Five years ago Sybil's sister had had a cone biopsy which revealed full-blown cancer: since the operation, however, it hadn't recurred. Sam had been diagnosed only recently, and she was looking for someone to blame. 'My advice to you,' she said, 'is keep your knees tight shut and go for alternative medicine.' Sam had become an expert on causes, contributing factors. 'Bloody

men,' she burst out at last. 'Never think of washing under their foreskins, do they.'

Kathleen wrapped her arms across her chest and stared at the tiger lilies, so whorled and glaring and exotic. So obvious. Quite slowly, figures started to move out of the shadows of last night's dream, move into the open. A young guy in sunglasses she'd rubbed herself against. A young woman student who'd come up to her shyly, asking for lessons in love. The student was naked and had no arms: symbol of powerlessness. She couldn't touch herself. Or daren't. Daren't touch herself? She thought of the women who had talked so freely about illness, and of the question she hadn't been able to ask: but what did it make you feel about your body, sex, the self which is female?

— We seem to be focussing on damage, lack . . .

— It was like a blight, I felt blue, frozen, like that little boy in the Snow Queen story, remember? Was it Franz or was it Hans, the little boy who saw the world twisted and ugly, and all because a chip of the Snow Queen's mirror had lodged in his eye? There was that palace with its tall cold halls, and the splinter-eyed Queen at whose feet Franz/Hans sat frozen-hearted. Little Franz/Hans was quite blue with cold, indeed almost black; but he did not know it, for she had kissed away the frost-shiver, and his heart was like a lump of ice. He sat dragging some sharp-edged, flat pieces of ice about, fitting them together in all possible ways. He was also forming figures of the most wonderful description, and that was the ice-game of the understanding. In his eyes the figures were perfect, and of the highest importance, for the piece of glass in his eye made him think this. He could form whole words, but could never succeed in forming the one he most wanted, which was the word Eternity; for the Snow Queen had told him that if he could form this one word he would be his own master, and she would give him the whole world. They flew on a sledge high above a black cloud, and below them the frost glittered and the wolves howled, and the Snow Queen wrapped him in a white bearskin and said that he must now have no more kisses, or else she would kiss him to death. . . . But after great cold came great heat, for little Gerda travelled far and braved many perils and gathered many helpers, until the ice-mirror fell from Hans' eye, and in the happy end he melted. . . .

– *I think you believed that only a little boy . . . only as a little boy could you have been perfect for your mother and father.*

– Phallic, you mean? Oh, yes, I envied Will, envied his power, ease, whatever the phallus stands for. But he envied me too, we envied each other.

– *So what did Will envy?*

– I've remembered now. He wasn't called Hans, he was called Kay. Little Hans was a patient of Freud's, the phobic one, remember? He was afraid of horses biting him, of carts, furniture vans, buses, of horses that looked big and heavy, horses that drove quickly. Horses that might fall down. It wasn't him at all, it was Kay: the little hero who melted.

This is how Joanna dreams, this is why her heart wouldn't melt, there has to be a reason. Joanna has a tune in her head, a silly jaunty tune nagging her about her father. She's lying in the bottom of a rowboat, going over the sea to Skye, it's dark, and the waves rock her. There's someone there, navy sweater, warm invisible face, and she has a tune in her head, a silly jaunty tune nagging at her. 'Every nice girl loves a sailor, Every nice girl loves a tar,' and she wakes up fusty-mouthed in the middle of the night obsessing about Harry, Harry the wandering sailor, the cliché to end all clichés, it would be hard to take him seriously if it weren't for the harm he's done, years of it, years in which her mother carried on as usual, that's what she'd say, you've just got to carry on, haven't you – wearily, for years, never looking at another man, never saying a harsh word about Harry. My lovely girls, she'd say, I've always got my girls. Remember the sly pity in the eyes of the women she worked with in Liptons: got a woman in Helsinki, poor Doreen, it's nearly done her in, and Nan with an angry pursed mouth thrusting pound notes into Doreen's apron pocket: now don't say a word, Doreen, it's just something for the girls. As for the girls, well, he didn't give you much of a thought, did he? You must have been eight when he left, you'd just started Brownies learning to make dampers with flour and water and a hole for jam in the middle. Remember scolding Lesley and Carol as they stood giggling in the kitchen with their hands dripping jam – it's important, it's a surprise, scolding them to clean up the mess before Doreen got back from work, unable to tell them why it was so very important that the doily be laid on the clean plate and the plate laid on the clean table, why every damper filled with jam was a wrong righted, an emptiness filled up. Before that there had been Harry's leaves when the kitchen would be hot with new baking, fruitcakes and Madeiras, steak-and-kidney pie, all Harry's favourites; on one leave he brought you a model of a reindeer in a jar and when you shook it the snow flew up and around and fell in slow hypnotic flakes. He taught you the numbers one to ten in Finnish, guttural syllables which sounded like coughs, remember how proud he was when you got them right? And yet all that time there'd been the secret other woman, the children even – little blond half-brothers who rolled the difficult syllables easily around their tongues. Although that was the part you didn't discover till later, ten years later, ten years in which Doreen kept mum and thought she was sparing you. Far better, surely, if she'd raged or fought or dyed her hair, taken up mini-skirts or bingo, God it makes you angry thinking of that generation of women, how little they asked for and how very little they got.

*

Of course you've always known you were selfish. In fact, looking back, what comes to mind is that probably the only truly unselfish thing you ever did was to let Will go off climbing. If you think back to the beginning, your first night, you remember running across the garden to the loo and banging your head against hanging lemons, pale yellow and hard as wood, and when you climbed back into bed you were crying because what came into your mind was, what you said was: wait till you find out how selfish I really am. That was Sydney, aeons ago, downtown Glebe with its famous cockroaches, where Will rented a shack he called the Summerhouse; it was under a mulberry tree and in summer the walls were streaked red from the fallen fruit. Inside, books were crowded higgledy-piggledy on ramshackle shelves: Borges, Pynchon, Castaneda. Books of an era. Books which accused you of ignorance. You can still remember the exact feeling, as if they had sharp whispering little tongues you drew back from, and you'd scowl at these books, scowl from some stubborn mole-like place that Will couldn't understand – nor could you, if it comes to that – but could only laugh at, because you'd insist on reading James Bond books or Alistair MacLean, it was wilfully stupid of course but you were fighting for your identity. Will found it a complete hoot, laughed about it with his friends, 'Hey, meet Joanna, she hates intellectuals' – laughed but went on loving so effortlessly, sometimes you thought you were drowning. In those days, if the truth be told – although at the time you'd have died rather than admit it – you hung on every word he said. Even after all this time there's a needling disappointment in the satisfaction you feel whenever you have to recognise that in fact he really can be quite a woolly thinker, lazy and erratic.

Memory: aeons ago, in the smoke of a Sydney bar, Will slaps a tray down in front of you.

'Two Fosters, three Tequila Sunrise, and . . . a Red Indian?'

American accent, you thought; not an Aussie, then. You hadn't the faintest idea what a Red Indian was, but you certainly weren't going to say so. You threw vodka and Cointreau into a glass, topped it up with grenadine and then – fuck it – jammed a slice of pine-apple on the rim. Will stood there watching your antics. 'I guess I heard him right,' he grinned, and with a wink that said, Yeah, you live by your wits in a dump like this, he snatched up the tray and vanished into the dark and smoke. You were exiles, both of you, two allies in a Sydney bar, a bottle's throw from the waterfront and the stout ferries plying across the harbour to Manly. You never did discover what the guy had ordered. It became a private joke, tacked on onto the end of every order from that day on: 'And of course, a Red Indian.'

So OK, maybe you are being too hard on yourself. So Will was selfish as well, you were both selfish; of course you were. Two strong personalities who wanted what you wanted, obviously it was going to be a struggle and obviously it didn't always feel as if the struggle was worth it.

– I'm trying to understand this equation, love-death.

– But it all begins with that. If I look back I remember, first . . . illness, fright. The abnormal smear. And I was going to be forty. It all came at once. As if being forty alone wouldn't have been bad enough.

–

– I watch my friends get to forty, one by one, and we all laugh and we're militant and we agree that we'll never be middle-aged in the way our mothers were – cardigans and grey hair and *invisible* – but beyond that, we don't discuss so much. Maybe it's too dangerous. Not just mortality or existential angst, but looks too, decay. Not looking in mirrors so much, because there's less and less to reassure you there. No longer a nice smooth concealing envelope of skin, but many marks, marks in which the woman shows, in which your death shows: insignia of experience, imperfections, incompleteness . . . bits of pieces which are best ignored, left to their own devices. . . .

27

– *Imperfections?*

– Sometimes I think, how awful to be a beauty like Garbo or Dietrich, imagine the heartbreak . . . to feel that long affair with your mirror foundering. To start thinking of it as a cold, withholding lover whose withdrawal makes you suspect it of flirting with this woman, that woman, every woman. . . .

– *You see the process of ageing as decay?*

– Isn't it? Certainly I felt that I was decaying, the abnormal cells simply reinforced that feeling. They were a shock, yes, terrible, but somehow not actually a *surprise.* . . .

– *And Will's youth?*

– Yes.

– *He seemed immortal?*

– I remember he told me how crazy gay he got up there in the mountains sometimes, thinking of throwing himself off. I could see it, too – a jump like a shrug, a faint smile saying OK. In my dreams it's like surfing, he said; I'm wheeling and sailing, the edge of my hand cuts the air . . . Oh, I know it exactly, that night-flying on driftwood or horses, but for me it brought vertigo, always vertigo.

–

– The impossible peaks of the heart. *Love's boat has crashed against real life.* That's what Mayakovsky said before he put the gun to his head. Then there was Tsvetayeva, dead in a wood-shed when love failed her.

–

– Love, the poet's disease, I can hear you thinking it.

– *I wasn't aware that I'd said any such thing.*

28

14 May

Works from the repertoire of Diaghilev's *Ballets Russes*, restaged by Nureyev, with the original decor and costumes – Laurencin, Bakst – and of course the 'Faune', which I'd never seen . . . well obviously I couldn't pass this one up. Joanna, on the other hand, could. 'The Palladium?' she sneered. 'Isn't that all conjurors and Ken Dodd?' And since Brian and Felicity's cultural tastes don't extend past opera at the moment I set off for my night out alone. Sat up in the gods surrounded by gold cherubs and grey-coiffed ladies in hairspray and listened to their bitchy comments about Nureyev. The woman right beside me kept peering through her opera glasses to provide a running commentary on every wrinkle: 'He's put it on a bit, hasn't he? Paunchy, almost. Of course, I saw him on television recently, and let me tell you he looked *extremely* tired, *extremely* weary. Well, at some point you've got to give up, haven't you. Say, it's time to go now, bye bye.'

I have to say I found them so vulturish that I had a strong desire to fart loudly or pick my nose or dig my elbows into their ribs. OK, so Nureyev isn't twenty any more, nor does he leap like he used to, and I did detect a certain lack of commitment in his Petrouchka, but in Nijinsky's 'Faune' the guy was something else. (Nijinsky, it occurs to me, got out just in time, went mad before he could go bald or old or otherwise despoil the image of the youthful genius/superman, and I guess that's one way to evade the vultures' claws, if a rather extreme one.)

As for the Nijinsky choreography – innovative is hardly the word. The audience seemed utterly stumped by it. And I guess it *was* puzzling. I sat there thinking, this is a faun, isn't it: non-human, right? So why no grace or fleetness of foot, no leaps or bounds? Why these truncated, two-dimensional moves with elbows sharply angled and hands held flat as fans . . . what on earth's he getting at? Then it

29

struck me, maybe what N was really trying to say is that *we*, not the fauns and nymphs, are the cut-outs who move only in one plane, *we* are the gawky ones, because of the forces we try to forget. So in fact he isn't representing some glorious nostalgic notion of pantheistic oneness at all, but rather the real maiming we've done by ignoring these personages in ourselves: the real conflict and disunity and underdevelopment in us. Only by looking at it in this way did the choreography begin to make sense. A choreography of incompleteness, distortion, missing links – sure, Nijinsky was a modern, all right. It didn't surprise me to read that the 'Faune' caused a scandal when it was first staged. In 1912, the shock of the famous final gesture (Pan, after all, was supposed to be the masturbatory god) seems to have stirred such hysteria that more serious appreciations and criticisms went by the board. The nymph's silk scarf for all the world like a pair of panties . . . quite gross even now, let alone back then! Crude and electric and, yes, even a bit terrifying. . . .

During the performance, memory couldn't help flashing up prochronous knowledge of the madness which overtook him only a few years later, and superimposing images of *la maison de Nijinsky* which Jean-Yves took me to see last year: a big pink stucco mansion on the road to Vallorcines with rotting shutters which we peered through: you could just pick out a dark ballroom, dust everywhere, chandeliers still. Jean-Yves' Uncle François, who likes to show off his English, told us the story at full tilt, embellished by plenty of dramatic arm-waving.

Nijinsky, he said, appears in a simple black practice costume and takes a chair facing the audience. 'I am going to show you how we artists live and suffer and create,' he announces, and to their discomfiture proceeds to stare at them in silence for half an hour. At last, taking some rolls of black and white cloth, he lays out a huge cross on the floor and signals to the pianist to strike up Chopin's 'Prelude in C minor'. 'I have danced God for you,' he says, standing at the head of the cross with his arms open – *Un croix vivant soi-même*, François said – 'and now I will dance you the war with its suffering, its destruction, its death. The war which you did not prevent and are therefore responsible for.'

By this time the audience isn't merely restive, but antagonistic. Nijinsky's friends are panicky, because what they've been fearing for some time has finally happened – Nijinsky's bouts of instability have spilled into the public sphere, there to be revealed not as some passing eccentricity but as out and out battiness. With each chord the pianist plays, Nijinsky makes a single gesture. First, he stretches out both arms with the palms of the hands raised stiffly, as if in defence. Then he opens his arms in a gesture of welcome, raises them in supplication . . . and then, with the fourth and fifth chords, lets them drop helplessly, as though the wrists had been broken. Again and again he repeats the sequence until, when the final chords of the Prelude have died away, he drops his arms, and looking blankly around him, murmurs, 'The little horse is very tired.' (I wonder how my blue-rinsed ladies would have liked that!)

Anyway, *une histoire très tragique*, as François said, although as a rendering of the great genius of the dance I have to say that when it comes to tragedy, portly Uncle François in his postmaster's uniform left a little to be desired. But I guess a comic edge can filter and fix an image of desperate vulnerability which might otherwise be experienced as just too much of an assault on the senses . . .

All roads lead to the Alps

The summer of 1909 finds Freud in the Bernese Oberland, preparing (although he has promised his wife that he will rest) the

manuscript of little Hans for publication in the *Jahrbuch*. His wife
has insisted on staying in Grindelwald, a clean village with an
inordinate number of bakeries, where housewives shake quilted
bedcovers over the balconies early each morning. The air is
wholesome here, crisp and dry after the heavy mists of the
Danube, and Freud has already noted an improvement in the slight
catarrh which has troubled him since the winter.

The lodgings they have taken are modest, but the views from the
windows are fit for the gods. To the north-west the Thun See
glimmers down in the valley, and to the south the shifting sun
throws into relief the subtle moods of that most seductive of
maidens, the Jungfrau. Every time Freud lays down his pen to
relight his pipe he finds that his gaze rests on her with the deepest
of pleasure, for, unlike some of his patients, she never fails to
surprise him. At nights under his thick quilted coverlet he dreams
of her, of being her, tall and still and broad-skirted, and all the many
patients he has known wear sturdy nailed shoes and cling on with
ropes to his wide, accommodating slopes, and then he chuckles in
his sleep, the hairs of his beard damp with dew from the chill night
air, and in the morning he wakes unusually happy, and does not
remember.

> *Hans' Father:* 'It seems to me that, all the same, you do
> wish Mummy would have a baby.'
>
> *Hans:* 'But I don't want it to happen.'
>
> *Hans' Father:* 'But you wish it for it?'
>
> *Hans:* 'Oh yes, *wish*.'
>
> *Hans' Father:* 'Do you know why you wish for it? It's
> because you'd like to be Daddy.'
>
> *Hans:* 'Yes . . . How does it work?'
>
> *Hans' Father:* 'How does what work?'

Hans: 'You say daddies don't have babies: so how does it work, my wanting to be Daddy?'

Hans' Father: 'You'd like to be Daddy and married to Mummy; you'd like to be as big as me and have a moustache, and you'd like Mummy to have a baby.'

Hans: 'And, Daddy, when I'm married I'll only have one if I want to, when I'm married to Mummy, and if I don't want a baby, God won't want it either, when I'm married.'

Hans' Father: 'Would you like to be married to Mummy?'

Hans: 'Oh yes.'

(It is easy to see that Hans' enjoyment of his phantasy was interfered with by his uncertainty as to the part played by fathers and by his doubts as to whether the begetting of children would be under his control.)

Hans' Father: 'On the evening of the same day, as Hans was being put to bed, he said to me: "I say, d'you know what I'm going to do now? Now I'm going to talk to Grete till ten o'clock: she's in bed with me. My children are always in bed with me. Can you tell me why that is?" As he was very sleepy already, I promised him that we should write it down the next day, and he went to sleep.'

(I have already noticed in earlier records, that since Hans' return from Gmunden he has constantly been having phantasies about 'his children', has carried on conversations with them, and so on.)*

*There is no necessity on this account to assume in Hans the presence of a feminine train of desire for having children. It was with his mother that Hans had his most blissful experiences as a child, and he was now repeating them, with himself playing the active part, which was thus necessarily that of mother. (S.F.)

It wasn't so much that he was handsome, she decided. You could see that face on any American soap opera or Budweiser ad – broad-jawed, light-eyed, with a honey-and-popcorn smoothness; an unfinished, motley face on which a dozen WASP nations muddled. The trouble was, no matter how hard Kathleen tried to keep him at a distance, he had a way of closing in on her, of doggedly being there, offering lifts, buying drinks, grinning his college-boy grin. All winter and spring she'd seen him only in class or in the pub afterwards; then, around Easter, the sightings had begun: like UFOs in the fifties, he seemed to float into view whenever she raised her eyes.

It was afternoon, and she'd been dancing. After an hour of aerobics the tutor had taught them a Hebrew women's dance, all cross steps and bobs – originally, she said, something to do with fertility. They rushed into the centre with hands raised, mouths breathing near and warm, arms sloping from the fulcrum of hands like ribbons from a maypole. They were married women, mostly, sensible, kids in the crèche: they came for the slimming. Stamping backwards into their former wide circle, they giggled and looked slyly at each other: it's a bit lezzie, but it's a laugh, isn't it?

Afterwards, as she went out through the main hall of the sports centre she passed the Climbing Wall, where a group of boys stood with a teacher, looking up. High up on the wall a boy was attached to a rope; beside him a man who was attached to nothing at all had splayed himself out across the fibreglass face and was pointing, indicating some invisible protruberance or fissure, tapping the boy's hand. 'Here, Gary, put it right here.' On the parapet of the wall another instructor looked down anxiously, making hand signals. It took her a moment to realise, first, that Gary was deaf, and second, that the instructor spreadeagled on the wall was Will.

Up from her stomach a flush of excitement rising as she watched him climb past the deaf boy, thirty feet up with nothing to save him if he fell, pleasure sharpened by vertigo as he swung himself up on to the parapet and stretched his hand down to Gary. Come on, you can make it. With a last lurch Gary heaved himself over the top, and

34

Will caught him and hugged him, and then he biffed him on the shoulder and laughed. A kind of cheer – strange, strangled – went up from the boys on the ground as Gary poised on the parapet and leaned out to scare them, flapping his hands like wings. From his mouth came inarticulate sounds of joy. When the applause died down Kathleen felt exposed, observed, as you do when the house lights go up at the end of a performance, realising now that in those last few moments before the catharsis she had been not herself but Gary; Gary in his unsuitable tight jeans and his visible fright, Gary trembling, wanting to emulate, possibly adoring; feeling also that in some obscure way Will had played a trick on her.

Will had spotted her now, and waved, but when he reappeared at the bottom of the wall she was sharp with him. 'I didn't know you were a climber,' she accused – meaning, a teacher, adult. She'd heard him say that he was a mature student – Literature and Philosophy, or Sociology of Literature, she'd never been able to distinguish these kinds of categories – and she had packed him away in that young safe box. But now he'd stepped out of it, and she was in a muddle, and complimented him clumsily.

In the pub Will sat easily opposite her, praising her in return – her teaching, her books: it felt illicit, early drinking in the shabby empty barn of a place, just after opening time with the sun so high and bright outside. Will's hands gripped a pint, his tracksuit pants stretched between the sharp splayed points of his knees. There was a knap of genitals too, which made her think how unself-conscious men were: they had their sexuality, they made love, maybe even lived with someone.

She thought maybe of touching his face and for some reason her arse opened and ached. 'That kids' book of yours,' he was saying. 'A man who turns into an eagle, metempsychosis on Midsummer's Eve . . . great stuff.' Children? she wondered: no, she didn't see him with children. 'Joanna liked it too,' he added. 'Joanna's my, well, wife.'

She nodded hard. She heard her voice ring out with assurance. She told him that all she'd done was hold the pen. 'It's like that sometimes,' she said.

Will grimaced. 'Not often enough for me, I guess.'

'Does Joanna write too?' she asked from a polite and frigid mouth.

'Sure. Well, mainly academic stuff at the moment, but yeah – a mile better than me. I keep telling her she should come to the workshop, she'd get a lot out of it.' Will turned clear, worried grey eyes on her. 'But you know the picture: the more you encourage, the more she digs her heels in.'

Mm mm mm, she said, touched and trapped and cynical. Your wife has no confidence in herself: yes, I do know the picture. She stared into her whisky, nodding very professionally.

On the way home she asked him why he never wrote about climbing. The canvas roof of the Deux Chevaux flapped as they jolted through the Finsbury Park traffic: outside, an apricot evening was beginning. Will's smile was canny. He gave her an appraising look before he answered. 'People leap to conclusions. They reckon you're either a basket case or a hero. Either way, normal conversation becomes impossible.'

On a cassette player wired to the dashboard, Lou Reed sang of the rain, always back to the rain. She told him that she could relate to mountains, but not to all the technology. Pitons. Crampons. The hardware. Will laughed. 'The masculine mystique? Sure, it's intimidating. Chamonix still makes me feel like a stranger in a strange land. Still, you learn to change your spots. I guess all that travel made me a good mixer.'

She looked at him, amused. No one she knew talked like that, but perhaps she'd led a sheltered life. 'Like a cocktail, you mean?'

Will grinned rapidly, recovering himself. 'Maybe it's the American Way. We get to thinking everything's too easy for us.' He gave her a quick sideways glance. 'I guess I get the feeling your life's more authentic or something.'

It was full-frontal flattery, serious bullshitting. She pursed up her mouth, seriously teacher-like. 'So maybe you ought to try something difficult.'

'Difficult?' Will flashed a ravishing smile. 'Well, so far, writing's the toughest damn thing I've come across.'

*

36

'America', said Will. 'Land of the Free. Doesn't know its ego from
its id. All teenage cars and heavy petting and terribly knowing
your own desires. My father was in the air force so we moved
a lot – Nevada, San Diego, Virginia. In school I was academic
but only just; I guess it surprised everybody when I passed
admission for Amherst, hockey scholarship or not. Ice hockey, we
did pretty well with that team. There was a lake in the grounds
and on winter nights we'd go skating: I remember the moon
big and frosted and us all shouting and how ice sounds in the
night and the echo. It wasn't till the second year that people
started coming up to me: Hey man, what d'you know about
Hawthorne? Or Melville, or Kerouac or whoever. I'd discovered
Liberal Arts, yeah, Literature with a capital L. So then I got to
thinking, Well, so maybe I can stack up the grades as well as the
next guy. . . .

'Meanwhile, before, there had been a revolution and I'd missed
it. For a long time I had "hippies and free love" mixed up with "the
baby boom", which I'd also been told I was a part of. The baby
boom seemed OK to me, I remember I identified it in some
obscure way with an upsurge in the stock market which I also didn't
understand but which was greeted with a hell of a lot of enthusiasm
on the news. I still find something lyrical in those monotone voices
who do the financial reports on the radio. . . .

'Anyway, a couple of years of Amherst, and then my ambition
lapsed: I always tended to think they left that bit out when they put
me together, and I can't say I had a lot of enthusiasm for the options
that were open to me at the time – medicine, law, accounting. Sure I
wanted to pay my folks back all the money they'd spent on me, but
you can earn good money in bars whatever they thought about that.
So you could say I dropped out.

'All the travel – yeah, it started round then: Europe, Sydney, Bali,
the usual. I'd already got into surfing in a big way in California. You
can get work lifeguarding, you can get work in ski resorts, you can
wash up or tend bar or be bellhop – I guess in those days I never
saw that it mattered that much. I even trained horses for a living

once, for a crazy Irishwoman in Kenya. Didn't know the first thing about it but I sure learned fast!

'There are these mountains in Zaire they call the Mountains of the Moon. Anyway, heading over the Kenyan border I got a lift with a government guy who knew a bit about climbing so he put me up for the night. So of course we sit down and have dinner with beers and I recount my adventures like you do, to kind of earn your keep, and he tells me there are three different armed factions out to topple Obote – this is well after the fall of Amin but the country's still in a pretty bad way. He's an Obote man himself, of course. And later when he has to go out to some meeting there's shooting nearby, and he comes into the bathroom while I'm in the tub and says, Here man, don't let go of this, just in case. So I'm sitting in the bathtub watching the cockroaches with nothing but a sub-machine gun for company . . .'*

There were books she'd said she would lend him, and he followed her into the bedroom. 'I'm really looking forward to your new one,' he said quickly, good manners remembered.

She laughed at him and at herself. 'It's about politics and passion and breakdown,' she said, parodying five years of work in as many seconds. 'You know the sort of thing.' The embarrassing truth being that the hero (a fiction) had undeniable similarities to Will (American, adventurous, etc). Clearly there was a place already laid for him, and it was enough to make a cat laugh – or Aphrodite, if she was listening.

When Will forgot to smile his stare was eerie. It was as if his eyes – so very light, all transparent grey iris and hardly any pupil – aimed straight through to a point at the back of her skull. Nervously, she pulled books from the shelves. If he was thinking of thriller writing, he ought to read Patricia Highsmith, quite brilliant, had he seen An American Friend? That was Highsmith's Tom Ripley – narcissistic, plausible, a charming psychotic . . . She pulled out poetry books too – Rich, Levertov; she wanted to give him poetry, something difficult. She showed him Rich's poem about Elvira Shatayeva and her team of women climbers, all dead in a storm on Lenin Peak. Will nodded; yes, he'd heard the story. 'The worst thing is,' he said, taking the book from her hands, 'the worst thing is that she died saying sorry. It came through on the radio at base camp: "We're so sorry."' He shrugged painfully. 'Abalakov had fought for an all-women's traverse so I guess she felt they'd let him down . . .'

Pigeons flicked across the windowpane, she heard them quarrelling in the eaves. Will was studying the postcards and photos which were pinned to the wall above her desk. He pointed to a black and white snapshot: the Galway hills, her, young and windblown and upright as anything beside her father. 'Do you get home often?' he asked.

Still shaken by that 'sorry', she answered flatly. 'Not since my father died. My mother emigrated soon after.' She wished suddenly that they could change the subject, she wished that he would think of leaving. She'd done what she could for him, filled his lap with books, so he should go now, since he was going to go anyway.

'Was your father, um. . . ?' He was looking at her enquiringly.

'Republican, you mean?' She heard the faint sneer in her voice, familiar scorn of the Irish for the outsider. 'He was Sinn Fein, actually.'

Will finished his coffee and zipped the books inside his jacket. She watched him, feeling dull and impatient. He was looking around distractedly. Then he spotted the car keys on the desk and laughed. 'Uh. Forgot I wasn't cycling.'

Only when he was at the door did some of the warmth return. 'See you Friday,' she said, but then, as Will turned to go, she stepped forward in a rush and planted a kiss on his cheek – not exactly professional ethics, she knew, but there it was, it was done, she hadn't been able to help herself.

'See you Friday,' Will repeated, blushing with surprise.

– How it feels . . . my words. At the swimming pond yesterday I saw a little boy blowing bubbles. They were big and

39

rainbow-coloured and elastic, they bounced on the surface of the water until the colours thinned and shivered and then were gone in a sneeze of spray . . . as I was saying, that's how it feels . . . my words . . . bouncing across the room and bursting before they get to you. No effect. Powerless. They can't get there.

– *They can't penetrate?*

– Yes, maybe. They can't get inside you.

– *Is there another language we should be using?*

– Yes, well, I've said it before, haven't I? Myth. Image. Gods and goddesses. Otherwise it's not big enough.

– *It won't contain?*

– Look, I'm tired. I work hard here.

–

– You could just tell *me* a story, and I'll lie here quiet as anything. And listen.

– *And put your thumb in your mouth?*

– A fairy story.

– *On the other hand, perhaps you could tell me one?*

–

–

– Dionysus is hot and slender. He is sweet upon the mountain, he drops to the earth with the running pack. He lies down under the blackthorn, by a cloud of yellow irises. At the shore the astonishing waves laugh for him, the pebbles grind hollow music under his feet. Dionysus mounts a quartz-seamed rock and lounges back on it, watching the waves eat deeper into the cove, where the fire is, where the fire waits for the water, where the women wait to claim him with soft enveloping hands which ask too much. Spray drips from his hair and his eyes are bloodshot from the glare of the sun and the flickering reflections of the waves, the flickering reflections on his golden arms. And he jumps from the rock and runs up the steep path away from the force of the tide and the rattle and drag of pebbles, leaving the fire to its fate, a fate which will not be his. On the quieter cliff top he stands panting, bees badgering at his hair. In the stillness an explosion of larks and gorse, a yellow flaring bush, Dionysus's colour, a bush so yellow and hot that it blots out sound, wind; a yellow so strong you could lean on it.

He is sweet upon the mountains, he drops to the earth with the running pack.

From down here he looks light and clear yellow and frail as a wand, and the two women are red, we two women, dark by contrast, dark genitals, the hidden red interior, the red we share, the red between us. Blood on our hands.

— *You believe your love destroyed him?*

— I took him in my mouth and he cried out.

20 May
Autobiography

At first Billy was sure that the moon had been full that night. Later he realised that this was wrong and that he must have mixed it up with the Earth, a fat blue ball floating on the TV screen: themselves, as others saw them. Streaked with seas and cloud. Scintillating. Mom put her hand on the back of Dad's chair and said Pray God they come home safe and Billy felt sorry because he kind of knew somehow she was thinking of Evan, Evan always wanted to be a spaceman. On the moon the sky was black and the whole world was watching. Billy wondered what would happen if their lines broke and they floated off into outer space, would they die or what?

41

His father blew his nose loudly. His father struck the palm of his hand with his fist. Well, Billy, he said. We certainly showed 'em. Billy blinked the tears from his eyes. He was twelve years old and proud to be American.

21 May
So she ticks me off last on the register, well, fair enough, I said to myself, noting nevertheless the slight sting of wounded vanity as K sits on the desk with her feet tucked under her, going through the punters one by one:

Sue
Arran
Gemma who just did a film with Fellini
Stiff-shirt Jeanetta we all love to hate
Gwylim (Sp?)
Crew-cut Charles, Beckett expert
Jess of the disarming admission: but I *do* pee myself when I laugh too much
Harold who can't see her marking off his name, Harold who punches out his work in Braille on small yellowish wafers. 'Harold,' she says, 'yes, Harold's here,' at which Harold smiles his secretive smile. Eventually she looks at me as if she's only just noticed that I'm back in my regular place at the front, large as life and looking, I'm damn sure, keen as mustard – 'Hmm, thought you'd abandoned us.' But then she sees the note which has found its way inside the register, my apology, my message slowed and re-routed by bureaucracy, and she says, Uh, OK, cutting off my eager explanation . . .

Tonight we were teased and bullied (an affectionate pantomime in which K springs something on us, we act bewildered, she gets bossy and sassy and a good time is had by all) through more stuff on metaphor. K asked us to consider the four elements – air, earth, fire, water – of which

42

the ancients believed all souls were made up, in varying proportion. A kind of primitive psychology, K said, and I guess it was as accurate as anything we've got now.

Charles, who avoids first-person writing like the plague, made a put-down remark about Automatic Writing, but as I pointed out to him, it doesn't hurt to suspend a little disbelief now and again; after all, we've got our whole long lives to be rational. After the five minutes it took to clear my head of mundane trivia, I got down to work and, while recognising that I'm no poet, I really enjoyed it. I am air, free and everywhere, inside and out. I cross frontiers, I enter mouths, everything quick and winged is in me, and so on . . . The others were already writing, in spiral-bound notebooks, reporters' pads, exercise books, with green, gold, blue and black pens. Frowning into a space which contained metaphors, if only they could find them. Or allow them. Maybe that's the trick. At Jeanetta's desk K was whispering, explaining the exercise all over again, and Jeanetta was nodding eagerly, her face set in that mask of obedience, that licking-to-be-liked look which never fails to make my stomack clench up and which obviously irritates K also, tho' she tries powerfully to hide it. Later, when K had gone back to her desk, Jeanetta started up this bizarre mime routine. Whenever K looked up from her notes or whatever it is she looks at while we're working, Jeanetta glances soulfully at the ceiling, as if waiting for poetic inspiration, and then opens her eyes wider than wide, makes an Oh with her mouth (Eureka! Illumination!) and starts scribbling furiously. Sometimes it gets to be a real pain to have to notice these things and be unable to intervene, to have to stay silent and hold on to my role of tactful, easygoing (dissembling) student.

In the pub after class Scottish Brian homed in on K.

'I see you've a new book coming out. June, isn't it? I read catalogues, you see.'

43

And Jeanetta swoops. 'How exciting, you must be awfully thrilled, aren't you *thrilled?*'

Seeing K's embarrassment, I cut in: 'Say, you mean you're not just here for our benefit?'

K looks relieved and laughs. 'Scandalous, isn't it?' But as Jess observed, it *is* kind of funny how possessive everyone gets, like kids who don't want Mom to paint pictures or sell Real Estate or do anything at all except be Mom. But now Brian wants to know what it really takes to write a book; the Recipe, he pleads; can't you give us the Recipe? To which K replies: 'Well, it's not talent.'

'Do I detect false modesty?' says Charles, arch as anything.

'I'm telling you,' says K with a grimace, 'there's so much talent around, it's *sickening*.' (Relieved laughs as she waves her hand to include all of us in this definition – which is of course what we really bargained on hearing.) 'Obsession's the thing you need,' she announces with a big grin, and of course then we the merely talented groan loudly; and so the game goes on, except it's also serious because I for one envy that inner-directedness of hers which I can only presume cost dear and which never fails to bring to mind a picture of my own paralysis and panic in the face of quite trivial day to day decisions like what brand of filing card to buy or when to renew my Sports Pass.

At the mention of the word Obsession, Brian sighs melodramatically. 'Dedication, you mean?'

But K just looks serious and reminds him once again that there's no excuse for not getting to grips with the novel he's always fantasising about and is perfectly capable of taking on – warm, stern, and, oh my, that Irish burr of hers. 'I mean,' she scolds, 'will you turn your life inside out and upside down, if necessary, to do it?'

Me: (sardonic) 'Mm, and that's *all?*'

K: (grinning) 'That's about it.'

44

At which point Jeanetta jumps up and makes a big fuss about putting her jacket on and collecting her briefcase and file and handbag. 'Must be off to catch my train,' she cries gaily. 'We suburbanites, you know.' As if she's sensed the challenge in what K is really saying – or what I believe she's saying – which is that in order to write well you've got to review not only your lifestyle and ingrained habits but also your values and prejudices, be they white male imperialist or simply bourgeois suburban or whatever. 'Oh!' says Jeanetta in mid-departure, one hand flying to her mouth: 'But Kathleen hasn't given us our homework yet.'

K: (tiredly) 'It's not obligatory, Jeanetta.'

However, Jeanetta insists, so K suggests that we all try observing a relationship in action, and off Jeanetta trips, having successfully killed the conversation stone dead, and K sits looking a touch depressed, as if she's blaming herself, at which point I come to the rescue by reminding her that if she can't win them all, she's nevertheless captured the hearts and minds of us the masses, and K looks cheered and smiles ruefully. 'OK, so I'm an extremist, don't tell me.'

On the way home from work Kathleen looked at her watch. It was late, after eleven; she'd hung around too long in the pub with the students and now the tube was crowded with Friday-nighters who unlike her were dressed up and festive and hadn't been working.

Opposite her, a young couple were entwined as cosily as puppies. The boy's knee touches the girl's pleated skirt, his hand touches his own denim knee, his thigh, her ear, earring, cups her cheeks and turns her face towards him, squeezes her cheeks, puckers her mouth up like a Pekinese. The girl quirked an eyebrow at her, and she had to laugh. And now she slaps the boy off, he rummages close again, picks and plucks dust or dandruff from her hair, his other arm loose around her shoulders. Then the

45

plucking hand reaches for the knee on which the girl's hands lie clasped, and he leans across her as if to peer out of the window at the cinema posters in the station, but in fact prods a kiss at her instead. The girl shifts her knee pertly, slaps, they wrestle, she wins, pushes her hand up through her hair, he rests for a moment, she rests with her finger in her mouth – hello self, me, taking space from possession, keeping his kiss out just for once, just for a little while, just till the next time.

She looked away, embarrassed, fixing on her face a smile more appropriate to her age. Mild. Indulgent. The smile of an outsider. When the train stopped she got out with relief and ran up the escalator with a determined energy that might have passed for jauntiness. She felt the ice move into place again: it was going to be a black night, for brandies.

The operation had been scheduled for the last Thursday in June. The letter said that she was to report to the hospital on the Wednesday at 10 am: she would need a nightdress, slippers, a dressing gown. On the phone to Louise she almost broke down. It's the thought of the slippers, she cried, it's being the sort of person who wears slippers.

She went to Giovanni's, had her eyelashes dyed, legs waxed: Louise told her to stop soldiering on, rely on her friends a bit. Louise thought she was too stoical; and Louise could well be right. But deep down she felt like an hysteric.

She decided to be firm with herself. Split the unified, animal fear into two. First, the facts: the diagnosis of disease, damage. Second, the deeper, long-standing image of decay, of time running out. Both halves fear death, yes, but one half – and this is a thought she can either turn away from or track down, follow – one half, in a strange way, also seeks it, this death of the self, ego, whatever. Is drawn by visions of a woman who on the other side of the mirror dances in red mud and spreads herself in the full moonlit forest under a dark May tree in the mulch of browned leaves and crushed

46

berries, who waits to submit to all the horned gods: Tammuz, Osiris, Pan; Cerunna, Lord of the Stags; Azazel, the Goat God; Dionysus, son and consort, who dies and ever is reborn. Left loose, her mind floats off on this craze (crazy?) to submit to someone/thing greater than itself and wider – the rock life green life star life, as if only when held inside out in some healing darkness can it know itself, exclude the excluded, the split off, the suppressed.

But always in the background the voice of reason argues back. Metaphor was all very well, but she could imagine what Louise would say, the long and the short of it. What you need is a lover. Romance. The swoon into his arms. Which, come to think of it, could simply be a trace, a vestige. Distorted. Like the plaster statues of Aphrodite which sat in Giovanni's cubicles – so smooth and white, and armless, of course.

– It happens every year. Regularly. Ever since then. Summer ending, autumn beginning sharply and Mummy Death scrags out her arms in a boo-halloo and I want to run, jump on a train, see my strong scratched still youthfullish legs stretched out. One of those swishing couchettes with nightlights, the train rocking you across frontiers. Only the Alps will do, for cheating this death, pre-empting it. (Pre-emptying?) You sweat up a peak and lose yourself before you can be stolen. You spread yourself before you can be narrowed. It's one way to stop the god dying.

– *You leave before you can be left?*

– He was the man I would have wanted to be.

–

– We search for our dead. I went to find him, a mad rendezvous.

Dream: Will's coffin lay in the nave of a church. Candles. There was a hierarchy of mourning. Joanna and I were still

47

arguing – which one of us was entitled to be the chief mourner, the second chief mourner?

Dream: 'Without an ever-present sense of death, life is insipid. You might as well live on the whites of eggs.'

Dream: there was a baby in a stable, a straw manger. Straining. Maxine Hong-Kingston tells the story of a Chinese baby born without an anus, a baby who dies straining to shit. But the baby in the dream is a boy baby. His small stomach is taut and convulsing, face hurt astonished furious; he's impossibly pregnant (no vagina), he's straining to give birth.

I'm in the car with my father, a little Austin Seven, in the front seat for once. Usually it's my mother's seat, but she's just come out of hospital, she's quiet in the back. So it must be Sunday, family outing day. It's winter, I remember pylons marching across the snowy moor, and I shout out 'Martians' and in the memory my father always chuckles and agrees. For he's got an imagination too, he knows poems and stories, sometimes even stands up and sings to Uncle Desmond's accordion, hands in his pockets, swaying back and forth in the black patent shoes he wears for weddings and best. 'Have you ever been in Garnavilla, or have you seen in Garnavilla, the gay young girl of the golden locks, my sweetheart, Kate of Garnavilla . . .'

– *And your mother?*

– Well, she just came out of hospital and she has no womb any more and I don't remember her saying anything.

– *You don't remember?*

– I remember her absence, that's what I remember. All those weeks I got the coal in and made the tea and pressed my own school skirt. I remember sitting in the front seat with my dad, guilty, but somehow rebellious, thinking, Well, we

48

managed fine, didn't we? Looking sideways at his profile and feeling possessive, proud. Almost as if there wasn't that third person in the car, but that was impossible, because of course there was my mother, in the back seat, all wrapped up in a tartan travelling rug.

 – *So she was the one who was swaddled?*

 – No. But there was something that fell out of the glove compartment . . . on to the floor at my feet. I'd opened the glove compartment to look for things. Sometimes there were coloured pipecleaners you could make cowboys or stallions out of, or even the odd boiled sweet, but this time a bundle fell out, a bundle wrapped in chamois leather, heavy, it went clunk on the floor. And then my father shouted out – I was bending down to pick it up – Leave it! He put the brakes on hard, swearing at me. And then I was frightened, I think he hit my arm. I was so scared that the chamois leather would come loose and I'd see . . .

 – *You were scared of . . .*

 – But it looked like a gun.

 –

 – His revolver, I think.

 – *But you expected?*

 – I expected . . . I was frightened of seeing . . . blood. A dead baby. Yes.

22 May

A Relationship Observed

W enters the flat and shouts Hi to J. In the kitchen he brews coffee and opens his mail from the morning. He

49

can hear J on the telephone next-door, arguing with her mother about mortgage payments.

'It's a mature student's grant, you know, and if Lesley's paying a third, I can manage my share . . . so I can get a cleaning job or something . . . Look, you've paid rent all your life, you've never had any security. Harry's not earning exactly. So will you just let me do this OK? Yes, Will's fine. Yes, I'll tell him to be careful with that awful climbing business.' (On this last remark J raises her voice ironically, so that W will hear.)

W takes the coffee through to the living room and sits down with a pair of crampons whose points need sharpening. It's a nice room, in the way London rooms can be – Victorian, tall sash windows, high ceiling with a sunburst of plaster acanthus leaves in the middle, a painted marble mantelpiece they kept meaning to strip. A three-piece suite which Brian and Felicity had jettisoned when money came along: nondescript, comfortable, the sofa covered in blue and white Greek rugs.

There were draughts in the bathroom, mice in the kitchen, and patches of dry rot; all the same, it was the best flat they'd ever had. J had found it when W was abroad, not through ads or agencies but by the simple if teeth-gritting expedient of knocking on every door in half a dozen streets until she struck lucky. Self-contained, rent-controlled, with a landlord who'd conveniently removed to Cyprus: in Inner London, it was more than lucky, it was miraculous. J had spent a whole winter stripping wallpaper and sanding floors; she'd built bookshelves and replaced the skirting and sewn new drapes, and when W finally returned from Kenya she was calm as a turtle in its shell and had forgotten that men or pain existed. W saw that she had dug a grave for him and covered it over, but he knew that distance could kill nothing for him, and however thin and worn he might be on that unfamiliar doorstep he was still alive and aching and kicking. It was a fair fight for a while and then it was over; inside J the clouds had parted and W knew that she hadn't stopped loving him.

A long streamer of dark hair dances across J's cheek and she sweeps it back impatiently. Hazellish eyes, one lazy wandering one. She squints slightly when shy but nobody ever called it unappealing. 'Yes I'll give him Harry's regards.' Her lip curls into a growl. Harry is her father, estranged but recently returned; as far as J's concerned, he should have stayed away. 'What a marathon!' She puts the phone down and drinks her coffee thankfully, in gulps. 'Good class?'

'Great, yeah. How was the New Right?'

'Oh, rampant. Want to hear what Clifford said about the Fightback leaflet? "We should have no truck with people whom we know are *not the sort of people* who belong in our Labour Party." So, the leaflet *was* a bit knee-jerk, but all the same . . .'

'Mind like a filofax, that guy.' Will chuckles. She had his sympathy. While not particularly parliamentary-minded himself, he had followed her into the party after the last election, and since then had pushed leaflets through letterboxes, collected subs, even sat through the occasional Ward meeting so that those with bigger egos would have someone to talk to. Holding office, however, was something he drew the line at – at least for the moment. Yes, you had to 'build the party'; more immediately, you had to work out how best to defend the interests of the working-class people who'd put the Labour Council in power. Rent rises weren't part of the manifesto, but then neither was refusing to balance the budget and putting the Council into the hands of the receivers. Given the real achievements of the Council over the past five years, abdicating responsibility at this stage just didn't make sense. But if policies were to be so drastically reversed, how long before principles wavered and followed? Joanna the pragmatist said he should dig in, get his hands dirty, and maybe she was right. But for the moment, to be perfectly honest, he preferred her anecdotes to the real thing.

'Sometimes I think he's really looking forward to pushing through the closures and the job cuts. Thinks it'll restore the Party's credibility!'

'Who with? The Tories?'

J flings her arms oratorically wide: 'We've got to get into shape, comrades, get it together, slim down to weather the storm.'

'The Party Beautiful, eh?'

'I wish you'd seen Valerie's face. "I've spent forty years fighting for the working class and now I'm supposed to listen to comrades talking about doing the Tories' work for them?" ' J mimes Valerie's strict chin, the way she leans into her speech, one hand tucked backwards on her hip like a little wing, the other flapping her Ward papers at the Chair. 'Anyway, sanity prevailed. The Fightback leaflet got the thumbs down, but so did Clifford's motion.'

Will laughs. 'Thank God for democracy.'

'So how's Teach?' asks Joanna, cocking her head at him. 'She's on our Women's Studies syllabus, or so I'm told.'

'You don't say?' Will grins and files at the front-point of his crampon. 'That should give her a laugh. She doesn't have a whole lot of time for Academe.'

'Well bully for her!' Joanna's voice is sharp: sometimes he forgets how prickly she can be, how easily put on the defensive. She runs her hand over the bookshelf, looking intent and cross. 'Have you seen that Dworkin?'

'Could be under the bed, I guess,' says Will, who should know better. We're talking sexual politics here.

'Where you left it.'

'OK,' he concedes, getting up. He finds the book under a pile of climbing books and Morality Plays and volumes of Augustan poetry. 'I don't know,' he says, handing it over with a frown. 'Women as victims of male lust. It's feminism gone retrograde, don't you reckon? Positively Victorian.'

Joanna bends again to her notes. 'Piss off,' she says nicely.

On the sofa, the cat noses her way onto Will's lap. Holding the sharpened points of his crampon against his palm, he thinks of K again. The points make small indentations in his flesh. 'She's just so kind of reserved, though . . .'

Joanna eyes Will. 'As long as I know,' she says crisply.

Later she reads in bed and Will feels ignored. It's rather like lying beside an empty oil barrel. He strokes her shoulder, which is warm and rosy. 'So how about the talent in the Lit/Phil class?'

Joanna's eyes don't leave the book. 'There's plenty of nice *women*,' she says. 'So can I read my book now please?'

'Sorry,' says Will, but goes on stroking her all the same – any response, at this point, being better than none at all. After a few minutes Joanna gets out of bed and fetches a packet of digestive biscuits from the kitchen. Will, meanwhile, has picked up the book. 'As if women didn't have any sexuality of their own,' he grumbles. 'It's a kind of Moral Majority line in the end.'

Joanna snorts with annoyance. 'Am I going to be allowed to make up my own mind, just for once?'

Will shifts in bed, irritable and uncomfortable. 'Christ, you're filling the bed with crumbs.'

In fighting mood now, Joanna chews a mouthful of biscuit and blows out crumbs, deliberately. The crumbs splatter over the bed. The mess is appalling. 'So are you going to shut up? I'm serious!' Then she bursts out laughing, and after a moment Will gives in, hooting at himself, her, the disgusting state of the bed.

(Joanna looks ferrety and bad-tempered, as if even in sleep she's arguing something out, debating something. She has a narrow back, and big breasts which loll quietly. I can look at her and say she's a bit po-faced, looks messy when she puts on lipstick, etc, etc. I can look at her and I can tell myself I'm knowing her, but she's already escaped, slithered out from under my butterfly-collector's pin.)

X Certificate

I was on holiday – seemed in the dream to be the Alps group. A beginning part where we post sentries, keep a lookout for . . . is it war? Is it the army? Or just mad murderers? Remember later sitting round a table in some kitchen, discussing how we might defend ourselves. I said, See, I've got this bread knife! Lee had an axe, someone else had a gun – we were counting up the weapons. Someone started tearing six inch nails out of the walls, maybe Tracey, I don't remember. It was an arsenal, anyway. There was a garden scythe I think. It made a suck suck noise going through the air. So we're counting our weapons but now it turns out – Andy is the one pushing this – that we're going to murder *ourselves*. The whole point of the exercise is a collective suicide/murder pact, a blood sacrifice, shades of Jonestown. Everyone's nodding and agreeing, even level-headed Tracey, so I figure I'd better pretend to as well or else all these madmen might turn on me. If I show disagreement I could be a traitor and therefore first for the chop. I do my best sociable laid-back act to cover terror and escape the axe, and wake sweating with everything twisted up horribly inside. Paranoia as a result of clinging to binary oppositions? (One cuts the other out, one kills the other in order to live: Aristotelian logic.) X on the other hand crosses over, changes places. Masculine to feminine. Love to hate. Insider to outsider. X trespasses, is heretical.

– Can you put Joanna on that chair?

– I look into her and can't find myself.

– Can you be Joanna now?

– Step into her shoes?

– Well, into her chair.

– She feels, well . . . strong, forbidding. Knows her boundaries. Articulate. When drunk she's a dogmatist, despising the politically ingenuous, the morally sloppy. She disapproves of people around her to the same extent that she disapproves of herself, her own lack of clarity. If I sit in her chair my mouth wants to speak . . . theory.

– And it would say?

– The woman, for Freud as for other Western philosophers, becomes a mirror for his own masculinity. Iragaray concludes that in our society representation, and therefore also social and cultural structures, are products of what she sees as a fundamental *hom(m)o sexualite*. The pun in French is on *Homo* (same) and *Homme* (man) – the male desire for the same. The pleasure of self-representation, of her desire for the same, is

55

denied woman: she is cut off from any pleasure that might be specific to her.

– *And you'd say?*

– I'd say, Where does Joanna end and Kathleen begin? It would be easier if there were clear marks of differentiation, of class or political outlook, but if what Will said was true, we're really quite similar. I'd say that if there's a difference it's in terms of time, the gap of years. At Joanna's age I also thought I could theorise anything, thought that intellect could strip reality bare and set the world to rights. At that time I'd had more than enough of Ireland, its myths and its murky heroics . . . some people have to exile themselves, I think, to claim their heritage. So I suppose you could say that Joanna represents a past me, the insistent rationalist I once was, a phase frozen in the flow of time, now suddenly thrown up to confront me.

– *Can you look at her?*

– If I looked at her I'd ask her about love, the irrational, disorder. I'd ask her if they'd ever been happy.

– *And she'll reply?*

– About happiness. This is what she'll say. That it's all a question of expectation. That I always expected too much, whereas she, on the other hand, always thought it was up to her to be happy. And insofar as she wasn't happy, she assumed it was her fault – *she* was difficult, restless, critical, discontented, she had terrible problems with work, she couldn't concentrate, she was no good . . . so her problem was *her*, not Will or anyone else, that's what she thought. And then she'll say that with him there have been times, many times, when they've been happy. When they first met, of course. Big patches. And now she's smiling and she's telling me how even Will's bad tempers could make her laugh, how funny she found them, how you've never seen such a baby in your life as Will, he could be so tight-lipped about something terribly tiny and trivial, it was hysterical. And likewise Will with her particular kind of mania. For instance, she'd be writing an essay or something and she'd say to Will, Look, I'm not going to be able to write this, you don't understand, it's impossible, I'm really depressed, I'm really going to have to go into psychoanalysis or something, and Will would say, Oh yeah, I'm sure you're right, Joanna, but on the other hand this is how you've been for the last nine years, so . . . and she'd be enraged, so angry at him: How can you say something so *insensitive* . . . so yes, she's telling me that they were happy like that, they got on very well, also they were happy in . . . oh, when two people just fix together physically and . . .

– *And?*

– I hate her I don't hurt I hate her I don't hurt I hate her I don't hurt

–

– Look, she's crushing me. Their warm automatic nights.

–

–

– *We have five more minutes.*

– Wait, though. This is Joanna's dream: she dreams that Will and Kathleen are in a mountain refuge, stone hut set high among the snows, a window unshuttered. The sky is dark. Kathleen's nightdress is wet from the sleet which drives in at the open window, and she and Will are laughing at the storm, leaning out over darkness, an abyss. Snow melts on their faces, their bare arms. And then a thunderbolt comes down and strikes fire from the metal bar on the shutters and they're thrown back in each other's arms, flat on the floor, bones clicking.

– Are they both dead in the dream?

– Oh yes. Twitching. The feeling of the sphincters released, orgiastic.

– I'm afraid we have to stop now.

15 June
In tonight's workshop we read the stories on the masculinity theme which K set last week. There were moments of humour. Arran, for instance, shaking in his shoes while Sue – who's as staunch (doctrinaire?) a feminist as I've come across – praised the way he had depicted the male character in his story as an absolute rat.

K sat listening to all this with a kind of doleful smile, shaking her head. 'But since Arran's a man himself,' she argued, 'couldn't he have provided more of an insight into this guy? Into what he's feeling, or trying not to feel, about treating his girlfriend so shittily?'

'Why bother?' said Sue belligerently. 'I mean, why should he make excuses for him?'

'A rat is a rat is a rat?' says K, to laughter and cries of 'Yes' from Jess and Gemma etc, but K isn't having it. 'As writers we have to bother,' she says definitely, 'especially the men.' Then she wags her finger at us guys, smiling a bit. 'So come on, men, there's your task. Decipher masculinity for us.'

Then Charles leads a debate on the difference between 'decipher' and 'deconstruct' and various confused and unholy alliances form and dissolve, until at last we get round to my Africa piece, which I really stretched my honesty on and therefore felt kind of edgy about. The general consensus seemed to be that it worked, although Brett's motivation seemed to elude one or two people, not to mention Kathleen herself. Gemma, for instance, had to ask if Brett bought the black girl dinner on the train just to get her into his

compartment for the night. Sue, however, from the un-
assailable heights of her radical feminism, was crystal clear
– 'Well, he didn't do it out of the goodness of his heart, did
he?' – and, I must admit, nearly succeeded in jeering me
into defensiveness. So I said, Sure, that was the point, Brett
had his eye on the main chance. At which K looked quite
taken aback, and we kind of gaped at each other for a
minute. (I don't know which of us was the more surprised.)

'Then you should have made him less plausible,' she
said. 'Let us in on his calculating side a bit more?' Well, I
thought I had, but as it turned out, K had been so touched
by the dining car scene, where Brett realises that Miriam
doesn't know how to eat with a knife and fork (a tough
scene I worked hard on and am to be honest quite proud
of), that she'd actually missed his real (dishonourable)
intentions. I could see that K was embarrassed. 'Evidently
I'm as gullible as Miriam,' she joked, and hurried us on to
next week's assignment, which will basically be the last one
before we finish. It's to be a love letter from a historical/
mythical character – a ploy designed to free us from the
limitations of our own voices, but also guaranteed to
provide a bit of fun on the last night if people's choices are
anything to go by: Sid Vicious, Richard Nixon, Marilyn
Monroe, to name but a few – sounds like quite a party.

In the car going home – I make a point of booking it on
Friday nights, for obvious reasons – K wanted to know why
I'd chosen Nijinsky. I said I'd been intrigued by the
'Faune' and by the other snippets I'd heard or read, but
apart from that I didn't know. I guess it's because he flew,
or so they say – for of course in the absence of film records
imagination enhances his famous leaps to mythical proportions. K told me that she'd seen a documentary about
Nijinsky's daughter Kyra, now a schizophrenic in middle
age. Kyra was describing how she saw her dead father fly
through her casement window 'like an angel', but the

interviewer, who was obviously quite familiar with Kyra's aberrations, laughed and chided her: 'Oh, Kyra, I think you have an angel fixation.' To which Kyra retorted: 'Fixation? Fixation? No, they *move* like *comets*.'

Telling me this, K laughed and said in that mocking but absolutist Irish way of hers, 'But then he probably was, wasn't he?'

'An angel?' I said. 'Yeah, maybe you're right.' Playing along, saying in that case I'd have my work cut out when it came to writing him, and indeed feeling less than angelic at that moment for it was late and she had circles under her eyes and was obviously tired out, but all I wanted was to stop the car and kiss her – which is only one among many things I want to and feel I could give her – but it's always harder than you think when it comes to the moment of decision. So I drove on with my head nodding and bobbing like a big party balloon, telling myself we'd be across the traffic lights and at her door soon enough. Then K starts talking about the Africa story again, saying that she must have looked pretty naive back there, and of course, not realising then that I'd already missed my moment, I rush in with colours flying, eager to take all the blame for any confusion that's been caused.

'I guess I flunked out on narrator distance,' I say humbly as we draw up outside her block. 'Didn't spell out his character enough.'

'Or else I flunked out on teacher distance,' she replies, but before I have time to digest this she grabs her bag and is half way out of the door. 'I'm having a party for the book next Saturday,' she says, 'if you feel like coming.' And she adds in a rush, 'I mean, bring Joanna, of course.'

– What I imagine is . . . that she didn't want to go to the party at all. I mean, why on earth would she have wanted to? When she had far too much work to do and, unlike Will, she had never been sentimental about Saturday nights. I imagine her, if not disgruntled, then teasing him; telling him that he's nothing but an old snob at heart, ideas above his station and so on. I imagine also that he badgered her, although she'd made it clear that she was quite happy for him to go alone, and that she taunted him: 'Feeling in need of protection?' or words to that effect, and that he laughed, but all the same she knew that she wasn't far off the mark, that he'd never have gone alone, that he'd have run a mile. . . .

–

– Well, yes, he needed her permission but he already had that, didn't he? What I imagine is . . . they're coming up the stairs to the flat, and Will says, Just don't get pissed and beat anybody up, OK? And Joanna says, You read my mind. And they arrive at the door full of suppressed giggles, like two kids, conspiratorial; Will even gets an attack of hiccups. Now maybe none of this actually happens, maybe the dynamic is totally repressed, unconscious, but there it is, this fantasy which is neither exactly his nor exactly hers, but which hangs somehow between them: Will makes a pass at Kathleen, and Joanna wades in and stops him. And then there's a wildly melodramatic scene in which she claws Kathleen's face and whisks Will off home like a smacked baby. And this is why he needed Joanna to go with him, because the fantasy – which is after all quite exciting – requires her to be there. For the thing about fantasy is that it must remain imaginary, and since Will doesn't quite trust that it won't become real – that Joanna won't actually erupt and shoot Kathleen down in flames – he needs to test it out. See if he really is allowed to have what he wants, see how far he can really go.

I don't imagine that Will would have made a serious move at the party in any case, I'm sure she wasn't worried about anything like that. And if she was jealous at all – well, envious, rather – probably it was of his excitement, of that frisson which must come from tugging at a bond which you know will almost certainly hold. So that when Kathleen opens the door to them they'll feel like two spies with a code of signals: touch your nose with your thumb if you think she's OK, pull your earlobe twice, that sort of thing. And if, as I imagine, Will very much needs this sanction; if, unlike Joanna, he hasn't yet developed a sixth sense to tell him who will threaten and who will not, then Kathleen has already been drawn into Joanna's aegis, and perhaps she even feels gracious, almost as if she were Kathleen's mother or sister, as if she'd stood beside her dressing table, advising: yes the broad patent belt, no not the flat lace-ups . . . Perhaps she feels, in some odd, megalomaniac way, that Kathleen exists because she allows her to, because she assents . . . And of course the other part of the thought process is: well, Kathleen's a feminist too, therefore honourable, trustworthy. This is the part I know is true, this is the part that much later and at screaming point becomes law and it's a law with no leeway: feminists don't poach each other's husbands, feminists don't betray each other.

–

In the gynae ward, midday, bright sunshine outside the window, Kathleen lay watching a man mending a lightning conductor on the hospital roof. White hospital bed, white gown. The nurses had already been round to strip her of everything: jewelry, her watch, make-up. She felt her edges dissolve in a white ground. They had even forgotten her real name and addressed her by the name on the records, her married name of years before. The man on the spire rested in his harness and ate a red apple as she railed at this cheating white which denied the hidden red interior (which was the real business, which was to be entered; that small cone to be cut from her cervix – so sweet and round, like a doughnut). A Sister bustled in to check on her. 'How's the pre-med, dear? Nice and sleepy?' She frowned at the pink varnish on Kathleen's toenails, the last spot of colour. 'We'll have to have that off.'

It was the last straw, and Kathleen fought back. What possible difference could nail varnish make? It seemed perverse, sadistic. She knew she was making a fuss, she knew she shouldn't be. The Sister insisted that it was the rules, the anaesthetist might have to check for circulation. She fetched cotton wool and remover and swabbed meticulously. Kathleen felt the alcohol cool on her toes. She tried to see but her head lolled. She burst into helpless tears. 'To see if I'm dead, you mean? I feel as if you're stripping me for a corpse.'

'Now now, dear,' the Sister shushed, as other patients turned their heads to look. She gave a sharp dismissive public smile, 'Oh, now, listen to her.'

Budapest, 1915

Imagine, my dear Serge, a city surrounded by hills. Imagine white marble rock so plentiful that even the culverts are constructed from it. I walk and walk these glittering slopes while above me two careless hawks wheel. Somewhere in the distance is the cough of bullocks; somewhere nearer, footsteps echo inside ribs like mine and my ears listen distantly, as if from the pines overhead, to the stones which crunch and spin away under my feet. A frieze of gorse blurs by, and long strands of mist obscure the city and its silver river.

The war is in my very veins, making all thoughts unfinished and rowdy, and I walk rickety and full of noise, for all the world like a wicker birdcage with light flicking dizzily through its slats. Were it not for the twittering gossip of memory I might be that hollowed dead sheep with the small protruding teeth, or that

guinea-fowl on the bank, raking the dust backwards. . . .
What am I saying, dear friend, is that there are times
when I lose a conception of myself as a being bounded
by skin; feel, rather, the interstices of me . . . I wonder if
it is possible that you, the most solid and certain of men,
will understand this? I feel, rather, like a hill of many
honeycombs. Do women, I wonder, live with this sensation constantly?

No doubt you will say that the enforced idleness of
captivity fills my mind with fancies, and it is true that
phantasms surround me here: phantasms, Serge, which
lie like truth. Your step imprinting beside mine like a
brother's on this unearthly marble which glitters like
the snows, your dear gruff voice remonstrating with me,
your shadow like a great bear accompanying my own. I
will say nothing of the flesh but that my soul flies up
once again in the dance which was of our making if not
God's; sometimes, Serge, my poor brain must only
conclude that it is indeed God in his punishing wisdom
who has led me into the exile which your silence so
bitterly compounds. (Not a word against my dear wife,
Serge, whose efforts with her countrymen in the highest
places may yet secure my freedom, and whose loyal
generosity lends her to comfort me with assurances that
in the high clarity of the mountains you will find it in
your heart to forgive our marriage. In more ways than
one, Serge, our hopes turn towards peaceful Switzerland.)

To return, however, to the pompous nationalism of
this muddle-headed country. They ask me, Will the
great Nijinsky dance for our brave Hungarian soldiers?
I cannot dance, I tell them, for those who are killing my
countrymen, even though I consider all mankind my
brothers. If I danced for the wounded, it would only be if
half the proceeds were given for the Russian prisoners.

Yesterday, Serge, a patriotic young poet and lover of

the dance turned his face away and spat, passing me on the street.

If only they would let me be! They believe, I swear, that I write in some arcane code, therefore God knows what elisions will obstruct your reading of this letter from

Your devoted Vaslav.

(Practice? Oh yes, my dear friend, to a mouldy gramophone record of – most fittingly – 'The Blue Danube', thrusting aside the rugs, the crystal, the grandfather clocks, shuffling around like an old sheep in bedroom slippers while my beautiful mother-in-law with the soul, God forgive me, of a turnip, screeches at the abominable, insufferable noise of the Russian interloper. Neither musicians, nor rehearsal rooms, nor collaboration of any kind is to be granted to this enemy alien. A curse on the madness of chauvinism which maggots at the heart of Europe, Serge!)

Night streets of London, hot, exhaust smell, sweat on your upper lip. The window flaps of the Citroën went bang bang as they jounced along: Kathleen's earrings – cheap, wooden, summery – danced against her neck. Will had come to pick her up in shorts, embarrassing her with his bare legs, legs which were long and young and ended in trainers and bright boyish white socks. She knew how to be his teacher, even his friend, but really, out in the city people did stare so. On the crowded pavements girls wore bare midriffs, their hair tied up in Betty Boop bows; Arabs drifted in white suits; women of her own age and upwards hailed taxis, immaculate women with slim faces and even slimmer shoes.

Still weak from the operation, she took refuge behind a barrier of fretfulness. Will, who hadn't known about the illness or the

operation, was shocked, solicitous in a high-speed kind of way. He shook his head in surprise. 'And you've been keeping this under your hat for how long?'

They were early, desultory. Killing time outside a pub near the cinema, they discussed a flamenco version of Carmen, which they'd both seen the week before. Kathleen had gone with Louise, it was one of a series of outings designed to take her mind off the hospital. They'd been riveted by the formalised aggression, jealousy, seductions. The lead female dancer – fortyish, frowning, powerful – had instructed a younger woman, later to be her rival in love, on the correct posture for the flamenco. Setting her hands on the younger woman's torso, she'd lifted it, thrust the shoulders hard back. Simultaneously Louise and Kathleen (Anglo-Saxon, slumped) had sat up straight, looked at each other, giggled. Squatting on the cobbles outside the pub Kathleen arched her shoulders back, mimicking: 'The breasts must be like bull's horns, yet soft also.' As Will laughed, she touched the cool wine glass to her cheek and saw the past weeks as no longer the whole truth and nothing but the truth, but as a pattern distinct from her, an almost gloating stoicism based on illness. She saw skin – Will's healthy leg with its fuzz of light hairs, her own freckled forearm resting on her thigh.

The summer feeling creaked in her and spread. Hot railway lines and the shadows of plane trees; midnight in Arles. Will drank down his pint and took a cigarette and talked; his voice drawled around her, amused, amusing. She laughed rashly. In the hospital labs they were taking cross-sections of tissue, staining it, but for once the thought stayed far off and neutral and couldn't harm her.

The cinema was spacious, air-conditioned. Southern France spread across the screen: bleached limestone and olive groves, and Depardieu hamming it up. The film fitted her altered mood. She liked the idea of a trickster daring enough to return from the wars and steal another man's wife, bed, pleasure, deceiving everyone. Besides, the real husband, when he finally reappeared,

66

had such a frigid pettish look; it was hardly surprising that the wife had preferred the impostor.

When they came out, the heat of the night hit them. Irked by that self-conscious moment in the foyer when the audience, having been entertained, racks its brains for intellectual comment, she said gaily, 'I loved the bed scenes, didn't you?'

Will fixed her with a look that was oddly dour and puritanical. 'Passion on screen's too problematic,' he muttered. 'The way it's set up, you end up feeling that if you don't have a relationship like that, you don't have one at all.'

'But it's a fiction,' she protested, 'surely.' And then she stopped short, transfixed by the chink – exciting, forbidden – which had suddenly opened in his marriage. She discounted the possibility that it might have been deliberate, which made Will laugh, later, when he felt free to document all the moves she had missed.

'Then I heard this disembodied voice dictating, "The patient is an anxious woman, therefore the anaesthetic has made her weepy." Well, screw you, I thought, but of course I couldn't get a word out.' Nervous, she tossed her head. 'Honestly, you're such a cipher in these places.' It seemed late. They must have been sitting there for hours. She got up to change the tape and saw her face in the mirror, tired and glazed and slightly deranged. It wasn't like her to blurt like that, about bodies, blood, the black pit of anaesthesia. This wasn't how she'd wanted to be at all. She'd wanted to be playful and intimate, ironic and easy, but somehow the turn of the talk kept darkening, as if Will were determined to tap the tragic in her.

'So when will you know?'

She fussed at the mirror, dabbing at her hair. 'I have to go back for the results on Friday.'

Will sat on the floor with his back against the divan, fidgeting the end of his shoelace in and out of the eyelet of his tennis shoe. His feet had rucked up the Indian rug, exposing the jute underlay. He picked up a book from the pile he'd brought to return to her and

flattened the pages back. It was the Elvira Shatayeva poem and he
began to read aloud; his voice was light and resonant and there
was nothing for it but to sit down again opposite him and listen. In
the poem the black hole was death, the final contradiction, the No
whose singularity could be outflanked only by the many Yeses of
the women, by forces shared and given, by dreams and by
choices. Kathleen willed herself to agree, to nod and be open and
grave, but at the same time she resisted, fearful that she might be
pushed once again to a point where everything mattered too much,
and then she would cry and what good would that do (for he would
not). When Will glanced up from the page enquiringly she frowned
hard at him, and then she was ashamed and looked away, for
perhaps he had simply intended to comfort her, and it was hardly
his fault if the words were too sombre and triumphal and drummed
in her like a lecture.

Cross-legged on her cushion, she watched him miserably. He
looked spick and span and bland and she had no idea what he felt,
how he understood the world, or, for that matter, what on earth he
thought they were doing here.

'I'm coming closer,' he said, laying the book face down on the
rug. Rapidly, he was on his feet, and she was shocked and shy.
Long bare legs flashed above her and then he was kneeling on the
rug beside her, absolutely unfamiliar positioning. When he kissed
her she giggled.

'I can't do anything. Doctors orders!' Then he kissed her again,
reaching for her, and she was immediately hot, vibrant, amazed.
Her body – this object of desire – bracing itself so ingenuously and
forgetfully for pleasure that she let out a great laugh at the absurdity,
the ludicrous prohibition.

'I've waited a year,' said Will gallantly. He grinned. 'I guess I can
wait a bit longer.'

'But what about Joanna?' she murmured, putting up a last stand,
protocol.

Will drew back and cocked his head at her. 'It's an open
marriage, we have an arrangement.'

68

She gave a blank startled nod. Carte blanche, *she thought. Easy as anything. She picked fluff from the carpet and tried to smile at him. There was something else she should do or say but she couldn't work out what it was. 'It's OK, then?' she said, wishing that he would stop looking at her, wishing that he would simply pull her to her feet, tug her into the bedroom, rush the thing to its conclusion. In an acute absence of desire, she caressed his back with small monotonous strokes. Until at last Will, wriggling away, stripped his T-shirt up, and hers.*

In bed they touched each other: bellies, breasts, toes, curve of neck, his straight clean hair. Will flopped back on the pillows and looked at her. 'I don't believe this.' She didn't believe it either. That he could want her. But he said he did, insisted.

'Remember Christmas, you were flirting with Jessica in the pub.' She'd felt like some old mother hen, boring as hell.

Will plumped up his cheeks and looked smug. 'Not true. I picked you out right at the start.'

In between memoirs, their smiles stretched to bursting. Happiness or anxiety made her talk helter-skelter. She couldn't lie still, and ran out to pee. When she came back her shoes and jeans lay in a heap where she'd left them, candle-lit, and she was glad that they couldn't make love, do it, perform. For men it was easy but for women one of two things happened and both were problematic: either you went down into the dark with them or you stayed out in the light, stranded and watching. 'I'm frightened of coming any way at all,' she said. 'I'm frightened of bursting the stitches.' Her laugh was girlish. She felt innocent and released.

Will's hand played in her hair. Stretching out a curl to its full length, he grinned at it. 'Well, as first nights go, it's certainly original!'

She laid her hand under the curve of his pectoral. 'Climbing makes you top heavy,' he said. His chest was packed with muscle, solid, like a weight-lifter's. Taking her finger he traced a line which demarcated two shades of skin, a diagonal from left nipple to right

69

hipbone. 'The top bit's fairer, from my mother. The rest's olive, tans easier. Evan had it the exact other way round.'

Next-door the tape clicked off, and in the quiet she thought she could hear the vibrations between them, twittering like birds. She knelt up and scurried over him, starved, licking. Will looked up at her, smiling and abashed. 'You make me feel so exciting,' he said, and she glimpsed Joanna again for a brief second, but this time only as lack, negative. She couldn't sleep now, not possibly. The limbo had become too pleasurable, addictive; she wanted it to go on all night, until dawn rose behind the green window blinds and filled the room with underwater light.

Late, around five, Will got up to take out his contact lenses, a small incongruous defect which touched her. She watched him bend over the desk, naked, and tear two strips of paper from the edge of a manuscript. He folded the lenses into two tiny parcels which made her laugh, made her think of the sixties, acid tabs, Detroit on mescalin, a jewel in the midnight plains. She told him about her trip across the States in a rackety bus daubed with women's slogans: Mayday and the Anti-War movement, he'd been in grade school then. 'These Americans,' she said. 'I was shocked. They ran all their political meetings on grass.' She thought of the NLF flag, so beautiful with its gold star. Tears came to her eyes and Will kissed her.

'It's the Fourth of July,' he said. 'American Independence Day.'

Kathleen laughed back at him. She thought that her whole body was probably shining. 'Stroke the insides of my arms,' she demanded.

7 July

Summer Pudding

Glutinous redcurrants, you pop them on your tongue: only the slightest pressure is needed. At first it feels like an unequal contest, brutal as squishing a greenfly . . . but then they get their own back with an explosion of sting on your tongue, sour, you suck in your cheeks: shit! Eyes watering. Shee-it! And the seeds inside stick in between your teeth, raspberry seeds too. All of this encased in a spongey mould made from bread, which isn't sweet enough to cancel out the filling – a grown-up pudding, an intelligent pudding, full of moods and contrasts that have to be deciphered. A macho pudding, even – I always did kind of prefer things that bite back. All that red, too, your whole mouth fills up with it, you worry that it might be running down your chin.

Met K at her street door Friday – I was putting a poem I'd written for her through the letterbox, and she arrived back from the hospital, where she'd had the all clear, so she was happy and chirpy and kind of weak-kneed with relief. I went upstairs with her but only briefly since I was supposed to be shopping for the dinner party and I was pushed for time. She made me a concoction of lemonade and ice-cream which turned to a white foam in the glass and which was so sweet I couldn't manage more than a mouthful: an iced drink, she called it, she used to drink it in Belfast when she was a kid and it was hot. Then she sat on the arm of my chair and looked at my poem – which was some four lines on leaving her flat Thursday am and feeling like a grass-blade trembling under lightning in the sky. Then she laughed because I'd spelled something wrong, and apologised for laughing, but she would only kiss me on the cheek. 'No, no, you're too nervous,' she said, whereas I sort of thought she was the one who was. 'In that case I'll head along,' I replied, 'and take my nerves off with me.'

Pembroke, Saturday
Flying ants, squads of them, doing a mating dance above the bracken. They get in your hair and down your neck, they seem blinded. Then I see one pair on a stone, attached

tail to tail and each one is fighting to crawl in the opposite direction – one drags the other a few inches, then she drags him, and so on – excruciating. Maybe the male was trying to escape, maybe the female was. Or maybe they were both having a terrific time, but you could have fooled me. Oily black segments of thorax which looked inextricably joined: I peered close but couldn't see any way to separate them. They had transparent rainbow wings and bright red thighs. Then one of them reared the front part of its thorax up and its wings whirred; there was an orgasmic tremble through its legs, a vibration that went on and on. I held out a stalk of grass thinking that it was over and that maybe they were ready to separate now and could do with a hand, but I guess I was wrong, for my advances were rejected and they stayed glued together for as long as I watched. This went for all the other pairs which were similarly enmeshed and pulling and pushing and shunting like some crazy marshalling yard.

Intercity, Sunday night
It was good to see Neil again. We'd talked two or three times on the phone but I hadn't seen him since we went climbing together back in November. I'm slowly developing his capacity for gossip which he artfully indulges in the pub. Being a barrister he's of course super-rational and subtle about it, so he managed to keep me cowed on quite a number of topics, but my developing familiarity with theories of irrationalism and indeterminacy has given me the words to redress the imbalances of his rationalist discourse in a way that brings the mess of emotions and egos more significantly into our discussions about women or the Labour Party or just where to pitch the tent.

Neil is very keen on crag-climbing, whereas my main interest is Alpine climbing – and, worse, he's quite competitive and self-conscious about the standard he's climbing at, something which he does acknowledge, if only super-ficially: he gets quite worried by the plethora of young climbers who take climbing E grades for granted. I try to remind him that he could climb to that standard if he was prepared to put in the time and take it that seriously, but I know I'm fairly lazy about rock-climbing and easily bored with talk of alterations to guidebooks, or the newest line in high-friction low-torque go-faster Italian climbing shoes.

I told him I might not be free to go climbing regularly again till September because of Chamonix. At first I couldn't figure out why this was an awkward thing to say but somewhere between the car-park and the train I began to realise how much having a regular climbing partner is like having a lover. I suggested he call Nick Rowthorne who has recently moved to Leicester and should be available thru' the summer, but this was a surprisingly difficult thing to do as it touched on feelings of jealousy in me and rejection in Neil.

And I realise now just how much Neil has dominated quite a major part of my life these last two years. I had always played the field quite widely before, with climbing friends not only in London but also Bristol, Bangor, Sheffield and Scotland. On the one hand I was pleased to find someone so personally amenable and equipped with very efficient car etc, so that I could have my climbing regular, as it were, but I realise now that because Neil almost always paid for petrol and most other expenses I developed a feeling of indebtedness which meant that I stopped climbing with other people – a sense of obligation not unlike that of a devoted but oppressed housewife. Of course 'playing the field' can be lonely and hard work because it's a matter of trade-offs and compromises, but it's funny how all this only occurred to me for the first time this weekend. . . .

Men do enjoy the patriarchal fruits of the big I Am but

they do so within a very tight box, even if it is one of their own making. Parting in the station car-park, Neil gave me a hug which felt a bit like being wrapped in the arms of an upright bicycle. He said it made him feel ridiculously self-conscious, and I laughed and said we'd have to work on it, but frankly I think it's hopeless. I've always felt stiff as a scarecrow embracing the couple of gay friends I've sincerely loved and so I guess it will be at least another generation before 'enlightened' but conventionally masculine males like Neil and me can genuinely show affection.

Wednesday, Clapton Park, *en route* from K's

Talking about what
is necessary as food –
the supermarket of relationships
Express check-out
Eight items or less
for those in a hurry.
And are you?
I'm sure I don't know

Not that
I don't care.
Carrier bags 4p each
I bring my old ones now
each time I go.
Something new
but not unexpected.
Someday I must
surprise myself.

You Spartan women
are fierce as an elite.

When I went in I couldn't see K at first.
'I'm making tea,' she called, from behind the screen of

climbing plants that separates the kitchen from the living
room. 'Ordinary or hippy?'

'Hippy?' She made it sound so aggressive that I laughed.

'Herb: I mean, it isn't even good for you. All it is is not
bad for you.' She came out of hiding then. 'Not a very
inspiring way to live, is it?'

I went to hug her but she held the tea out at me with a
rapid laugh. We sat down on the rug and I told her about
Neil and the weekend but she picked at the carpet and
would not look me in the eye. Then she threw her fists in the
air and she was trying to smile. 'Married men!' she said,
and I thought, Uh-oh. 'I suppose you think I've got a lover
already,' she went on, 'and it's all cool and easy for me too;
I suppose that's what you think.'

To which I replied (truthfully), Sure, with her being so
attractive I reckoned there had to be men around somewhere, and then she really seemed to get angry and said,
Well of course it would be convenient, wouldn't it, but it
wasn't so and therefore she was *vulnerable*. She seemed to lay
great stress on this word vulnerable but from my side it felt
like being hit on the head with an axe-handle and I sat there
pretty confused, trying to think how to say I cared for her
(which I do), just wanting to hold her and being told this
was clearly out of line. It turns out that K was pissed off
because I'd called by casually when she was in fact going
out, and she told me in fairly strong terms that if I wanted a
relationship with her I'd have to book up like everyone else
since she wasn't going to sit around on the off-chance –
something which she knew from experience would make
her hate me. Which made me feel cold all over but also
somewhat annoyed because it sounded like a threat. I
have to confess that this London appointments system of
meeting has always got me down; on the other hand I don't
want to lose her (which I said). Apart from anything else it
would be like stopping dead and retreating just when

you've crossed a frontier post. Maybe someone ought to start a School for the Management of Relationships; they'd be severely over-enrolled. I do see that we've got to be a bit more organised about it, OK. It's hard, though, to put myself in her place and almost into an economy of scarcity (which is what I think she was saying) when I feel – perhaps self-deceivingly – that I have plenty to give and then some, but I realise that this leaves me open to accusations that it all comes back to the privilege of the male. Whereas women are more down-to-earth and always suspect they will be cheated or short-changed, and I guess I can bring my mind, at least, to an understanding of this if I try hard enough, or if it's thrust under my nose often enough – which is after all what you have to expect if you prefer autonomous women – (and which I can rely on J to regularly do).

'Stay cool, but care,' Will said to Kathleen much later. 'That's what I meant to do, that's the mistake I made.'

One morning in the holidays, shortly before Will was due to leave for Chamonix and Kathleen for the Hérault, they were lying in bed together when the telephone rang. Kathleen picked it up without thinking and heard a deep, rather brusque voice she would hardly have recognised if it hadn't been asking for Will. Automatically she handed the phone over. Automatically, too, she disentangled herself, withdrew, but Will snatched her hand back and replaced it, flattening it along his thigh and holding it there as he smiled tensely into the receiver. Afterwards he shrugged and said he had to go. The gas men were coming to repair the Ascot and he'd forgotten that Joanna had to leave for her cleaning job at eight. He was matter-of-fact about it, and Kathleen gasped. 'You young yuppy couples,' she accused. 'You've always got things under control, haven't you?'

Later she could still see herself, the strained aghast face trying to handle it, the face she hid under the bedcovers, laughing abominably: it was a nightmare which would go away if only she could make a joke of it. When she refused to come out Will thumped on the duvet and burrowed under; in the dim light his face was greenish but glad, because her playacting had let him off the hook, that playacting which allowed them to laugh together, quick disordered shrieks of excitement before he dressed and left, before she got up too and ate a yellow pear, slitting thin slices off one by one with a bone-handled knife.

Later she stood at the window and thought and thought of his penis, how it grew monstrous and lovely in her throat, how there was memory and fantasy and each mingled with the other: his leg, loose somehow, jerked ecstatically in her mind like a stroked cat or even death throes – she'd dreamed, definitely, of a white horse senselessly dismembered. She felt a tingling in her jaws, teeth. Incisors, incise, incisive: Will had said he had a vision of her at her desk, very distinct – typewriter keys stabbing the page like knives.

Outside the rain came down straight as a pencil. She gripped the sill of the open window and rocked slowly on the balls of her feet, her heels slipping in and out of her shoes. She knew that she ought to be disciplined, get on with it; knew also that she wouldn't, that everything conspired against work – the fine rain, wet sparrows tussling in the full gutters, the heavy greenness of the garden below.

His eyes meet hers to the hilt and they both tremble. She's sitting with her back against the wall, wet from love, wet between the legs and he touches her exactly there where she's so wet and wide; the tears seem to have to come first before she does and he lets out a starved sound, a growl, like relief; he says it's right, the tears are right – she has to be that open. A statement of intent: he wanted the tears more than anything, he wanted them most of all?

Her mind picked up the memory, teasing out its possibilities. Made him lay his finger tender and straight as a moustache across her upper lip, a finger which led back to an image, a sensation of her nose being held, coercion, medicine . . .

... and tests her cunt with his finger: no, she's not wet enough, he'll be the one to say when she is, he'll be the one to decide. And this is the way she must always be, this wet and open before he'll enter her. His full penis thrusts against her teeth like a spoon, he's puckered up her cheeks around it, he holds her hand to her own spread slicked wings, his neck/cock in the dark of her throat/cunt, and the white manic horse they become sweating ...

There were inkstains on the bedcover, and for one crazy moment she thought they'd come from her: blue-black juices she'd leaked like a squid on the white soaked bed. There was an image of herself the night before, keyed up. Waiting for Will and pretending not to. She'd pushed the button to open the street entrance, then picked up her pen – fraudulent – so that when Will made it up four flights and into the flat he'd find her bent over her manuscript, fecund, chaotic, one hand forking abstractedly through her hair.

She was hot, strangled, moving about the flat restlessly. Envying marriage for a sharp convulsive second. Marriage which is safe. Nurturing. Louise and Geoff, who'd lasted, even without children to weld them. Terry, who had fought for what she wanted and got it, and in doing so had allowed Colin to bloom into a late soft surprised fatherliness.

Whereas what, in the end, had she fought for? Space to write, dream, think? Space to float like Peter Pan, head in the clouds, while all around the grown-ups went about their business, buying and selling? These were harsh times for idealists, after all. Not so many people singing about revolution; instead, so often, money catching you out like an insect, calling you ugly: before you knew it, there you were in the mirror, yelling at yourself. So here she was, a remnant of more collective times, looking at her old leather jacket slung across a chair, her thick city skin, neither fashionable nor unfashionable. Her life spread out in postcards and maxims on the wall: 'Press on' and 'Despite fear' and 'Play with a loose arm'. There were freesias on the table, cherries in a bowl like red silk, and here she was, still comforting herself with plurals, thinking *we*, thinking *of the other single women who were erratically employed and artistically inclined, the we who worked quietly in empty rooms, read poetry when requested, went on holidays to France, maybe, to a stone house with a terrace among vines . . . And now she was standing in the centre of the room with one hand pressed to her cheek, for she was thinking of Will again, and how he must come to the Hérault, he had to, it was too possible, tantalising – the autoroute via Geneva, Lyon, Montpellier – suddenly it was obvious that he must come, that they could and should have that. Outside the rain came down harder, splashing in at the open window. 'You can always see your cup as half empty or half full,' she read, and now she was laughing, screwing up her face – ugh, God, love, what a nightmare – sure, but it didn't take much to up-end the whole damned thing.*

The rain had gone on all weekend, the elderflowers in the garden spread great white plates to catch it. On Sunday evening Kathleen was deep in a new chapter when the doorbell rang unexpectedly. It was Will; he had been in North Wales climbing a cliff called A Dream of White Horses, and he was soaked and sweating and needing a beer. Hunched under his rucksack, he looked heavy-shouldered and delicate-legged as a goat. 'Joanna thinks I'm still in Bangor,' he said, looking at her shiftily. 'Are you doing anything?'

'No,' she said immediately. It was a lie but a pale one next to his. For a moment she was too excited to speak. She put her arm round his waist and led him into the living room.

'I get so anxious hitching back to you,' Will said, with such a stark look of relief that she flushed with pleasure. It was as if life hadn't yet taught him the need to dissimulate, so that, at thirty, he was still the well-loved child with a plain faith in his right to be exactly himself and have exactly what he wanted. It was amazing, it was enviable, it was an enigma.

'In case you find a fractious mistress waiting?' She brought cheese out of the fridge, salads, whatever she could find. Will ate in the American way, fork in one hand, holding her hand with the

other. She broke away, laughter bursting out of her. He had a new yellow climbing harness, festooned with karabiners and nuts; she buckled it round her waist and paraded on an imaginary catwalk, clowning – mmm, bondage – jingling like a reindeer. Will laid his hand across the curve of his chest and laughed and laughed. In bed her manic mood continued. 'What's a handsome lad like you doing with an old lady like me?' she demanded, flying up on to him, bearing down, baring her teeth. 'What you need's a cool little twenty-year-old, all clean limbs and quick thanks over breakfast.'

'Oh no,' said Will, 'it's you I want all right.' Quick glint of an accusing smile. (Her fault? That he had lied to Joanna?)

In the night she woke to find him watching her, curved over her like a harp, his pale stare on her. 'It's a small village, not even a bar,' she murmured. 'I'll kill you if you don't come.'

In the morning she opened her eyes and saw Will sitting on the edge of the bed, notebook in hand, frowning at lists. The separation rose up suddenly, swelling in her, billowing out in waves. He was on the coach already, he was crossing Paris in the night, he was hunched over a chocolat chaud *in some Chamonix café while the patron apologised for the weather,* incroyable pour le mois de juillet, incroyable. *She let the tears roll down her face, excusing herself: it's my period, I feel like a whale, no skin, etc etc.*

'Uh,' said Will, stretching himself out on top of her and pressing his face to hers as if to blot up the tears. 'I hate leaving you like this.'

'I'm OK,' she said, 'I just need to wallow. Don't look so anxious.' And it struck her that she was OK, that in fact she felt quite contented, and safe, if only because for once she hadn't thrust the sadness away, defended herself against it. She lay there under him, surprised, trusting, no envy in her.

When Will left, promising to return at some point to look at maps, she got up dreamily and did things. After supper she felt clumsy and sleepy and lay down on the divan. There was a mirror on the wall beside the window, an oval-ish mirror with fluted angles around the edge. The mirror reflected the light of the table lamp on the shelf behind her, but without revealing its source, so that all she could see was gold, a gold oval against a pinkish wall. And as the sun faded, all the objects contained in the mirror began to glow – the red-ribbed paper lampshade on the ceiling, the buff of a faded Steinberg poster, the dark cedar colour of the wood shelves. Along the fluted edges the reflections wavered, distorting, like so many ribbons thrown down and fallen askew. She closed her eyes for a second and when she opened them again it was as if the mirror, in that instant of not being observed, had taken on its true colours and what hung now on the wall was a shield-like artefact worked in pure metal with crimsons and reds enamelled on it, sunk deep and molten into the surface, and although she had never been a person who liked gold, its colour or meaning, she was shaken, illuminated, overtaken by this gold, this mirror she couldn't see herself in, this mirror-for-itself. She the irreligious one, shaking her head and lighting a cigarette and feeling herself beginning to bleed.

Will came back at ten and peered at her. He was smooth-shaven and had the compressed look of a man who was supposed to be elsewhere. 'I can't stay long,' he said, 'are you OK.'

She was fine, and said so. She'd already forgotten about the tears. 'Are you packed and everything?'

'I guess so.' Will put his hands in his pockets and shrugged wildly. 'Look, I'm used to people who're more reserved, that's all . . . I mean, if you get a bit down you go for a beer or play a game of tennis or something.'

He looked angry. She said, 'Are you angry with me?'

Taking a cigarette from her pack he lit it and sucked hard. He gave a fast laugh. 'Hey, this pre-menstrual thing – can you catch it or what?' He put the cigarette out with a grimace and stretched out beside her on the divan.

She was laughing. She said she thought he'd survive. Separation anxiety, she said. Will shut his eyes and lay back, shoulders imploding, hands tucked childishly between his thighs. 'Uh. Is that what they call it.'

'Pub,' she said, heaving him up. 'You've got to go off and be the hero, remember.'

Will looked at her suspiciously. 'Well, I guess none of Joanna's friends go to that one.' A heavy glowering guilt came off him in waves. Kathleen felt murky and resentful and excited. She wondered what excuse he had given to Joanna, but couldn't bring herself to ask. Complicit, yes, certainly she was complicit, but she drew the line at conspiracy.

'Come on,' she said. 'I'll get the maps.'

30 July

Like looking into the mirror and seeing someone you never even knew . . .

Once or twice – it started after Evan died – I was dreaming or thinking a dream that Mom showed me a wallet she said was mine but I wasn't allowed to see what was in it; when I think of this there's a jolt. It was the kind of wallet Dad kept his plane tickets or passport in and I remember thinking that she'd let Evan see his, which was the same as mine so I asked her why I couldn't see inside mine and she just laughed and said later, Billy, when you're grown.

My dear Serge,

Today I worked in the onion room – so-called because of the green cupola on the tower – all morning without disturbance. My hand flew across the page, my notations flickering like semaphore in an extraordinary melding of time and space into a dimension which is neither, being linear . . . how many *entrechats*, to which beat, where executed . . . Can you imagine the complexity of a *pas de quatre*? Even the rictus of Bournonville's choreography is a nest of snakes to classify on the page. And as for the Faune, Serge! Discarded papers snowed the room, I was beetle-browed with ink, the coffee cooled unnoticed on the desk, and then at lunchtime

I was treated to a *grande folie* – the boiler has burst, Nijinsky has sabotaged the boiler! Romola interceded and eventually succeeded in calming my *belle-mère*, but the servants have already become xenophobic enough without eruptions of this kind, which only encourage them to new malice. Kyra's nurse, whose fiancé was called to the front, has vehemently refused any more milk for the babe. I have taken her care into my own hands and am fast becoming an expert in feeding her from a bottle like an orphaned lamb. She is indeed the jewel of these dark days, her strong limbs and the sound of her laughter. We build snowmen together on the pure white lawn and wind mufflers round their necks and place flowerpot hats on their frosty heads. Sometimes we steal barley from the kitchen to fill their outstretched hands so that the birds come down to eat from nowhere, from very heaven, and that is lovely; we watch from behind the windows and Kyra puts a finger to her lips in droll imitation of my commands and I could weep for joy, Serge, weep. Please do not falter in your petitions to M. Argeles in Geneva, and pray that the war will end soon,

Your grateful friend,
Nijinsky

On receiving within the last hour your telegram detailing the kind efforts of Lord Islemere in London, what can I say but: *everything is changing. The sky is becoming beautiful. How happy I feel, the soul can't explain it.* The words you will recognise from William Tell, but the sentiments are my own. As you say, I will try to have patience, but already I feel that the high mountains lie in wait for me like some special province of the heart, cloudless and boundless.

Part Two

The Ice Mother

But you see, when I'm pre-menstrual I don't think your way and I don't like the fake wood-panelling on your walls or your wife's stiff forbidding English voice on the phone or the language you use or anything, specially not the language. Needs. Demands. Negotiations. An economics of emotion. Some day I think you'll start talking about stocks and bonds and futures.

–

– You see, when I'm pre-menstrual I think of my mother as my dark goddess the crow and there's no goodness in her. I see her hopping hunch-winged over some field and I'm the afterbirth trailing bloody across the grass, the ragged remainder, womb-scrapings. I'm the red bundle she took to the river and skimmed like a flat stone, she took me to the high window and threw me from her with a shriek; something in me is absolutely sure of this, her negativity, her terrible rage I feel inside me. The red compression of women, the rage that throws me away.

– *You think my wife will put a stop to . . .*

– What I want to know is . . . how analysis accounts for all this!

– *You're asking – am I powerful enough to keep my wife at bay?*

– One day you'll lose patience with me and I won't blame you.

– I'll lose patience and throw you away?

–

–

– Listen, this is my letter to the Ice Mother:

I'm looking at photos on the wall and they don't add up to much: me, my father, the Galway wind, words scattered. In the absence of God I need you to add me up. I want to tell you my difficulties, as Yeats the mystic wrote to Leo Africanus, dead Moor and poet, his shadow self, reflecting him. Yet in this mirror of yours there's nothing that's benign, it's like some fairy tale from which I wake like a fist, seeing that seam of a mouth and I can't pronounce the word 'love'. I think of opening myself to take you in – your breast – and I shudder with longing and distrust, imagining the ice in my mouth, its sharp cutting edges.

In the night I climb the sycamore tree to her bedroom window and ease up the sash. On the pillow, her shoulders, a white old-fashioned nightdress with a scalloped frill at the neck like a Pierrot's costume. And she holds his head on her breast wondering why men must always make love before they make confessions.

I need you to add me up. I need an adversary, struggle, winning, jealousy. To have been named bad and made it come true . . . then fate fits snugly and one can be comfortable. Only your pain completes me, rounds me out, so that I can become magnanimous, tender; my heart melts, thinking of making reparations.

And this is what the Ice Mother replies:

You were so neat in white, I always loved white: vests, mittens, small bootees the size of cotton reels. But now my hand isn't big enough to hold any part of you, no part of you is small and all the parts are turned against me. Nothing anyone can do is ever enough. This is my excuse, the excuse I make to the mutinous face which taunts me with my failures. Yes I wanted to murder like most mothers but not *you*; it was the impulse, the instinct that I wanted to tear out at the root. I admit, however, that I wasn't prepared for an intruder. In my sixth month I could no longer dance, for your body lodged in me, prohibiting the usual torque of waist and hips; I was rigid as a weld and left the dance floor abruptly. In the lavatory I beat my fists against the whitewashed wall until my knuckles bled and the priest said to me it was a sin, but I was only young, remember: I couldn't see why your time should come so soon when mine had not, couldn't see why my body should be home to you when it was hardly home to me. I wanted you to be small, to stay small, small as a belt-buckle and no obstacle. Then you were neat as a small saint in your christening shawl which folded transversely across your chest like an envelope to keep you from scratching your face with those tiny sharp fingernails I couldn't bear to cut in case the scissors slipped, and though Grandmother Farrell said that I should nibble them short with my teeth, that was the old way, the safe way, I couldn't bring myself to do it, I was afraid of biting off a whole small finger. Grandmother Farrell knitted your small white mittens for the hard winters, and as we walked to early Mass her long black coat swished against the snowdrifts, you were so neat in white against the black bosom she carried all the more haughtily because your father would not come, your father who made no secret of his indifference to the Blessed Saints.

It was the morning after Will had left; it was Saturday. Outside Sainsbury's people were selling Socialist Worker *and* The Next Step; *against the railings which separated the crowded pavement from a traffic jam of red buses, placards were propped:* Free Nelson Mandela *and* Boycott South African goods. *Kathleen was standing in front of a fruit stall wondering about melons when a* clear deep voice hailed her. Spinning round, she saw a woman in a reddish anorak who might have been a hiker or a head prefect, but it was Joanna and she had a clipboard and she was coming towards her. With her frank face and her collecting tin she looked dedicated and terrifying and grand.

'How's business?' Kathleen nodded at the petition – approval, solidarity; her mind was wayward, however, outrageous, ticking up points. At close quarters Joanna's mouth was quite small, not sensual; her skin looked dry and was already lined around the eyes. 'Sorry,' she said, 'I've signed it already.' Her regret – genuine – sounded forced, hollow.

'Never mind. Most people have.' Joanna looked amused. 'How're you?'

Just then the stallholder caught Kathleen's eye and brandished a cucumber, grinning. 'Come on girls! Come and get yours!'

She lowered her shopping bags to the ground. 'Fine,' she said, appalled, for suddenly it was as if Joanna knew everything, sex and farewells and the long hot talking nights, and was saying nothing, making light of it, and the vulgarity was all part of the joke, and suddenly she was panicky, determined, hating the English and that pall of politeness they hid behind. 'Did Will get off to Chamonix OK?' she asked, because someone had to come clean.

Joanna raised a wry eyebrow. She didn't look flustered at all. 'Well he hasn't reappeared since I dropped him at Victoria, so presumably.'

Kathleen shook her hair out of her eyes and stared wildly around, saying good, great, darting hopeless little smiles at Joanna. Nothing could have been crueller than that composure, in the face of which her challenge had fallen away like a stone deflected by the armoured shell of a tank. She fumbled fifty pence into the collecting tin and backed away. 'Better go,' she muttered. And then she started dropping things, oranges rolled out of her bag and she was desperate and laughed. 'God, I'm so pre-menstrual I can't believe it.'

Joanna clasped the clipboard flat against her chest. 'See you,

then,' she said, with such a cool curious look that Kathleen felt like
begging for mercy.

Wed, Aug ?
Bar Terrasse, Chamonix

Dear Kathleen,

Well, I managed to overcome my separation anxiety, or
whatever, enough to pack my bags and get on the bus
Friday, and arrived here on Saturday noon-time to grey
skies, low cloud and an ominous forecast: all of which only
further contributed to my deteriorating resolve and dis-
integrating personal sense of the world. Met a climbing
comrade from Liverpool on the bus and confessed I didn't
much feel like being left alone, so he came to my camping
wood in Chamonix before moving up to Argentière the next
day where he's doing a week's course. When the cloud is
low the valley is so dark and sheer and I get this softening
foreboding knowing that the peaks and summits are
towering above me somewhere invisibly. As I was pitching
my tent I became afraid my body was sprouting roots into
that soft woodland grass and that I might never get up into
the white and rocky mountain valleys above. So weak I sat
down beside the tent as I pushed each peg into the turf and
tried to pull the sides of the tent taut like they should be.
We'd already been to the bar, met some friends, smoked
some dope, and I finally crawled into the tent and had a
slow constipated weep – and although I tried, I still
couldn't figure out why. It was just too quick being back in
the dank(dangerous?) melancholic valley. Definitely not-
so-Zorro.

We had steak frites in town and Chris and I went to the
Bar Nash where I renewed my spotty relationship with my
climbing acquaintances and caught up on the gossip. We

moved on to the Europa Disco about midnight and I was just beginning to enjoy myself when my survival instincts told me it was time to beat a hasty retreat back to the tent, which of course wouldn't stop spinning until I got up and vomited under the flysheet, fortunately picking the spot where I hadn't stowed any gear . . .

I eventually located my Swiss mate Jean-Yves to climb with and after nursing the hangover on Sunday we went up the Aiguilles Rouges under a doubtful forecast and solo'd La Chapelle and the Index in very short order, so planned and succeeded on something more ambitious yesterday: the north Face of the Peigne, 300 metres E.D.Sup (Extrême Difficile Superieur). It's a new 'modern' route, one which was put up only last summer and which is quite stunning, magnificently sustained at a level of technical difficulty I've rarely experienced before in the Alps: all the same, Jean-Yves and I pawed up it like cats.

Started *Annapurna: A Woman's Place* on the bus out and just finished it last night – a magnificently told story and good for generating a few emotions in my current watery mood. Also looked at your book again and once again admired the clarity and poetry of the writing which gives it such palpable depth, because I for one as a reader needed that sort of warmth to get involved with a character whose story is so chilling. At first I didn't believe your male characters could be quite that awful or that, if so, the protagonist could carry on building and colliding with all those stone and mortar walls, but looking at it again it seems to me too tragically true and I strangely enjoyed something melancholic rather than depressing in recognising something of myself in their portraits.

With that thought, time to debunk to the Brasserie Nationale to suss out the lemmings. See you gathering rubies on the banks of the Rhône on Tues? Wed?

Love, Will

92

At the river beach the municipal sand was brassy as a bleached blonde, and so shallowly spread that a finger idly digging, or the rain driving pits in it, revealed a mud dull as dark roots. Kathleen smoothed the bright surface with her hand and could no longer convince herself that she wasn't waiting. Louise and the German family had coaxed Geoff on to an airbed and were towing him around the shallows; at each turn his knees gripped the bed hard and his gaunt back was a rictus of alarm. 'Jesus wept,' he kept saying. 'Jesus wept.'

By nightfall she had waited long and secretly and hard – he would enter the square by this or that road, he'd find the three of them drinking Campari on the stone bench under the window, he'd burst in at dinner time through the clack clack of the plastic strips which dangled over the door – and she began to worry about her face and smile a lot. A careless belay, a snapped harness, a sudden storm: there were so many ways to fall, and if he had decided, after all, not to come, it was the least, yes, the least he could have done, to write.

At 4 am, the rat hour, she decided that all was lost and felt somehow better. The anticipation had been unbearable, and it was a relief to discover that once again she was alone, abandoned, men always let you down, etc, to drift, tranquillised and peacefully adjusted to misery, into sleep.

A persistent knocking woke her. It took her a moment to decipher what the tall ghost in the doorway was trying to tell her. 'Someone's kicking up quite a row in the street, hadn't you better let him in?' Geoff looked amused, sleepy; she realised that he was bringing good news. There was a faint noise down below, hardly a row, only slightly louder than the other night noises, and she said, 'What?' as you do when everything changes so fast, utterly, and stumbled down the stairs to let Will in.

In the morning, at the bread van, the village ladies were waiting. Madame Elise, who lived in the house opposite, touched Kathleen's elbow lightly, as if delegated. The jeune Anglais in the night, he had arrived safely?

'Je regrette,' *she apologised.* 'Mon copain a voyagé des Alpes hier soir.'

'Un Alpiniste?' *the ladies murmured, and she blushed for the myth that sparkled in their eyes. Wanting to boast about him, wanting to tell them how he'd come calling her name through the sleeping streets; clammy from night trains and hitching, he'd burrowed under her nightshirt, he'd prattled, he'd sighed. He'd caught a midnight train from Marseilles, he'd begged, yes, begged a lift from a late chef going off duty; he would have crawled into a ditch to wait for daylight, he said, if his sense of drama hadn't forbidden it: to arrive like an idiot in the rational glare of morning (he laughed) – imagine the anti-climax. Oh no, he said, a story like that had to end in the dark, in bed, before the moon set, it was the thought of the bed that kept him going.*

She saw them pushing the single beds together, making a big square platform which filled the room. Bleary at the bread van with her arms full of baguettes and the early sun stunning her, she thought of it as a bed wide as the sea, a bed you could drown in. It was impossible, yet it was not impossible: back at the house Will lay on the bed, splayed, dead to the world. The proof lay in the morning, the fur on her tongue, the village opening its shutters on another steel-blue day.

Two kilometres away across the vineyards, at Pezenas, someone began to test a PA system for the fête. She hurried back to the house, eyes down, humble, like a nun scurrying to Vespers. Upstairs she stood in the doorway and gazed at him, his large sleeping feet. His hands clutched the sheet up under his chin but from the waist down he was blatantly bare. Sunlight ticked on his skin. When she set a bowl of coffee on the chair beside the bed he stirred and opened his eyes. He looked at the coffee, the pain chocolat. *His eyes moved round the room: shutters, the dressing table with books, her clothes hanging in the alcove. Then he looked blankly at her breasts.*

'The name's Kathleen,' *she laughed,* 'in case you've forgotten.'

'I dreamed I was falling, I don't dream that, ever.' *Shaking his* head, he sat up with a start. 'No, not last night – I dreamed it in Chamonix. I fell into a room where you were, a room with a window just there, and the bed here, like it is, and our skin was darker than the walls, just like now, it's incredible.' He passed a hand over his eyes.

'Don't say things like that. I'm impressionable.' A light touch, sensible. Someone had to be. Her mouth smiled but her eyes wavered; she felt embarrassed for him, for this self-exposure, so young and innocent and full of little hooks. She sat on the edge of the bed, hiding her face from him, and unbuttoned her dress. Will smiled as his arms went round her, a deep smile which disappeared into his body, softening the muscles. She looked back at things in her life and tried to remember closeness, risks, but all that came to mind was a picture of her mother, tight-mouthed and turbulent. Outside the window cicadas trilled, and in the garden across the street Madame Elise's chickens scuffled over their feed. Enfolded, she wanted to tell him everything, to be completely understood. Tears pricked her eyes with the urgency of it: what she envied was his artlessness, the artlessness of someone who can't conceive of humiliation, rejection.

Conflict: that bright ugly smile.

Two days later, on the stone weir which jutted out into the river, Will was cutting up a melon. Poplars were blue in the late afternoon light, and the shadow of the mill tower had begun to slide across the barrage. Jean-Paul Belmondo had been filmed on the parapet, or so the village ladies had told Kathleen, patting their cheeks in a fret because oh là là they simply couldn't recall the name of the picture. Next day at noon they were triumphant. 'Cartouche,' they cried at her from their bench in the square. Oh yes, she said, she'd seen it, years ago. 'Vraiment?' they cried, clapping their hands in the deep lilac shade of the plane trees. It was a small excitement in a village where little happened. She hoped that Will wasn't going to be bored.

Downstream the four small German children raced each other

tirelessly, fighting the current. They were fearless and lovely but Will wasn't watching them. Since morning he had been moody, and the quieter he became, the more she found herself straining against him, resentful. She stared at the mirroring river, at the red earth of the vineyards stretching west to the village with its flood dyke and its church spire where birds circled. Only two more days, she thought, can't he see how perfect it is? She began to talk about poetry – one trance, she thought, that they could safely share – telling him, half-teasingly, that all around things speak for us, you only have to look and listen. She pointed to the deep dreaming angle of fishing rods, the sudden streak of a watersnake. 'Objective correlatives for the unconscious,' she said grandly. She waited for Will to laugh or scoff: either would do, if only he would talk to her. But Will wasn't laughing. He was holding the knife loosely, with the blade pointing up, and he was staring at it. She watched him touch the point of the blade to his calf. His face was expressionless.

'If I could dig this in,' he said. 'If I could just feel the pain.' He pressed harder, and the skin indented. Her imagination saw the puncture, the flower of blood.

'What?' she said, 'What?'

'Instead of this blankness. Instead of . . . nothing.'

Distantly she felt the hurt, the erasure. She touched his shoulder. 'Don't,' she said.

Will turned away with a black shrug. She couldn't catch what he said next. She thought she heard the word Vietnam. Then he looked at her and said distinctly: 'I would have gone, OK?'

'I don't think I heard that,' she said, 'I don't want to hear that.' He had clasped his arms across his chest and he was gripping himself hard.

'For the intensity, OK?'

She was frightened now. 'What's the matter? I don't know what's the matter.'

'You don't really want to hear this.'

'Yes I do,' she said numbly. She had never seen him smile like that, with the corners of his mouth pricked up tightly, like a

vengeful puppet. He opened his hand and let the knife fall in the dust.

'Well, for a start, you don't touch me enough.'

Her mouth fell open. He was too ridiculous and she wanted to laugh. 'But that's crazy,' she said. Didn't they make love all the time, didn't they kiss and caress and walk everywhere entwined, the village ladies were quite delighted with them. She thought of how she had lifted her red skirt on the flat road to Charolles, he'd seen his fingers glisten. In the orchard he'd tasted her; impossible not to laugh, afterwards, at the split nectarines which rolled in the dust. Her mind raced, her mind ran through the story whose pages Will had suddenly ripped out, deleted. 'When you're like this,' she cried, 'I wouldn't dare. You'd only push me away.'

Will shrugged. His face blamed her. 'I always thought risks like that were part of life myself.' She turned her face to the sun and closed her eyes. Tears welled up under her lids. She heard his breath come out in an angry sigh. 'I know I haven't the right to ask, for Christ's sake.'

She looked at him in confusion. She could hear the hurt, but it wasn't as if she'd made the rules. She knew she ought to be angry, but instead she felt dull and awry, like a failed hostess. 'Look, I'm happy when I see you, I'm sad when you go. Can't we leave it at that?' Two dragonflies coupled with delicate balance above the shallows. She watched them miserably. Yes it was a lie, but who had made lies necessary in the first place?

'So you can't have everything?' The bright ugly smile flashed at her again.

'Exactly.' She forced herself to fall in with his cool sparring tone. 'I can't get everything I want from you, so I content myself with what there is.'

'And what's that? Marriage, I suppose? Kids too? Going the whole hog?' Will's eyes narrowly bitched at her. 'Well, that's fine by me, I've always been into kids.'

Kathleen jumped up and stood on the end of the barrage where the broken rocks fell away and there was only rushing water. The

97

river was high after the night's rain, and lost objects floated in the current: a Dr Scholl sandal, an Evian bottle, a red and green apple. Madame Elise had said that before the dyke was built floods had submerged the village most winters; marooned in her bedroom, she would listen to the hollow noises of her furniture in the room below, floating and bumping. At the thought of the abandoned furniture a violent self-pity filled her. She threw a stone at the Evian bottle and missed. 'Excuse me,' she cried bitterly. 'I thought you were already married.'

'Uh,' said Will. 'I am, aren't I?' She stared at him in disbelief, and for a moment saw a capricious little boy whistling down at the dirt, sifting for flat pebbles to skim. He cupped a stone in his palm, curled his wrist back, and threw. The stone leapt and skidded as many as a dozen times before its leap-frogging became an even tail of spray like a comet or a perfect slalom, and it arced into the shadows under the mill tower. Stretching up straight, Will shook himself quickly, like a dog. 'Pretty good. Must be because you were watching.' His grin was white in a wary brown face. 'You with your intimidating poet's thoughts.'

He was happy, she could see it. Now that he'd succeeded in provoking her. 'Fuck you,' she said, without conviction. He was being childish, cruel: she could allow the thought to creep into a corner of her mind, but she couldn't make it make sense. It was far easier to let her own failings rise up accusingly in front of her. Wanting what he couldn't give, wanting – oh yes – too much, she'd punished him with coldness, distance, dissembling. She'd thought that she had already faced the bleak facts of what she couldn't have, but perhaps hopes like hers weren't so easy to dislodge, and clung at the very roots, tenacious and illicit. Will walked away from her backwards and grinning until his heels hung out over the edge of the barrage, and she felt her focus blur, the thoughts twisting into a pure dark pain inside her.

Will turned abruptly and dived into the deep water above the barrage; surfacing, he shook the wet hair out of his eyes. 'Come on,' he cried, 'Let's sink our moods.' She watched him swim out to the centre, his arms chopping the water easily. 'Peace!' he called from *far out, beckoning, but she shook her head, suddenly timid as Geoff and as convinced that she would sink. It was impossible to imagine plunging in, thrusting herself through the current face down and powerful; like a holed boat or something porous she would take in the weight of the water and the weight of the water would haul her down.*

Suddenly she was desperate to be with him and she cried out in panic. 'It's too deep.'

Out in the river Will trod water. 'Oh yeah?' he said, and stood up. The water barely reached his thighs. 'Thought I was brave, eh?' Standing in the rich evening light, gold on his body, bleached strands of hair sticking up.

'Oh,' she said, mortified. How idiotic to lose confidence like that, to think that she couldn't swim the short distance, when she could no more have forgotten how to ride a bicycle. The water was cold but neutral, and shocked sense back into her. She struck out strongly, feeling it give back her boundaries: that slick envelope of skin into which her feelings fitted, proper-sized, instead of that clamorous, exaggerated ache. When her feet touched the sandy bank she saw that Will had dredged up a rock to throw and drench her. She understood that it was horseplay, and groped down for one to throw in reply. They beat the water with their hands, they ducked, they dived, they scooped handfuls at each other, and so it went on, an escalation of splashes and shrieks which drew dour looks from the fishermen upriver, until at last they were tired, and Will took her hand and held it tightly.

'That's better,' he said, with a mock-petulant look which forbade her to let go. 'That's better.'

'So you reckon you can manage two more days?' she said, laughing with relief.

'I guess I can think of worse things,' Will said wryly.

Joanna and Ann-Marie lay under circling thin cloud at the top of the grassy bank which overlooked the Ladies' Pond. All around them the park was murmuring. Dramas. A woman with cropped hair sat with her head in her hands while her lover huddled miserably over her. 'Come on, Liz.' The painful indrawn breath of trouble, break-up.

Ann-Marie cupped her hand over her mouth. 'And we always thought it would be simpler with women. Silly, isn't it.'

Down on the jetty there was laughter, a splash. Joanna gazed around her. Bodies, breasts, Sunday papers, cast-off bikini tops. Hardly anyone was touching. Or if they were it was discreet: fingertips, a foot strayed over the edge of a neighbouring towel. Casual enough to be accidental and not to invade, offend. Here and there she saw women sitting up cross-legged, smoking, frowning into the sun. A trailing, idle glance. Maybe that's how it was done.

'Well, nothing but middle-aged lust down my way,' Ann-Marie said energetically. 'It's disgusting, I can tell you.'

Joanna grinned. 'Wyndham, you mean?' Wyndham was managing director of a software company in Swindon. He had an egg-smooth face, small blue eyes, and a wife whose sidelong glances spoke loathing. He sang to himself in his Audi and was quite certain that he was handsome.

'Wyndham, I mean. I ask you. You know what the fucker presented me with last weekend? Second-hand sweetpeas! I'm not kidding. He arrives down for the weekend with his wife's sweetpeas to make his little place nice, then on Sunday when he's leaving he knocks on the door: "Still a few days left in them." And I let this man into my bed?'

Joanna listened and knew better than to interject. This was the agit-prop version, crude and colourful, to be hissed and booed and cheered at. The truth was more complicated and not amusing and would take longer than they had.

'It's not as if I'm asking for much. Just the normal privileges of the mistress, right? I mean, he comes back from Paris and says, "I've brought you a present, Ann-Marie." But is it French lingerie? Is it Chanel No 19? Oh my goodness no. Turns out it's two little slivers of soap; you know, the kind you get in hotel bedrooms!'

Joanna laughed uncomfortably. 'The man's a monster.'

'You've said it.'

'So why not dump him? No, really.'

Ann-Marie rolled onto her front. Her face was droll. 'Would desperation do?' She sighed. 'Seriously, though. When are you coming down to see me?'

Joanna shut her eyes and heard the vroom vroom of a decelerating plane, the elastic flip-flop of sandals. 'I can't risk slacking off on the dissertation. Not yet.'

'So bring the dissertation with you. You're such a slogger, I always work well with you around.'

Joanna thought of the winter Ann-Marie had moved in: a bitter winter punctuated by Will's letters from Kenya. Ann-Marie had been between homes, jobs. Thatcher, she complained, had succeeded in making her feel her age at last, and she was going to decamp to Cornwall and dig in until the Decline and Fall. I won't take up much space, she'd said, angering Joanna, who had wanted her to. That was the year Will had climbed the Diamond Couloir – the first American or first British or first solo ascent, she couldn't remember which. At the time, to be honest, she hadn't much cared if he'd climbed it standing on his head and pulling his knickers up and down . . . Oh, an exaggeration, perhaps, but she certainly hadn't felt like supplying the congratulations his letters seemed to expect. Ill with bronchitis, she'd lain for days in a strange haze of fever while the words from her 'A' level textbooks leapt and jiggled in her head: the exams were the first she'd ever studied seriously for and the spectre of failure was terrifying. Meanwhile Ann-Marie, motherly, brewed Friar's Balsam in steaming bowls and sat drawing her, hour after patient hour, the sound of her pencil soothing as a stroke on the cheek.

Out in the centre of the pond two women swam in tandem, a gentle, conversational breaststroke. 'But aren't you lonely?' Ann-Marie asked.

'With books up to my eyeballs and my blessed mother on the phone every half hour?' Her voice sounded impatient, snappish.

'Sorry,' she apologised. 'It's murder at the moment, that's all.'
She fought off a momentary resentment. Seriously, Will had said.
Come to Chamonix. Knowing that she couldn't, and even if she
had, what on earth would she have done with herself? Holidays
were for splashing out – tennis, the piscine, the eighty franc
menu sometimes – not for scrimping and saving. In the Alps Will
hoarded: prioritising, he called it. Money was for téléférique fares
and refuge fees, and no compromise was possible – unless it was
hers. Which made it even more remarkable that he could still make
her feel guilty for saying no. On the day he'd left she'd come back
from the library to find chaos in the kitchen. Two machine-loads of
washing were heaped on the ironing board, and ropes festooned
the door. The tent, half-folded, covered the table, sleeping bags
were draped over the chairs, and an ice-axe had fallen into the
cat's dish, spilling a puddle of milk. Will stood in front of the
spin-dryer, naked except for a tea-towel tied round his middle.

'I reckoned I might as well put my shorts through while I was at it,'
he's said with an anguished grin. She felt depressed, remembering.

'Maybe later,' she said. 'I promised I'd go cycling with Will
before college starts back. In Ireland, maybe. Just for a week. We
ought to be able to manage that without squabbling.'

Ann-Marie looked at her quickly. 'How is Will, anyway?'

'Oh well, you know . . .'

'I'm telling you, it's the incest taboo. Never fails.'

Joanna sat up and rested her chin on her knees. She heard
giggles and chat from a group picnic; in her other ear there were
more voices: she was hemmed in by conversations. 'Self-hatred,'
she heard. 'Waves of it. Months of torture hanging on to this man.'
She turned to look and saw a woman in a black T-shirt, peeling an
orange. 'That's when I decided, That's it – enough. I went into this
absolute trough then, of course . . . I've been seeing a therapist,
yes, at long last.'

Oh, therapy, she thought. What about psychoanalysis, why not
do it properly? So tell me, doctor, where desire goes, why Will's

body so close and warm becomes an abstraction, urgent unequal cliché of married sex. That want want want, the reproach of the shoulders which shift towards you a faint inch and settle back into the pillows like a sigh and you actually want to kill him. 'Sometimes I think, well, men, what have I got to say to them?'

'Look,' Ann-Marie said exasperatedly, 'Kathleen or no Kathleen, he worships the ground you walk on, anyone can see that.'

When he'd come back that morning she'd smelled the smoke in his hair. Fags, she'd complained, pressing him lightly away: that woman's a bad influence. That night they'd made love like in the old days, strong, strange. It was the sort of erotic thing that always worked, perversely, whether you wanted it to or not, like the fantasy of being taken in sleep when your mind was sovereign and miles away and your body could just please itself.

A towel was thrown down, overlapping the edge of hers, and withdrawn with a murmured sorry. The picnic group was growing, adding children to its numbers; the expansion made ripples across the grass: small accommodations of arms, legs, sandwich baskets. Half a yard from Joanna a tanned woman sat up in one smooth movement and ran her hands irritably through her short blonde hair. Bending her head she began to examine her thighs, touching them lightly with long fingernails. Her absorption was absolute. Watching her, Joanna frowned. 'What I want is honesty,' she said. 'I have to have that.'

Slow train from Carcassonne, Aug ?

Somewhere on this never-ending journey I've dreamed of descending the hill with Jean-Yves, glissading, then a slip, can't brake with my ice-axe, and as I slide down the snow, out of control like Andy, there's a window on the other side of which a man is watching me. A calm room littered with brightly-coloured toys, and a small girl takes me by the hand.

103

In the practice room Nijinsky merges with his demanding God. One two one two goes the beat of the silver-topped cane, that clean discipline, Diaghilev beating time to the harsh modernist music of 'Sacre du Printemps'. Again, he cries, cigar sending up swirls of blue smoke. Again, again. And Nijinsky in his black practice clothes must repeat each move over and over.

In climbing, an *enjambement* is a long stride across nothing. And so I have to admit it, drop it in with not-so-disarming casualness – actually, I called in on Kathleen in France, 500 miles, yeah, no big deal, remember we hitched to Antibes that year just for a party? (Who are you trying to kid? I hear your utterly alert and sceptical eyebrows challenge . . .)

To divert myself from the sick pit of nausea in my stomach, read of Nijinsky's arrest in Budapest on charges of espionage, a story about as surreal as I feel:

> 'The matter is very serious, M. Nijinsky. We are advised by patriotic people that you take long walks around the city. And now a manuscript is found which looks like mathematics but is not geometry and is not music, so what can it be? We believe it to be the fortifications of Budapest, M. Nijinsky.'

Nijinsky retorts that it is a system of notation of the dance, tells the Chief of Police:

> 'I am a pacifist. I believe in man's brotherhood. I know nothing of your fortifications.'

The Chief of Police isn't convinced.

> 'We believe it to be code, M. Nijinsky. Let me remind you that we are at war with your country.'

Eventually the intercession of N's aristocratic wife Romola and two professors from the university convince the police to drop the charges, and after a few days Nijinsky is released from custody. But, as a sympathetic captain said, with hindsight, perhaps the damage had already been done, perhaps history should see this cruel farce as a contributing factor in N's madness.

The artist stranded in the middle of an incomprehensible war . . . It's savage and touching and affecting, but there's also an irritant in the romanticisation of the victim, of N's very ingenuousness . . .

Wishing I could tear out this eye with which I watch myself and K, wishing I could be not in this pitiless angularity of ice-slopes but on the other side of some two-way mirror, on the other side in that calm soft darkness where two merge as one.

Why should I kill myself over you, what do I get out of this anyway except a few laughs and a good lay . . . OK, so I got over that feeling I had by the river and struggled back to normal to have you say this morning in the middle of your parting hurt, I love you – you say you said 'ridiculously', so why did I hear and would swear to have heard 'madly, wildly? Your instincts had always kept back the word before, its noticeable absence a hole in my skin I knew I couldn't ask to be filled. I can't remember now – your having said it is blotting everything else out – but I think I prodded you to say it or hinted or just ached so much to hear it that you had to say it. I hope that you don't regret it now, sitting at the *barrage* in the one o'clock sun; I don't regret it and don't think, hope I can, will use my heart and willpower not to abuse it.

I'm on the train now, north, as you sit there at the river with your poet's thoughts, and my mind goes back to the awful time of leaving. Cars were passing me by on the RN9 out of Paulhan but most filled to overflowing with families as one might expect on Sunday, and the odd single man, or other good prospects like young couples looked at me like I was a freak or painfully ignored me, I could have been a heap of grit at the side of the road. After half an hour of this neglect and building paranoia I decided to head back to Pézenas and try to pick up the *péage* at Béziers, and soon got a ride with a French communist in a beat-up Renault with Solidarity stickers. I'm not at all surprised that I didn't have any luck. I felt on the verge of tears (and still do, but I'm happier now that I can indulge the fatigue accompanying this pain) and must have looked utterly miserable. I knew I'd never get anywhere looking so out of control but it was impossible to concentrate. All I could see was the pain in your eyes and I knew you were trying not to cry. I could only hold you and kiss away the damp salt round your eyes, for every time I kissed your mouth you started to cry. I could only hold you and pray, beg for you somehow to know how I felt because I couldn't say 'love' except obliquely or with disarming matter-of-factness. It was what I meant when talking about last night sitting up with Louise and Geoff – I said how lovely it felt to be there with other people who would see how much I loved you, people with whom I didn't have to conceal it. That was the best I thought I could do, as much as was permitted between us; I could not tell you or ask you if you knew how much I loved you.

I was aggravated – no, I was disappointed and angry, at first, that the train to Paris was going to take eight hours – but now it seems to be flying by, as even eight hours of enforced stasis, eight hours of this effortless, idle motion won't be long enough to resolve my emotions. I wrote some initially, trying to exorcise or capitulate to the power and depth of my four days in the Hérault with Kathleen. The recent experience on this day of parting has become memories which generate painful emotions I would not normally indulge or tolerate or simply be lucky enough to have, and it's new and scary to see them as nurturing elements instead of clinging leeches.

6.50 am. Dawn and Dover. The beginning journey having just touched the edge of England and speeding for London. Me. Stuffing love into my stomach and empty pockets. You. The pink rising light behind me, burning off the morning damp, turning the grey slate sea blue and green. You, still soaking the continent of your feelings in the water of the river, there where the depth of these emotions was a threat to me in a way no river could ever be. I ached loving you, but hating my undeveloped self, hated you. The water, and the knife I didn't use, deadened all that. Until the night and the madness of the *Fête*, you dancing in the street with wild bare brown shoulders and laughing. Then, walking back in the soft dark darkness we were lost, drunk, idiotic, wandering in circles through rows of new bungalows. Avenue Jean-Paul Sartre, the sign said, and we stopped to look at it. You told me how you and Louise had cried on the day Sartre died, half a million people followed his cortège through the streets of Paris, you said, that's how important he was to your generation . . . and I who can cry only for myself – and so often not even that – felt even more strongly than at the river that death was the closest way to get to my life, that the pain of this life without pain was unendurable, terminal . . .

At breakfast Kathleen was clumsy and elated, miscalculating distances, convinced that she had all the space in the world. She dropped knives, she dropped spoons, she wanted to talk about Will, she wanted to draw everyone in. In the cramped kitchen Geoff chuckled at her great energy. 'Fuck me,' he said, 'this holiday's turning us all into teenagers.'

107

Last night she and Will had sat, limp as pensioners, on the stone seat outside the front door. They'd danced till three the night before, and so now it was their turn, they joked, to wave Louise and Geoff off to the Fête, to wait up late and worry. The moon and the church clock hung side by side and yellow; disco music swooned in the distance beyond the spiked maize fields. They'd drunk a good deal, and eaten oysters which Madame Elise's daughter-in-law had brought from the beds at Sète. Will launched into whisky stories, erratic and rambling, while across the street Madame Elise knitted quietly and nodded through the twilight at the lovers. But then Will started to talk about the Australian girl. He had picked her up in the Brasserie Nationale, where foreign climbers went to gossip over steak frites and pression. 'We had a few beers,' he said, 'talked about Sydney.' His voice went on and on, she couldn't stop him. 'She seemed keen enough,' he said, 'but then when it gets to closing time and I'm assuming we're leaving together, lo and behold her bloke appears – ropes, climbing gear, just off the hill.' The street light on the corner came on red and heated to a bluish glow round which moths clamoured. 'I couldn't figure out why she didn't say anything,' he complained. The stone wall of the house was rough against her bare shoulders. She didn't like his mouth. His mouth looked spoilt and mutinous. And then he'd needled her. 'You're not going to tell me you disapprove? I only do it for the affection . . .'

'One-night stands are hardly my department,' she'd snapped. Transfixed, angry, wretchedly moral.

In the end it was Colette who'd rescued her: Colette past fifty but thoroughly besotted. On the bed strewn with dog-eared paperbacks, river sand ran from the pages and trickled down between her breasts. As she read to him, Will raised a hand to brush the sand away, tidying her jealously.

'Oh là là and là là again,' she read. 'Your friend is very proper, believe it. She is in a fine, agreeable mess, and up to her chin, her eyes, and farther than that. Oh, the satanism of tranquil creatures –

and I'm speaking of the kid Maurice. Do you want to know what he is? He's a skunk and a this and a that, and at the same time a chic chap with a satiny hide. That's the mess I'm in . . .'

Louise came in from the bread van, twirling a pain de campagne the size of a lifebelt. At the breakfast table Geoff spread his bread extravagantly and she wagged a finger at him, lecturing. 'In France they eat either jam or butter, they think us Brits are babies.' She tore a piece from the new loaf and smiled at Kathleen. 'So, how were the goodbyes?'

'Wonderful, actually.' She watched Louise spoon apricot jam on to the side of her plate and knew that she was blushing. She would have liked to know what Louise thought of it all – Will, love, the whole glorious folly – but she couldn't bear to ask. Nights and whisky made Louise skittish and lovely, but in the mornings she was always sensible. She stood up, put her plate in the sink, drank more coffee. Then she sat down again, smiling from ear to ear. 'But what did you think, Louise?'

Louise fluttered a hand in the air while she chewed, swallowed. Her intelligent brown eyes weighed Will in the balance. 'Even for his age,' she said carefully, 'he seems young.'

Joanna stood still at the sink. Outside the window it was a dour day, cold enough for cardigans. Two black skateboarders rode past, bumping over the rough waves of the pavement; on the other side of the road an elderly women made slow, laboured progress with an aluminium walking frame.

Sometimes as a child she'd played a game with herself, pretended to be lame, dragged her left leg mournfully behind her, feeling the sympathetic eyes of strangers transform her into paraplegic or polio victim. Only later, when she'd fallen from a vaulting horse and broken that same leg did she realise that sympathy never came free, but had to be paid for in the hard currency of disablement.

Will let out a gruff laugh. 'I said, I saw Kathleen . . .'

'I heard you the first time.' She slit a pea-pod with her thumbnail and stripped the peas cleanly out. Somewhere in her a small voice was ready to cry out for reassurance but a greater caution quelled it. Will's eyes followed her as she dried her hands and set the pot of peas on the cooker. 'So when I met her in the market the plot was already hatched, was it?' She thought of Kathleen's face, so shy and sly, butter wouldn't melt in her mouth. 'Pre-menstrual,' she snorted. 'I'll give her pre-menstrual!'

'Listen . . .'

'Listen *to what?*'

'Oh bugger it.'

She took a bottle of wine from the fridge and began to fiddle with the corkscrew. She imagined them sitting down over a drink, discussing it. For a start, she might ask why he'd had to sneak off like a schoolboy. He knew she didn't mind him having other people, he knew she'd never stop him. If she hadn't been so sure that old scores were being settled here, she could have been very bloody angry indeed. 'Well,' she said, 'I thought something was up.'

Will shot her a look of gratitude. 'I should have known you'd suss it.' Just what he'd wanted her to say. She scowled and stabbed two-pronged fingers at him. His hands went up, palms turned to her, a game.

'I know you too bloody well, that's the trouble.' She threw down the corkscrew in disgust: it didn't work, she kept telling him it didn't.

Will took the bottle from her and wedged it between his knees. 'Wait till the arms go up by themselves, OK?'

'So how was it?' she said brusquely.

The bottle was open now. She watched him twist the corkscrew in reverse to free the cork. He shrugged. 'Fine. She was in a gîte with some friends.'

Outside the window a low car full of black youths swung past, stately, like a hippopotamus, its stereo pounding bass. 'So what about the sex?' Her voice sounded crude, challenging. She was *shaking. Of course, normally, she thought, normally I wouldn't have to ask. She looked at the wine and thought of throwing it and her mind fogged and she hated him.*

Will's shoulders were hunched and his face was hidden from her. At last the cork lay in his palm and he held the bottle out to her, his lips pressed into a miserable smile. 'Look. I just can't talk about it. Not yet, at any rate.'

'Oh, suit yourself!' she shouted, and turned on her heel and fled into the bathroom, slamming the door behind her. There was a stack of lino tiles under the sink, a tin of glue, a Stanley knife for stabbing him with. She ran the shower hot and stripped off her clothes and stood in it with her fists clenched and her face turned up to the spray, waiting for the panic to pass. Will knocked on the door once and she swore at him; if he wanted a fight she'd give him one, he ought to know that well enough by now. Steam condensed on the shower curtains and misted the mirror above the sink. Her mind spun through old grudges, settled on Michel. He never forgave me for that, she thought. Whatever he says.

Memory. Will drunk and grinning and frantic, a monkey swing up onto the top of someone's bay window. Then he'd shinned up a drain pipe, walked along the parapet, four storeys up, as if it were a pavement. They'd been on their way home from a party, back together again after that great love, supposedly the love of her life except that it had lasted exactly two weeks before she'd admitted to herself that it was madness. And she'd come back, if not humbled then sobered, and they'd looked at each other, wry, and Will shrugged, and although she hadn't promised never to leave him again, she hadn't promised to stay forever, somehow that was it, end of Act One, Act Two beginning. If there was hurt or anger Will had kept it to himself, and things had been calmer, closer, until that night and that outburst which seemed to come from nowhere and which Will claimed to have no memory of afterwards. Nothing. Expunged.

'The neighbours called the police,' she told him next day, as he shook his head bemusedly. 'They thought you were a suicide or

something.' He'd run across the rooftops until he reached the flat, and kicked his way in through the skylight. The police had burst into the hall and rushed up the stairs towards him; she could remember their red faces, their adrenalin sweat: how they hated being made fools of. When Will saw them he jumped straight down the stairwell, two flights – God knows he should have broken his neck. Next day when they let him out his face and hands were covered in sticking plaster, and he said the only thing he could remember was her voice on the other side of the cell door, yelling and screaming, demanding his release. The incident had passed into myth long since, to be laughed at with friends over late-night brandies. Whenever the tale was told, Will would listen with the fascinated smile of a child whose mother recounts some forgotten escapade from babyhood. To this day he'd never admitted what she'd suspected then and was convinced of now: that he'd known exactly what he was doing.

When she went back into the kitchen Will was still sitting in the same position. His arm hung over the arm of the chair, the corkscrew dangled from his fingers. He looked up at her, and a reluctant grin spread across his face. 'I wouldn't envy anyone who tried to rival you,' he said.

'Bullshitter!' Joanna turned away to set the table. 'I just hope you know what you're doing.' And then she held up her hand, enough, her last word, finish. He came up behind her and put both arms round her waist, and she leaned back against him. They stood there for a moment, rocking a little, but when Will began to kiss her neck she drew away, her body refusing him; after all, they'd been loving and hating long enough for him to know that some things had to be forgotten, rather than forgiven.

She was on her knees in the bathroom laying lino tiles when Will called her through to watch the nine o'clock news. The cut tiles lay all around her like a puzzle but Will's voice was urgent.

'Look at this, for Christ's sake.' He put his arm round her shoulders and they stood side by side, watching. There had been an accident at an air show in Germany. The planes blossomed out and up in two groups, while one maverick cut away at right angles, but at the bottom of the loop where the planes interlaced the maverick miscalculated by one red exploding microsecond, and now three of the planes fell in rags, spinning, ploughed through the crowds of onlookers. The voice of the commentator was rapt: numbers of dead, injured. Then came the analysts – air safety officers, veteran pilots: again and again the screen filled with the moment of impact. Will's arm on her shoulders was loose and his face was spellbound. Tears of rage rose to her eyes. The footage was perfect, unmarred by camera-shake: a testament to utter professionalism and utter fascination.

'How many times is that?' she cried. 'It's obscene.'

'I guess they're trying to figure out what happened,' Will said defensively.

'They were in at the kill and they can't believe their luck!' She twisted away from him angrily. 'You love it, you men. You just love it!'

Many times since that chance meeting in the market Kathleen had pictured herself running into Joanna on the street, had pictured each road and park and playground between the Square and the long curve of the crescent where Will and Joanna lived. On her way to Louise's that night, she'd jumped on the first bus that had come along, forgetting how near the route would take her. Finding herself suddenly at the end of their street, she'd almost turned back, and would have made a lengthy detour if embarrassment at her cowardice hadn't stopped her. She'd hurried on, imagining her face as bright as a pumpkin: she felt blatant, awful, a hussy. It was impossible to avoid noticing the door numbers, to avoid seeing wrought-iron railings, a tall sycamore, a half-plot of garden where Michaelmas daisies grew untended. There was a glimpse of heavy dark curtains and perhaps – she looked away too quickly to be sure – a chink of light. But having risked this glance the fiction of illicitness grew to such proportions that, if challenged, she would *have been hard put to remember her real (accidental) reason for being there, and would have had to rehearse it in her mind like a terrorist under orders in some foreign city. If her eye had seen nothing to speak of through that slight chink, her heart had filled the gap with visions of the legitimate; from making a pot of tea to balancing a cheque book, the most banal of scenes took on a positively mythological power. For a moment she could hardly breathe. Hitching her small rucksack higher on her shoulder she strode out hard and fast as if to put as much distance as possible between herself and that wicked, empty, envious stranger. Her legs were wooden and walked, but if she'd ever had any notion of a contained self (had she?) it had been scooped cleanly out and was sealed in now, somewhere behind those impenetrable velvet curtains.*

Out on Louise's balcony the evening air was luminous and swelled in her. 'I could just about survive,' mused Louise, 'if I had a regular photography column.'

Kathleen yawned and stretched. She'd hardly been attending at all to Louise's autumn angsts. Freelancing, the shortage of work, the collapse of so many radical outlets. In the summer you could always forget, persuade yourself that you'd get by, but as the nights drew in it was easy to get dragged down in the general malaise.

'Why not just junk it?' Geoff grumbled from the kitchen. 'Get out. Leave the south-east to the estate agents.' His head came round the door. 'Or better still, cede the lot to Argentina . . .'

'Fin de saison,' Louise said ruefully. 'We could always finish off the Cognac.' In other years this would have been a signal to spread out the holiday photographs and gloat over shots of bleached rock and brown skin and all the blue permutations of water. But this year, on their last morning at St Croix, Louise had spilled the entire film out of its canister, exposing it – a blunder she simply couldn't account for, she the professional with years of photo-journalism behind her. For days afterwards her eyes were wide, dark doors accusing herself: how could I? It's just appalling. On the boat after too many brandies she had even morbidly declared it a bad omen.

Kathleen and Geoff had teased her out of it, but it was sad, all the same, to lose these images of Will, images whose absence tantalised by leaving her free to imagine how many questions they might have answered.

High up in a tower block someone was playing an electric guitar. She put her feet up on the balcony rail and let the light lift her out beyond herself to an optimism which would last at least till the sun set and the first Septembery mists rose from nowhere to hang over the rooftops and the brittle, still leaves of the trees. This winter, she decided, I'll definitely put my own house in order.

Bank Holiday pubs wedged their doors open. Walking by, she wondered if after all she was a survivor. In the park starlings ate elderberries and the circus had arrived. She saw the ringmaster off-duty in bathing trunks, socks, plus these black immaculate eyebrows hamming up his face. Somehow this image of the ringmaster compounded the sensation of being kept hostage: lady in a box bright as shellac to be sawn in two while all the white horses pawed circles in the sawdust. At Will's pleasure and only at his pleasure he would come and open the lid and fluff up her skirts and play with her. The image filled her with a deathly excitement which she couldn't associate with love. The possibility of phoning – which no one had actually vetoed – crossed her mind more than once, but dread kept the box tight shut. She moped and paced and, unable to work, was drawn to the windows. They were dusty and streaked and she cleaned them fiercely, hoping to gain a clear view on the future. The twentieth car, she told herself, the twentieth car to enter the Square will be blue and yours. This wasn't a good idea, she knew. This way lay madness. But again and again she found herself at the window, counting and cheating.

Part Three

The Sea of Ice

– You take a train to Geneva, and then a narrow gauge to Chamonix, and then you cross over to the Montenvers, the mountain railway which goes up to 7,000 feet. Then, if you can, you climb another 2,000 feet up the Mer de Glace, and another 2,000 feet up zigzag paths and fixed iron ladders in the rock, past snow banks pitted with marmot tracks, and behind you is the Charmoz and before you is the Dru, and there's a solid stone refuge perched high above the glacier, a helicopter pad, and then there's no one.

–

– Maybe it doesn't matter what really happened, and if the trajectory of the love story is irresistible, you should give in to it, go blindly. It's like a joke Terry and I had when we used to go hillwalking. We'd hope terribly for good weather but never mention it in case the Narrator overheard. Then of course it would rain, and we'd say, OK, sorry, we cheated. And then there would be that relief, acceptance, giving in: all right, we'll take whatever the Narrator serves up, be it hail or sleet or thunder. And when you think that way you start to laugh, silly, light-hearted, because you've made yourself the right size; puny, but partaking in grandness, and a marvellous in-tune feeling. You yield, you don't resist, and then you have an appetite for every light and shade and gale in the face, or even being beaten and retreating. I can't tell you what a release it is to recognise that we only ever have the frailest control over our lives, the smallest margin of free will. It's like being in a state of grace.

*

I had keys cut for Will, when he showed me what he'd written. The gift of myself, space, availability, dropped into his palm; I had keys cut and I stood in the ironmongers picturing his pleasure; reluctance and eagerness clashing in laughter because I knew it was a risk I was meant to take, and I accepted it. Rain slashed at the shop window, the cutting wheel whined; there were sparks. He could come in and go out of me as he pleased, fall into my arms with a sigh and make love, this is how I imagined it. I was the white wool of his mother's arms and the underneath bleed of his dreams, the promise that this time he could have everything, and no one would set up boundaries beyond which he couldn't venture, limitations on what he could have. Because I had to give myself away, once and for all I had to. Disregarding all instincts which told me that someone must say no to children, show them a resistance, a law outside and beyond them (a law Joanna in her wisdom always knew how to uphold). For don't you think that if promises are too all-encompassing they can reactivate childhood fantasies of omnipotence?

You say that one construction I may have made is this: if I could have surrendered utterly to my mother – if I could have made myself passive, quiet, adoring, obedient – I might finally have won her. Magic thinking. I wouldn't have, of course.

Maybe I was hell-bent on making a sacrifice of myself but I still don't see how you can have love, desire, without that kind of surrender.

Maybe it doesn't matter what really happened, if the trajectory of the love story is irresistible.

And then Will came into the bathroom where I was washing my face and announced that he was going back to Chamonix. I felt immediately half dead, but didn't throw any tantrums, didn't even imagine my wrists cut and bleeding down the sink, for we'd agreed early on that no one in this drama was going to kill themselves, we were pretty strong, all honed and bent on survival. The glass of the bathroom window was dimpled and opaque, and behind it was a sunset, birds. The sound of the water running was very loud. 'I could come,' I said. 'I could come to Chamonix.' At that moment I didn't care if he refused me, I didn't care if I ruined everything as long as I tore up that internal rule book which says that if you ask for something from a man you'll certainly never get it. As long as I wanted, as long as I asked. I made a bold face in the mirror. I said that I wouldn't be a bother, I was a fair hillwalker, just wait and see. In the mirror Will shook his head and laughed and shook his head again. 'I'd give a lot to see you taking on the climbing fraternity in the Bar Nash,' he said. Tilting his head back and pinching his eyelids between finger and thumb, he put in his contact lenses and left without saying yes.

Next day he came in silently with his new keys, startling me. 'Am I coming then?' I asked. Yes, he said, so low that I could hardly hear him. Hectic, I recited the names, all the lovely names. The Aiguille Noire, the Mer de Glace, the Valleé Blanche, until his smile grew stiff and wounded. He took my hand jealously and slipped it inside his shirt against his chest. 'I feel like a bloody travel agent,' he complained. 'It's me you're supposed to love, not the damn mountains.'

He was positively pouting, and we both laughed. He opened my shirt and started to kiss my breasts. There was no time to make love but couldn't we do it anyway, do it quickly? I hurried my clothes off; beggars can't be choosers, I almost said, and of course it was too fast, almost sensationless, both of us speeding from coffee and whisky. I held him, I watched him sweat and sigh and say beautiful under his breath. Afterwards he stretched out his arm with its long blue veins and gazed at it in a trance. 'I knew I couldn't go without fucking,' he said. 'I wonder why?'

'The time!' I said. I reached for my watch but he stopped me.

'I don't want to know.' Then he was dressed and gone,

leaving me with instructions, lists of everything I would need – thermal underwear, boots, sweaters; above 6,000 feet, he said, when you stopped walking, the cold was punishing.

Next day was a day of nerves and novocaine, and the whole idea seemed like folly. 'It'll be wonderful,' Louise said. 'I think you'll be bitten by the bug.' We sat on her balcony looking at the leafless pear tree, the roses, tired and few. Overhead grey clouds ran north-south, and dust and bus tickets blew about the streets. The city looked impoverished, beaten down, and more than ever I wanted to leave it, but on the brink of leaving I cringed back, full of the sort of vertigo that Will the American would never understand. Louise plied me with questions, but I heard my voice come dully from a frozen mouth. I don't know what response I'd expected – that mockery, perhaps, that stems from envy. 'I keep sounding so *serious*,' I apologised. 'I don't meant to sound so *serious*.' By this time I was nearly in tears. 'Just tell me I can *do* it,' I pleaded.

Can I tell you why I'm frightened? Because in the fantasy *cul de sac* someone always has to die. I dreamed of my mother, she'd taken up residence in my flat. Ill, bedridden, she called me back indoors to care for her, this was my duty – but outside the snow swept transversely through the streets, piling up against the windward gables of houses, and under the lamplights a streak of pavement had been polished to fine gleaming ice for sliding.

I see/don't want to see what writing will reveal: an attack on my mother? A step out and forward? A bid to seduce, to steal Daddy away?

At the same time it feels like an attack on Daddy. I take his pen/penis from him, I take what I need, but if I do he could be left without defence, disarmed. I see and don't want to see that if he can't defend himself he can't protect me either, he goes down, he holds on to the toppling hedge, he can't hold on, can't stay alive, can't hold on to my hand.

Can I tell you why I'm frightened?

Aiguille Verte – For Kathy

I don't know what I think of mountains. Convenient cracks from which to take a running belay on my long slings, they surround me nudgingly, such big blocks, twisted, but the rocks are too heavily iced and hammered and they hurt you, fingers, sometimes you live solely on your wits and knees, they rough you up if you force the passage. Gloves are on if you care to climb in them, axes alternately bite the cold and can kill you then dangle, and the ice is variously fairytale on a steep V groove which bars my way.

Last August it was hot and perfect yet Jim and Sheila were gripped or stripped. Two friends who sang Cole Porter and looked alike, and that delicate love for their cats. Jim was straight and firm and this delicate mixed climbing absorbed him; he wore purple fleecy tights we roared at. However now they are dead friends, a vital hour has slipped away leaving their skulls empty as dead horses. The rope had tangled round Sheila's neck on the upper ice-field, the *agent* had advised me not to lift the white sheet and look.

They would have seen dawn moving in from the left over the Grandes Jorasses, the endless pink string of traverses wavering under the Aiguille Sans Nom, the original Charlet-Devouasseoux route of 1928. The sun kissing them years later as they unwrapped their sandwiches and removed their crampons on a whim of safety, maybe they thought of their cats at home and well looked after, black fluffy balls along their memory of the route.

Sheila always said that Jim her lover looked like a cat, and how momentarily maybe, but only momentarily, she doubted her choice, looking bruised and soft and inbrooding as she looked at him suddenly through a barrier. Maybe safe at that summit she convinced herself that the correct finish was to joke at him and push him flying face down in the snow like children, forgetting the snow-ice slope just visible on the right, forgetting the fact that you can't fly anywhere, there are no birds to lead you out on to the Sans Nom *arête*.

This is the *voie normale* on the Nant Blanc face, so I stick with vague memory and keep the sun on my right like an eyepatch which makes motes dance on my retina, endlessly tacking up hard ice-slopes. A cone of snow at the foot of a gully collapses under my weight, a drama of small but magnificent isolation enacted under my left boot, and I think of Sheila's hair veneered with granulated snow; as the Aiguille Sans Nom at 3982 m lowers by infinitesimal degrees I see her kneel up and kiss him, her disobedient joints suddenly pins and needles under her, and my calves sing out in a crescendo of pain as I reach the rocks and grasp the friendly flakes and spikes which clutter the *arête*. It hardly bears thinking about but my ragged mind, exhausted, thinks it anyway, although I don't know or want to how maybe she flailed and sent him roped and sliding, how she dug in her impotent cramponless heels while the surface mat of snow gave out glorious ease and security but slipped all the same and then surely it was all over and she followed him. First and foremost I hope for a more viable alternative finish, although we're friends in this and every dawn I dearly wish for protection, knowing we must first cross under the seracs to reach a comfortably angled exit and race up all triumphant to the sunlight summit vista.

– Chamonix. Shops full of cuckoo clocks, carved wooden edelweiss, chamois skins. I had travelled all night. Beside me on the coach a shy nun in grey nibbled hazelnuts and fingered a bus timetable. In the dawn we left the maize fields and vineyards of the plain and began to climb. The limestone escarpments which bordered the valley were pale breathtaking towers at first light; later, as we climbed higher and glimpsed the blue-white ridges up ahead, they faded to a memory of foothills. The gorges grew deeper and the rivers yellower, their silty torrents gushing in deep clefts far below the spanning bridges. It was a fast road; as if sucked on some funnelling updraught, the traffic streamed on, up towards the high mountains. Most of the passengers had left the coach at Geneva and there were only a handful of us now, mostly climbers with unlaced boots and crampons strapped on top of their rucksacks. Two Yorkshiremen pored over *Le Monde*, trying to decipher the weather map. An anti-cyclone moving across France from the west, a cold front easing towards Austria: bad in the Alps but clearing. They looked at me doubtfully when I asked about the Mer de Glace. No, they said, it was really far too dangerous for beginners.

Darkness of a tunnel, and then we swooped round a bend into full sunlight. Ahead lay a narrow valley, wooded on the lower slopes; faint spidery lines of cableways festooned the steep sides.

'*Voilè le Mont Blanc*,' the driver said, but I couldn't see it. For that, you have to lie along your seat or crouch down in the aisle, you have to go down on your knees to crane up at the white dome of the summit and the spindly towers which rim the Massif. I muttered and marvelled with the others, but I was tired, frightened, all romance leached out of me. All I could see was that it was cold, and beautiful, and miles above me.

There was no sign of Will in the square. I asked directions: '*Excusez-moi, madame, où est la Brasserie Nationale?*' Will would have left a note, surely, to tell me how to get to the campsite. There were new hotels, five or six storeys, but the mountains made everything minute. I walked through a shopping arcade, past crêperies, curio shops, Le Drugstore. In a small *place* by a narrow torrenting river a statue of a mountain guide pointed up at the great blue mushroom of Mont Blanc.

The Brasserie Nationale was smaller than I'd expected, tucked away in a narrow street behind the *poste*, and quieter. The walls were washed yellow; there were plain black Formica tables, and in the corner two weathered old men who could have been guides played a slow game of chess. On a baize noticeboard near the door, messages were pinned.

'Phil Kemp. We're camped up at Snell's Field. Your gear is sodden but safe.'

'Don the Dosser. Walt's taking another shot at the Peigne, thought I'd go along for the ride. Beer on you Saturday if we make it. Cheers, Charlie.'

Behind the bar counter two pale girls were watching me. I ordered hot chocolate and asked in bad French innocent of subjunctives, *Si quelqu'un m'a laissé une lettre*, it will be here? *Oui, madame*, they shrugged. *Bien sûr*. I was shivering. I meant a message, not a letter. Letters were what Will wrote to Joanna before a serious climb and left out plainly for posting. Letters meant endings, a last summing up. I didn't want a letter at all. I went downstairs to the *toilettes* and leaned against the wall. I was tired of trying not to tremble and tired of eyes on me and perhaps if I did ordinary things – cleaning my teeth, putting on mascara – an ordinary explanation would pretty soon present itself.

There was a film I saw once – I don't recall the name – in which the body of a *guide de montagne* is recovered from a crevasse fifty years on. He had been in the Resistance, ferrying refugees across the Alps into Switzerland; as the years passed, the frozen body was carried down from the high mountains inch by inch, at the painful crawl of the glacier. In the village square doors open and mourners with long memories come out to pay their respects. Among them is an old woman who loved the

126

guide, who had been his fiancée all those years ago. Although this incident was only a sub-plot in counterpoint to a main narrative, it's all been retained. The film as a whole has faded and I'm left with that close-up of the ancient face, expressionless, bent over the cruelly and fabulously preserved young one.

We flew into each other's arms . . .

This is how I couldn't help imagining it, beforehand. And so, long afterwards, this is the memory which insists: the relief from panic and waiting, all obstacles removed. Two birds in blue space, easy. Needless to say, under the dream-image was a tiled floor slippery from wet boots, and stray coffee cups, and the jutting edges of tables . . . When I came upstairs I saw someone from the back, leaning over the bar, asking something; then, in three-quarter profile, a youth with gangly brown legs. When he turned fully – unfamiliar blue anorak – I shivered, recognising that this face which was so young was certainly his. As we moved clumsily towards each other our voices flew ahead of us, full of accusations: where did you wait? Which street did you walk down? We were laughing but in our secret selves under the coats we were full of rage, like children who in the mid-stream of welcome thump little fists against their mother.

Against my cheek the material of his anorak was slippery and inhospitable. I remembered what he'd said on the telephone: I'm desperate for company, he'd said, and I'd replied brightly, very brightly, Company's coming. Taking on the plural with a laugh, hoping that way to hide my suddenly sole stark possessive self.

The chess players were staring now, and Will drew back. Taking my hand he hurried me out of the bar and led me through the streets with stiff quick steps, into the railway station, across tracks labelled *Danger de Mort*, to the edge of a main road where traffic seethed and signposts shouted ITALIE, SUISSE, TUNNEL MONT-BLANC. On the other side of the road was a birch grove, firs straggling up a steepening mountainside. There was a blue tent pitched under a rowan tree, a low table and bench made from planks and cut logs.

'My home,' said Will, grinning at me intently. A plastic mug filled with dog daisies sat in the centre of the table. I saw at once that a) this was for me, and b) he felt it was far from adequate. 'Strictly *sauvage*. Jean-Yves says the police cleared it a fortnight ago. The way we figure it, they won't be back so soon.' At the far end of the clearing, beyond a patch of wild raspberry bushes, I could see a green patched tent. 'He's OK,' said Will. 'A bit weird, I guess.'

I rested my head on his shoulder. There was a fresh damp smell of firs. I was waiting, I was light-headed. I'm here, I thought, wondering what I was waiting for.

'Someone sent him a rose, a red rose in a plastic box.' Will's voice was abstracted, a million miles away. 'He took it to the café with him and sat it on the table, plain as day. So he's reading and every so often he picks up this rose and looks at it, as if he wants me to ask who sent it, you know?'

'So why didn't you?'

Will tucked his hands into his sleeves and shivered and stared at me, a narrow shy distancing stare which fought recognition. 'Why didn't I what?' On the north side of the valley, just below a line of toothed peaks, a small orange cable car inched upwards. There was a noise in the undergrowth, a faint crack of twigs. Then someone started whistling, and Will took himself away from me by six inches, leaving a cold gap. 'He's coming back.'

Jean-Yves had a coiled rope over his shoulder and a fresh *baguette* under his arm. '*Salud*,' he said gravely. When he shook my hand he left chalk dust on my palm. 'Rock-climbing,' he apologised, brushing himself down with small fussy strokes. 'I have read your book, Will has given it to me.' He stood there, nodding at me. 'It is very good, I think.'

'*Merci*,' I said. 'Thank you.' When he smiled I could see that something was wrong with his face, a skin-graft, perhaps: his right eyelid crinkled normally but the skin at the corner of the left eye tugged downwards, shiny and taut.

'You will climb here in Chamonix?'

'Oh, I don't think so.' I glanced quickly at Will. The thin fanatical face intimidated me. I'd seen faces like that in Ireland and I reckoned I had a fair idea what climbing with Jean-Yves would involve.

'I thought I'd take Kathleen up to some of the huts,' Will said.

'I'm just a hillwaker,' I said. 'A complete amateur.'

'*Nous sommes tous amateurs*,' Jean-Yves corrected. '*C'est seulement l'armeé qui sont professionels. Tu as compris?*'

'*Oui*,' I said meekly, reproved.

'*Bon. D'accord.*' Jean-Yves turned to go. 'Enjoy it.'

'*Oui*,' I said again, although I couldn't imagine Jean-Yves enjoying anything. I waited for Will's arm to go round me. 'Hey,' I complained, 'don't mountaineers cuddle, then?'

Will shrugged, defensive. 'Well, you don't want to flaunt it, do you.'

'Oh my,' I said, and started to laugh. Will covered his eyes with his hand for a moment, then he lifted his hand like a visor and peered at me. 'You're like a dream in this place, I still can't believe it!'

I folded his hand in mine and nodded at it. Dimly I saw the spiked points of crampons stacked under the tent flap, an ice-axe with a bright red wrist sling. Blood ran in my arms, my legs, my own good pulsing blood. I'd forgotten the cold, I would probably never be cold again. 'You could always try kissing me,' I said.

– Yes. Empty in. That was the exact sensation. That feeling of clasping your skin tight around you like a jacket with a broken zip.

The cable car jolted upwards, swaying on its rigging. All

around me were perspex windows. Rigid, I stared straight ahead, into the soft, still green lower shoulder of the mountain, the safest place. Not back across the valley where Will was pointing, where that bowl of whitening space invited me to pour myself into it.

'Look at the new snow on the Aiguilles Rouges,' Will exclaimed. 'It's that *mauvais temps* I told you about.'

The storm had come the night before I arrived, punishing thunder rocking the roots of the valley, white lightning, he said, pinning him to the floor of his tent. That night, he told me, he'd dreamt that his father was buggering him, angrily, silently; suffering under him, he couldn't work out what on earth he had done to deserve such punishment. 'So what do you make of that?' he'd demanded, with such a crafty, hungry look that it was hard not to smile at all the insights he expected of me. But now, well, now these underneath streams were quite forgotten, now he was high and dry and headed for the clean top of the world. The pressure of his hand turning me to admire the sheer face of the Index, which he had soloed some weeks before, and I was shaking my head, feeling my lips dried out and gumming together, and then the cable car, passing a pylon, dipped like a swingboat, and I fell against his chest, my hands crabbing at him.

A hard grip. A chin clamped on top of my head. A 'Hey there'. Speechless, I nodded him away. I'll be all right. Just getting used to it. Soon I'll stand loose-legged as you, and crane like you, and we'll both shine as we rise. Just watch me.

At the first ski-station the summer slopes were greasy and rutted, and the café was closed. I had to agree that it wasn't worth stopping. I followed Will on to the connecting cable car and held my breath again as we rose, juddering, over tumbled moraines and the browned snout-ice of the glacier to 11,000 feet, where I had certainly never been.

'Bad conditions,' Will frowned, as we stepped out on to the concrete platform: the snow looked new and deep, and the wind was cutting. The téléférique station was built on a jutting high rock, so that to reach the snow-field we had to descend an ice-crusted iron ladder. At the bottom, in slight shelter, Will pulled extra clothing from his rucksack and, without a word, began to dress me. His blue fisherman's sweater went darkly over my head (smell of oiled wool, smell of candle grease and paraffin from the camp stove), his red fibre-pile waistcoat was zipped up to my neck, tight and tickling under my chin, my hair petted out over the high collar . . . I stuck my arms out straight like a scarecrow and submitted to – oh, fittings for a first party dress, the cold slide of taffeta, the rasp of towels after the bath . . . a voluminous duvet jacket followed (snap of studs one by one all the way from hip to throat, enclosing me), mittens, a stupidly huge balaclava. I took a few steps in the cumbersome mountain boots, flipping my hands in the outsize gloves, a pantomime, but instead of laughing he shook his head and drew me back, and now he was wrapping my waist with webbing slings, clipping karabiners on, knotting rope through the clips and coiling it over my shoulder, until at last he patted my cheek, kissed my cheek, it was done, I was a doll, and it was almost an affront, that pleased fatherly smile of his, turning the tables on me.

I twisted away to squint up at the slope. A beginner's climb, he'd said. Conjuring up forested tracks, some rock scrambling, perhaps: a chance to show him that I was agile and attuned to the land as an infant to its mother. Perhaps this is what I'd been trying to tell him on that silver river day at St Croix, when I'd talked about essences and expected him to laugh at me. But of course he had not; instead, his racked regretful frown had told me just how seriously I was admired . . . but now, staring up and up, I saw nothing that was benign. Saw instead a snow land where air and all that falls from it was in the ascendancy. Saw white slopes wind-moulded to bird shapes, blue wings of ice-ridges, folded overhangs insubstantial as cloud banks. Where earth took over, and rock spires forced their way

131

through the snow, they were spiked like beaks, their sharp angles shocking. I thought of weapons, of missiles, and suddenly I was angry, believing that I'd understood something about Will, and climbing, and masculinity.

'Is it because it's so hostile? Because you can only conquer it? Is that why?'

Will looked up from strapping on my crampons. 'Hostile? You have to calculate the odds, sure.' For a second his face faltered; he looked very young. He swept an impatient arm towards the mountain. 'But Christ. Look at it. Don't you find it absolutely beautiful?'

I hunched my shoulders against him and all his foreign worlds. Beautiful? Oh, beautiful it was, certainly – if you had a death wish. And here I was, trussed like a chicken, clumsy, defenceless against it.

Will had finished with my crampons now, and he stood up. 'Practise walking,' he said, 'this altitude takes a bit of getting used to.'

I remembered, now, that Will had mentioned the possibility of dizziness, mood swings, the weird effects of the thinner air. In the high Himalayas ghosts and visions were so common-place that no climber doubted them. Nor did I, if it came to that. When the body was fragile and in question, I could imagine how the spirit, sensing the shutters which had been left open, might move closer. At those heights, Will said, even the British army wore prayer scarves: at 7,000 metres, 8,000. But at 11,000 feet? I scowled back at him. Was he trying to say that it was altitude alone which was unravelling me? We were linked by rope now, and I wished I had never come, for it was quite plain that he had only brought me here to make a fool of me. This man. This place. That black hawk flying a steep diagonal off rocks like scissor points. All paring me down to a mere dunce.

I marched a few yards up an ice hillock, until the rope stopped me, and stood with my back to a great howl of wind, watching him. He was going through the same tedious performance with his own equipment now: careful crouch in the snow to adjust his crampons without soaking the knees of his salopettes; each strap hauled tight, each end tucked away; the rope coiled, uncoiled, coiled again. He had red ears, raw hands, and a drip on his nose. I shook my head grudgingly. I had to admit he was patient.

'Slow,' he instructed as we started up the slope. 'Plant each foot firmly.' I saw that he intended to teach me the technicalities whether or not I wanted to learn them; I could also see that he was serious. I fought an urge to joke, romp, fool around in the ridiculous rope and tackle. Practice makes perfect, I thought, resigning myself. I plodded on, following in the footsteps of previous climbers, as Will had told me to: that way, he said, there was less risk of stumbling into concealed crevasses. Slow, sweating, ungainly, I lanced with the shaft of my ice-axe for balance; my face stung from the spindrift which came at me in flurries. 150 metres of this to zigzag up, and above that, in cloud, 150 metres more, or so Will had said, and I had no reason to doubt it, although I could see nothing, for even through sunglasses the whiteness of the snow was blinding; but if Will believed I could do this extraordinary thing, then evidently I could do it.

Ten minutes later I felt a strange ache in my right hand, the hand which held the ice-axe. It felt like a bad rheumatism, and when I took off my glove the skin was a bruised colour. I called Will back. 'Is it frostbite?' I asked very humbly.

Will laughed and chafed it. 'Frost nip. But we should stop it before it gets worse.' He stripped off his mittens and began to chafe the hand roughly, blowing on it. Rub rub rub, he went, Daddy making it better, and I swam into him, and we were kissing mad inside each other's mouths again, the hottest place. Red haze under my eyelids, salty drips from our cold noses mingling. When I opened my eyes again, over his shoulder was so blue.

133

At the edge of a snow ridge Will's piss left steaming yellow holes: beyond the edge was nothing, was cloud. 'There's a *bergschrund* on the left, so keep to the crest.' His voice was matter of fact. I looked down and saw a blue slash which fell away into darkness; ahead of us the crest of the ridge ended in a steep corridor of ice which rose up into the mist. 'We have to climb the couloir,' Will said, 'but it's only twenty metres and not sheer.' His smile was encouraging or challenging, I wasn't sure which. 'Just give me five minutes to get a belay fixed.' Then he was off up the cliff of ice, cat-footing on the front points of his crampons, a tail of rope dangling behind him.

I waited, while the white mist soaked in and in. He had vanished into cloud, cloud which denied all sound except a lonely whine in my ears. I stamped my feet and beat myself with my arms to keep warm. So small, I thought in a burst of childishness, and not a bit brave, and what if he'd gone forever? I felt like crying, a sudden fierce despair at the expectations he had of me.

A shout. Action. Was I ready?

Nothing for it, then. One hand grips the ice-hammer, the other swings the ice-axe. Batter with the right front point. Again. It's hard as hell, not ice at all, surely: pick of the axe won't bite, it's hopeless.

'Scamble up,' Will yelled. 'Do it any old how. I'm pulling you.'

The rope tightened round my waist. Banged again, wildly: axe hammer left crampon right crampon. I swallowed at the thin air but the lungs were starving, blood and muscles too. I was a teddy bear bundle without agility shouting at the dank cloud, that inbetween element neither water nor air, and wasn't this what drowning would be, this scarcity, the puddling straggled hair floating into the eyes, the scourged hot effortful lungs? I was all hurry hurry before the slight energy ran out, hating that grace and grip of his, hating also the taut rope which encumbered me, dragging me flat against the wall when what I wanted was space and swing.

'Hang on,' Will cried, 'I'm taking a picture.'

So he can see me, then, coming up like a crab? Don't think about it. Spear with the pick, drag up the heavy body, rest, breathe, spear again.

A heave of the rope and congratulations, I'm belly-flopping at the top of the couloir. 'Not bad for a beginner,' Will laughed, and then I was rolling over in the snow beside him, a snow now blinding blue, for suddenly we were out of cloud and looking down on it. No longer watery, it was a wedge, lit white and dry-looking, an insulating roof over the valley. Only the summit of Mont Blanc pierced this upper atmosphere which was entirely mine, oh, and I was fizzing now, pulse racing as the heart tried to work with too much space, too little air, I'm drenched in blue all through, I don't know who I am . . . I looked over at Will, who was nodding, damn him, like some old sage. 'Good enough for you?' he grinned against the starched white snow and the impeccable sky, and I was dancing, dancing. . . .

– It's now, though, when they're kissing and pulling at each other's clothes, seeking entry, that Will becomes convinced that he's being watched. Turning away from Kathleen he stares blankly over his shoulder. He can see them as if framed by a window. He hears the clear scratch scratch of a pen moving across a page. He is convinced that Nijinsky is watching them, and that the diagrams he's working on are choreographic notations of their every move.

   – *Will is convinced or Kathleen is convinced?*

   – Will, definitely. Because he wanted to be discovered. Seen. Caught out. Otherwise why would he leave pages of his note-book lying around for Joanna to discover, in London, in the desk drawer, as she searches for file-cards? This part is true, this is what he did, this is what happened.

– And Kathleen? Does she want to be seen? Or to watch?

–

– Perhaps there has to be some kind of interruption, before the excitement becomes too intense?

–

–

– I can only imagine it as a film. Joanna glances idly at the dislodged pages. Then she stares. The camera could snoop here, could decipher a few sentences, but this would only replicate what we already know from the journal about Will, and in any case we can tell from Joanna's expression that the subject is Kathleen. It's night, she's reading by the light of an anglepoise lamp, she's aghast.

And now on the illegal campsite in the birch grove it's night too, and Jean-Yves sits in the mouth of his tent, reading by the light of his head-torch, the red rose beside him in its plastic box.

On the other side of the grove, beyond the raspberry bushes and spiders' webs a small brass lamp illumines the low trestle where Will and Kathleen are. The shadows of the birch trees swerve sideways as Will picks up the lamp and shows Kathleen an inscription engraved on a metal strip set into the base. We would need a close-up to see that the inscription reads: William Ryan, Eiger North Face, 1985. We would hear Will tell Kathleen that his parents gave the lamp to him, and Kathleen's exclamation: 'You never told me.' And Will's response, halting. 'I couldn't before.'

Tilting the lamp in his hands, he talks in a low voice, to make sure Jean-Yves can't hear, to make sure he isn't boasting.

'We walked around for a week, just trying to pluck up the courage. Checking the Météo, Eiger-watching. Shitting ourselves. Then in the end we kind of looked at each other and said, What the hell, let's give it a go.' (He laughs before continuing.) 'I wrote a dozen postcards and left them at the campsite with instructions to send them if we didn't make it. Guess I really thought it was all up. But yeah. Three days of it. Two nights hanging in our harnesses. It's what you'd call a fairly committing route . . .'

And now, in London, Joanna holds a glass of whisky in one hand and the telephone receiver in the other. What I haven't said so far is that Joanna drinks, periodically she hits the bottle, loses control, drinks half a litre of spirits at one sitting and becomes confident, belligerent, it's her one obvious weakness. Anyway, in Kathleen's empty flat the telephone rings and rings – at this point, remember, Joanna has no idea that Kathleen is in Chamonix with Will, no idea at all. On the wall above the desk we're seeing familiar images; the postcards, the photograph of Kathleen with her father in the Galway hills. The telephone stops ringing, leaving an abrupt silence in the empty room, but the image of the father is sustained, and there'll be a poem now, Kathleen's voice in the birch grove, stumblingly reciting; it'll be Goethe.

> Distance does not make you falter
> now, arriving in magic, flying –
> and finally, insane for the light,
> you are the butterfly and you are gone.

> And so long as you have not experienced
> this: to die, and so to grow,
> you are only a troubled guest
> on this dark earth.

Cut now to the dark needle peak of the Aiguille du Midi silhouetted against stars, the tumbled seracs of the Glacier des Bossons, the summit of Mont Blanc lit blue by moonlight.

Night surrounds the campsite, blotting out the town and its hotels, its ski-lifts, shop windows, pottery beer steins, alpenstocks – a fiercely selective vision. In the same way, by torchlight and with the covers over my head, I could sometimes imagine that downstairs there was no angry mother knitting in the kitchen, and outside there was no Belfast, no borderline, no guns, no gable ends painted with dreary effigies of King Billy on his cross-eyed horse . . . Anyway, for the moment Kathleen has forgotten that earlier she was afraid, and that tomorrow she may well be afraid again, high on the rutted ice of the Mer de Glace . . . as she and Will sit silently in the pool of lamplight, as moths flutter, as Will puts his head in his hands, as she rests her fingers gently on the back of his neck . . .

Cut now to London, to Will and Joanna's flat, where Joanna wrenches one of Kathleen's books from the shelf and rips it up, tears the pages from the spine, tears them in half, tears the halves to shreds and throws them into the air, the air full of falling white scraps. This is the bad movie, the clichéd image – a slow motion shower, fabulous as ticker tape. Actually I'm convinced that even when furious, Joanna would be icy, focussed, deliberate. Never helpless. This, yes, I'm sure of.

    – *But must Joanna cut in here? Interrupt? Can't you stay with the love story, with Will and Kathleen happy in the lamplight with the moon high over the Aiguilles?*

    – I'm afraid.

    –

    – It makes me afraid. All the things I yearn for scare me.

    –

    – Space, silence.

    – *Love?*

    – The télécabine was all windows, yet tiny. At the same time constricting and exposing. How can I convey to you the sensation of the valley floor falling away, the grunt and grind of the tackle overhead, the stricken tightness in the diaphragm as all your great dark feelings rise up but mustn't, because it isn't safe, because the cabine is too small, too fragile to hold them?

– The mother who can't contain?

– It'll fall apart, shards of metal and perspex. I remember how my glacier goggles filled up with tears, how humiliating it was. Everything around me was so huge and beautiful – the twisted spire of the Blaitière, the white fang of the Dent du Crocodile – but the heart smelled danger, a shadow from the deep past, if I let myself swell to take it in, all at once. Now I see that I can only grow bigger slowly, stretch in small stages. I need to climb at my own pace on my own feet, I need ground to stand on, ground from which to look around, absorb, make things particular and familiar. A close focus first, then, slowly, the distance, the gradual widening of the shutter to infinity. I see it now, but then, no, I didn't know this, I only knew that I couldn't give myself to that sweep of space and I felt . . . I began to feel . . . I looked at Will and felt myself a failure.

– In Will's eyes? Or your father's?

– I wanted him.

– But you never felt entitled to . . .

– I shouldn't . . .

– Have him?

– It's autumn. Herbs shiver in the pots on the windowsill. I feel the cold, the decay. There'll be snow showers on the hills around Belfast already.

– But if you did *have him?*

– We were like bees. So intimate, buzzing.

– *With alarm?*

– I always knew we didn't have long. I took my notebook to the Alps, you know. I made notes, I said it was my insurance policy, in case he left me.

– *You believe something will always interrupt your happiness.*

– Mother in the rug, in the back of the car. She might pretend to approve, smile at us, so close in the front, she might pretend to congratulate, like when my periods came: 'You're a young lady,' she said. And when I asked if I was pretty she said, 'Every young girl with clean hair is pretty.' Non-specific. All I was that was specific was a specific fly in the ointment, trouble, flotsam, drifted up on her shore. I'm pretty sure she must have fought her guilt, probably took it to confession all the time – this is what I imagine: I am trying to be a Christian mother and I hate my daughter. To her I meant illness, being out of action. I don't know if I mean this word action literally – in terms of her youth, Republicanism, what she might have been doing when I came along. But whatever it was, she'd repudiated it. Bunch of cowboys, she'd hiss, anger kept low over the cooker. Mutton bones boiling with that dreadful depressing smell. And to me it meant: stop admiring him, stop aping, stop idealising, *stop taking him away.* Being so close meant taking him away. My mother simply needed so much attention but I think it would have killed her to ask for it. Probably he adored her but just couldn't show it, like so many men. And anyway his own trajectory was too absorbing – stories, romance, bitterness at the English, organising, there wasn't a single community pie he didn't have his finger in, he was a very popular man . . .

– *The ideal object.*

– He'd do anything – run the fancy dress competition, roll up his sleeves and do the bar, lead the dancing at the Ceilidh, play Santa Claus in a cotton-wool beard at the Christmas jumble sale . . .

– The image of your mother in the rug . . . for some reason I'm reminded that the IRA – correct me if I'm mistaken – wrap the coffins of their members in the Republican flag?

– Drape. They *drape*. I don't see what that's got to do with my mother. The rug means . . . illness, impotence, whereas the flag . . .

– The flag means?

–

From the crowded terrasse of the Montenvers, I stared across the Mer de Glace. Coming up on the mountain railway we had squeezed on to slatted wooden benches with tourists from France, Belgium, Italy, who filled the carriages with cigarette smoke and held their small children to the windows to gaze down at the Chamonix valley. *Chouette, ah, c'est chouette,* they cried as the small red train laboured up the steep gradient through forest and cloud layers and finally sprang out into the sunshine of the Montenvers shoulder. On the other side of the glacier rose the symmetrical pyramid of the Grand Dru. Sun lit the pinkish granite of the west face, but the north face stayed in deep blue shadow. I scan the vertical pillars, searching for bird or bush or goat, for any yardstick which may give a clue to the scale. Am I looking at 1,000 metres of precipice or 3,000? Are these rock spires on the north *arête* the size of chimney pots or cathedrals? I plied Will with questions which he answered patiently enough. Without a starting point you can't begin to set one thing in relation to another, compare, contrast, the essence of the place evades you. 'And I suppose you've climbed it, too?' I said.

Will grinned back at me. 'Fraid so. I've still got designs on the Charmoz, though.' He pointed up the glacier at a shadowy tower abutted by a gut-wrenching *gendarme*. It struck me that he was testing me, noting my reactions. I found myself wondering what Joanna's response would have been. She would not, I was sure, have been speechless with admiration.

'All in a day's work?' I said drily. Will had turned from the Charmoz and was gazing longingly up at the bright red specks of hang-gliders which wheeled in the air currents above the Aiguilles Rouges.

'Quite exciting, huh?'

I gave a shudder which was both protest and defence. Because I knew all too well that Will would do it for the sheer thrill, make mere sport of the elements, which as far as I'm concerned is asking for it. But Will didn't think like that, this is what I was learning about him. He might be meticulous with his equipment and careful in his planning, but humble he wasn't, the very word meant nothing to him. To be at the summit, to be the size of the sky, to pit himself against the mountain – with all due respect for its capacity to shrug him off, yes – but to pit himself against it, and win: this was his meat and drink, his elation and desire, and the arrogance of it both excited and repelled me.

Scusi. Grazie. I moved aside to let a man in a Campagnolo cap aim his camera at the glacier. In half an hour the tourists would re-embark and be carried back down to the valley to lunch on fondue and the pale green wine of the region, whereas Will and I would go on, higher up the glacier, with our back-packs and our camping gaz and our small store of food and drink. Will said that we would walk on the glacier, we would climb fixed iron ladders set into sheer rock. And yes, probably I would be afraid, but the fear and the revelations it might bring belonged to some future time, not to the present and the sunny bustling terrasse, where, for the moment, it was enough simply to look the part. I drew on my cigarette, enjoying the glances. At my glacier goggles, the great Koflachs on my feet, the ice-axe strapped to my rucksack. Will stood relaxed, boots planted firmly, hands in the pockets of his salopettes. In the mountains he was so quiet and contained, as if the experience itself were enough for him; as if, by implication, it should also be enough for me. Or of course he could have been posing, for he was as self-conscious as the next person, and as narcissistic. The difference was that he could move fluently from the glamour of the image to the demands of the act itself. Which would have been hopelessly intimidating, if I hadn't already decided that I couldn't and wouldn't be entirely serious about this climbing business. Will leaned loosely against the balcony rail, keeping his secrets. His mouth widened into a smile.

'Could be a great yuppy sport one day, shooting down hang-gliders.'

The path down to the glacier was fringed with heather and blueberries. Gradually it steepened until we were down-climbing backwards on iron ladders smoothed by hands and weathers. Even in sun the surface of the ice looked grey and gnarled and heaps of boulders and rubble littered the edges, like debris left at the side of some enormous roadworks. I put my foot on a shelf of ice undercut by mud and trickling waters. Nothing could have felt more precarious. 'Relax,' laughed Will. 'You've got a grade A instructor at your beck and call.' On my right a crevasse yawned; deeper in I saw narrower blue jaws. We won't need crampons, Will had said, our boots should grip. I took a few steps on the rutted hilly surface and found that he was right; the ice was pocked and gritty and hardly slippery at all. I was walking on the frozen folded skin of an immense animal, perfectly alive yet bound to a time-scale slower than anything in the world except the rise and flux and fall of mountains. Looking closer I saw tones of green and blue and turquoise; somewhere deep inside the ice there were faint creaks, like muscles straining. And I thought that if you could slow down time enough to enter the rhythm of its life, you'd see its true slither, the undulating movement which began above

143

the tossed white *séracs* on the skyline and ended in torrenting meltwater far below in the valley of the Arve. A few centimetres a day, Will had said. If we stood on this hillock until it carried us down to the snout-ice below the Montenvers, it would take decades, we'd be old and grey. 'It's beautiful,' I said, and meant it.

Will stood on a small boulder, waiting for me. He seemed to be singing. 'You know I used to be in a tone-deaf barbershop quintet at Amherst? I'm not kidding.' Unslotting his ice-axe from his pack he tucked it under his arm like a baton and began to camp it up.

> When I fall in love,
> It will be completely,
> Or I'll ne – ver fall in love . . .

I held my hand to my mouth and doubled up, for it was awful, yes, dreadful, a grinding hopeless drone like nothing I'd ever heard.

> In a restless world like this is,
> La da da da da da da da da . . .

And as I bent over, split by laughter, and as my laughter echoed hugely against the scooped sides of the valley, it was as if some distorting glass had been shaken from my eye and for a split second I thought that I could see myself clearly. The suspicious, envious familiar who measured and observed and kept accounts did not do so simply out of fear of Joanna. If I held back, it was because I was afraid that if ever I aspired to the mountains as Will did – fervently, hungrily – if ever I came to share this obsession which, far from being a sport, came dangerously close to poetry, if ever I tried to compete and win, my cause was lost and my heart was broken. The taste of that envy hollowed me out, it was a blight on the day, and I blamed myself for it. For if the mountains made us temporary blood and bone, then wasn't it enough that we should be together,

144

that Will should simply be alive, from the pink skin under his fingernails to the stolid soles of his feet, that I should simply feel the tenderness which rushed up through belly and throat and burst out on my face at the lovely stupid sight of him dancing on the dirty ice of the glacier?

We tacked on up the humpback of the ice, singing, ridiculous. Will took my hand as we jumped small crevasses and skirted huge ones. The glacier veered right and steepened; the crown of the Dent du Géant reared up on the southern skyline. Will led me through moraine boulders to the edge of the ice, where sheer slabs of rock were daubed with vertical red arrows.

'Don't look down,' he said, starting up the ladder. I tightened the straps of my rucksack and tiptoed after him. At the top of the first ladder a narrow ledge led off to the left; a metal rail had been bolted into the rock, for handholds. And then another ladder, another traverse, and so it went on, until I crawled to the top of the last step and flopped down in the heather, my legs limp as strands of wool. Will held out flasks and chocolate but his face was concerned. 'Sorry, we've got to make tracks.' The sky had furred over with grey clouds, and these were not the *petites nuages elevées* that the Météo had promised; these were low and ominous and at that altitude could only mean snow. Above us the path rose narrowly up the almost sheer mountainside: 300 metres, 400. Will packed up and set off up the zig-zags, moving slowly and steadily. I hurried after him and stopped, breathless, at the second bend, feeling the altitude like an illness. Will beckoned me on, and I scowled at him. The land was high and cold and barren and the direction unremittingly up. Masochistic, I thought: it took a masochist to plod on like that, never stopping to look, never seeing. Rebellious, I stooped to pick blueberries, raced on, stopped again, panting. The distance between us was increasing, and now Will had vanished behind a rocky buttress; I knew that I wouldn't catch up. I sat down and sniffed away tears of fatigue, thankful at least that he wouldn't see my purple face and this intense, despairing loneliness. The scrub had thinned out now, and patches of frozen snow lay in the ice of the rocks. I was too furious to call out to him or ask for a rest stop; instead, I would push on, push harder, just to show him. I jumped up and rushed on, flurrying round each bend quite certain that I'd see him there, waiting, until at last he came into view, sitting cross-legged on a boulder, grinning at me. Ravaged by temper, I ran at him with my hand raised. 'Why didn't you wait, you might have waited!' Will warded me off, laughing. I couldn't believe he was laughing.

'You're just like a little puppy. You rush and rush and then you stop and pant like mad.' He rocked back on the boulder, hilarious, and then I started to laugh too, seeing my red pursed face through his eyes, the silliness of it.

'I was going to slap you right across the face, I promised myself.'

'I could see that!' Will unhooked the water bottle from his belt and passed it to me. 'It's no good, you know. You've got to go slow. Fix your mind on something else. Anything except how far you have to go.'

I lit a cigarette and waited for a scolding which didn't happen. I tried to take in the wisdom of what he said but the wisdom had barbs. A shadow question: where in his life had he learnt about the long haul? Marriage came to mind, the mystery challenge. I couldn't afford to think about that.

'It's only another thousand to the hut. Look. Lean back.' Will held me against his chest as I squinted up; his breath was easy against my cheek, the air of the mountain moving lightly in his lungs. The mountainside was a steep waste, colourless under the dull sky. At last I picked out the hut against the dun-grey rocks. From down here it looked like the Snow Queen's castle, perched, grim, fabulous. And far too high. Unless of course it was small, shed-sized, that too was possible.

The rock shelf was six feet wide and greasy with ice, but at least it was level, blessedly easy on legs and lungs. Streams fanned out across the smooth granite slabs to fall 2,000 feet to the glacier below. I began to feel safe again; my heart settled, my limbs began to glow. Colours came into focus in close up: orange lichens, one pure blue gentian with a yellow eye which glinted against the quartz-veined rocks. After the misery, it was miraculous how your eye could become so quiet and harmonious, how the spell of the mountain could make space in you, if you let it. I held my hand out over the precipice and the cold air of the glacier rose to meet it. I felt rather than saw that snow had begun to fall. Will looked up towards the refuge, cursed.

'*Fin de saison*. I should have thought of that. Could mean a night out.'

I strained to see. The shutters seemed to be closed. 'Will we die?' I asked comfortably: a rhetorical question. On some inner scale of safety and danger I felt positively immortal.

Will didn't smile back. 'No, but we'll be pretty damn wretched.'

'So what do we do?'

'Eat all our food, drink all our whisky and hug each other like mad.'

It sounded like a game, childish and adventurous. All we had to do was survive. Simple. Simple as love or this bare pared monochrome landscape. I felt like laughing, but propriety stopped me. We roped up and began to climb steeply again; the path was loose and treacherous, slippery with new snow. The snow was serious now; across the valley the mountains flickered and faded, merging into the sky. Whiteout. The silence was intense, windless. I saw a trail of paw prints on the path ahead, and something brown and furry stood up like a squirrel, sniffed the air, sped away. A marmot. I was glad that something else was busy and alive up here. Above me on the path Will's feet made no sound which could muffle the rasping of my breath or the inner echoing heartbeat. Once again it was as if I'd never exercised, never trained; only my geriatric will

147

forced a racking rhythm on my legs, and comfort was a thing of the past, fading into an abstraction; pain was the only, the exclusive fact of life. Caked snow clung to the wool of my mittens in slabs which split open when I flexed my hands: a wintry, childhood image, with fires to go home to. Think about something else, he'd said. I was using the ice-axe more for support than balance now, leaning heavily on it. I saw myself hobbling like an old pilgrim, a hag, maybe, stoop-shouldered and tubercular, making slow progress across a flat field. One foot simply went in front of another and the mind drifted away, for there was no room for it in a body so full of pain. The flat land stretched out ahead, the land was flat, it was my body which was angled, leaning into it as if for takeoff, borne up by some updraught which took the strain from my legs, thighs, which lifted my feet easily from their prints, which made me weightless . . . Remove the horizon and you obliterate gravity; was it as simple as that? Without the rope that linked me to Will, I might fly off and away.

Hallucinating, yes, maybe I was hallucinating, like those Himalayan veterans with their ghosts and their guardian angels, but it was a necessary hallucination, a trick of the mind to outwit the body and take it past the limits of the possible. The possible? Limits? Somewhere close by there was a strange choking sob. Frightened, I stopped and stared into the whiteness. When I moved on it followed me like a dog on a leash and drew level, and now it was inside me, in my own chest, and I was doubled over and gasping down at my boots. Will skidded down the slope and stopped in the snow beside me. 'Up,' he ordered, 'get up.'

'I'm sorry,' I said, and found that I was on my knees, leaning along the curved pick of the ice-axe. 'Did I faint or something?'

'Look, it's not far now. You're doing fine, OK?' Will's smile was urgent.

OK, I said, Right, and giggled – such terse buddy words – but a part of my mind said, This is serious. Either this was a war movie in which my body was weak and misplaced or else I had good strong legs which could get going.

Will tugged on the rope, dragging me to my feet. 'Only a few hundred feet and we've made it, OK?' OK, I thought, we'll have done enough then. We'll have done the stoical, the impossible, we can give up. Above us the refuge flickered briefly through a break in the cloud: grey stone, brown shutters. Locked. Will said nothing and I didn't look at him. Locked and barred. It was a dull thought in a dull head and it hardly distracted me for a moment. There were no hungers or desires now, only my ransacked lungs and the mean mechanics of up. My massive boots followed Will's, my legs meekly took their orders. The snowcloud closed in again, thick as milk. A black bird swooped across the path, yapping, and I stumbled again, fell. Felt Will's hand supporting my head. The scald of hot tea. He was saying something, he was saying that the path was easy and wider, he was walking beside me now, giving little glances. And then there were rough rock steps, and Will put his hand out to pat the top of a wall. 'We made it?' I asked weakly. But he was already half way across the terrace, leaving a trail of footprints in the unbroken snow, and before I had time to start hoping or hurting he had pushed the door open and stood waiting for me, smiling, under the long icicles which hung from the eaves.

– In the fantasy I am always outside and I am spying, nose just propped on the windowsill like the old WOT NO? cartoons from the war; rationing, scarcity. I'm spying on something I never actually saw: the ideal marriage. I'm trying to solidify an image which sets me definitively on the outside. Mummy and Daddy in the bed. Oh such a good time they're having, such a very good time is being had. Kisses and cuddles in inexhaustible supply, for a lifetime, I insist on this in the same moment that I envy it. Daddy has a hairy big stomach under his too-short vest, Mummy has a pretty nightdress. Probably her nose is cold, for we lived always in cold bedrooms. And there are the daisies I stole from O'Halloran's allotment, straggling over the dressing table; their stark white heads look on in hypocritical sweet welcome: Mother is back and God's in his kitchen and all's right with the world.

Imagine that refuge in the high Alps, the meaning of it. I was in the bedroom I had no right to be in. Perched, we were perched, like the Snow Queen's castle. Black choughs nested in the rock spires above the hut and marmots scurried on the snow cornices below it. There was a helicopter pad a few metres square to which a chopper might come speeding with that curious predatory sideways swoop, swinging up the valley of the glacier with its red belly lights flashing, the clearest possible symbol of a call for help, and a call answered. Our mountain boots stood side by side at the door which no one would open, in the high refuge which no one would visit, yet precisely because of this – or so it seemed to me, I was strangely sure of this – that dusty bare-boarded room was populated not only by the two of us, but in essence by everyone, everyone was already there, belonged there, in their keenest and widest and most deep-dreaming selves. I was swaddled in blankets like a baby – I had a fever, shivers from fatigue and exposure – and I was dreaming of a rescue, but if love is the rescue then it had already happened. Will rested his palms on my cheeks and stared at me as if I were the source of all happiness, and in the flicker of candle flame his face was both young and old and neither, all ages made fictive by the transforming love on it, the individual features – lovely enough in themselves – taken now to their limits and blurring out beyond and past the walls of personality into the collective, history, the myth, I don't understand this, I will never understand this.

In the beginning we'd talk about our lives, poetry, the Big Chill, whatever, and yes, the words were . . . what we said was important . . . but the vibration, the echo that we picked up was more so. His eyes would open in an inner strange way and I would look at him and feel it . . . Sometimes – at first – I felt that there was some intense, constant note he was listening for, a frequency which emanated from me, and that if I wasn't careful he would shatter like a glass. But later I saw that of course it was something we both made, some insistent fundamental sounding. Even when I was still sceptical of what he actually said – he was difficult to follow sometimes, his mind would make great arrogant leaps, but then he was young and the young so often have an over-intellectual, even a cold way of coming at things – that same note was there, and it was as if we were both circling, stilling, listening for it, and it had to be there or we wouldn't be satisfied; we knew, always, when it was there, that particular note, that echo which prolonged the pause before the future came to be. And we'd wait there, alert, until we felt the filaments of our present, our past, knitting together into a no-time, a linking of dead souls and live, of gathering and dispersion: brother to sister, son to mother, twin to twin, daughter to father, a cross-hatch across darkness and beyond.

We argued, oh yes, sparred, but our eyes never left each other, our eyes were too intelligent, our eyes and our noses and our skin just went on with the business of loving, they knew no other . . . and the light would come and go in his face and the words would come and go, and if as time went on there were fewer words it was because we didn't know them for this.

When Will opened the shutters I saw a man's room, full of dirty ashtrays and bottles lipped with candle grease. At the far end, trestle tables and benches were stacked. The door to the kitchen was padlocked, so Will had set up the camp stove on one of the tables, and set about cooking the food he'd carried in his rucksack. He had boiled water for tea, brought out candles

and cups. His finger and thumb had tested my pulse and found
it too thin and fast – effects of fatigue and altitude – so he had
wrapped me up and poured liquids down my throat, and now I
sat like a barley sack, wedged between table and bench-back,
quite idle and more than happy to die if this was dying. Every
time he passed my barley sack he pinned the blankets more
tightly around me, so that I couldn't move my arms or help
with the cooking, and laughed at himself for doing it, and at me
for tolerating it. And I imagined that one day he would do just
this with his child, as playfully, and that I was standing in for
the child he should already have had, needed to have, the child
which Joanna hadn't given him but which I would . . . So there
we were, the snow was falling outside, and inside Will was
singing and stirring a pot of beans with a Swiss army knife and
chuckling and darting secretive little looks at me. 'What?' I
said, but he wouldn't answer. 'What's up?' I demanded, falling
into giggles myself, for his cheeks were puffed up with pride
and he looked as if he might positively strut. He shook his head
and wrapped his lips up tight in the silly way he had when he
was bursting to say something. Then a great hysterical whoop
came out of his mouth. 'It's because I've got you *utterly in my
power*', he yelled, laughing and aghast.

We made up a bed in the upstairs dormitory, nostalgic ritual of
mattresses being wedged together, like we'd done in St Croix.
A candle, whisky, chocolate. Water in Will's canteen. We
stretched out in our thermal underwear on the shabby
mattress-ticking and held each other. My limbs felt bruised
and trampled from the climb, and my pulse ran wild still, a
rushing constant excitement with no place to settle or hide. I
fell into spasms of sleep while Will watched me, and I dreamed
of a man on some hot coast, beach-naked and golden, with
streaks and runnels of blood on his legs. He held a surf
board-shaped shield of goatskin stretched tight on a bamboo
frame, a shield he hadn't used to protect himself, or else my

huge dark feelings could never have scarred him so. I woke, for love and more love in the hot restless bed, and when I ran out at last for a cold pee on the snowy terrace I felt so lost and far gone in him that I was almost transparent. The snow had stopped falling now; the sky was vast and dark and empty of cloud, and the stars were wet white holes in it. To the south the ridge of the Grandes Jorasses jutted up at the moon, the moon which cast my dwarfish shadow on the snow, the moon which could have shone right through me with such little effort, and I swore fervently on that moon that no matter what happened or what was to come, as long as I lived I'd remember that he had given me this.

When I crawled back into the snarled nest of blankets Will's eyes were open and glinting and there was a sweat of triumph on his forehead. 'Of course,' he announced with startled authority, 'I love you so very much, it's inconceivable that you wouldn't love me!' A look of utter satisfaction crossed his face, as if he'd just grasped some irrefutable truth of the universe. And then he gathered up my hand in both of his and curling himself around it like a squirrel round a nut, he quivered once, and sighed, and slept.

When we came down through a bank of mist and saw the town and the flat valley floor far below us, it was like that shock you feel when, after elastic hours in the air, you land again on some finite continent, in some finite time zone, and before you're ready for it the present has slipped into the past, and the future with its limits and decisions closes in around you.

Will had let me sleep late that morning, to recover, and when we set out the sun was already high. The snow on the steep path down from the refuge was a soft slush through which red mud oozed, and the surface of the glacier was slippery. To make matters worse, we had missed one of the cairns which marked the route back to the Montenvers station and found ourselves in a sea of transverse ridges divided by wide crevasses. Some of the ridges were too narrow to balance on, so that we had to kick toe-holds in the slope and inch along hand over hand.

Will had just reached the end of the traverse when my feet began to slip. I tore off my gloves and scrabbled for a finger-hold, only this wasn't rock, this was ice which the sun had melted and smoothed, and I knew it was useless. I saw my gloves roll down and disappear into the narrow blue mouth of the crevasse below, and although I flattened myself against the lip I could feel myself sliding. Will heard my weak cry and spun round, but when he started back along the crest towards me he slipped and went down on one knee, cursing, his left leg sunk thigh-deep in a melt-hole. And then everything was fast slapstick, as Will jerked his leg free and, straddling the ridge, lunged forward to grab my hand, hauled me sideways along the soaking slope, and landed me like some fish, gasping, on the safe shore at the other side. If I found it farcical at the time – Will's shocked red face as his leg vanished from sight – it's because lying there I felt more stupid and helpless than afraid. My mind, leaping ahead, had already calculated that the mouth of the crevasse was too narrow to swallow me, and if the worst came to the worst I could wedge my body across it. It would be tricky, yes, to climb back up the glassy slope, but I'd face that if and when I came to it. Thinking about it now, I can hardly believe such cavalier optimism. For it's quite possible – I can see it now – that my judgement was completely haywire, that my mind, dazzled and trusting, simply turned an illusion of safety into a certainty, when in fact the danger had been very real. It isn't as if Will said anything afterwards, but then it would hardly have been his style to dwell on past mistakes or dispense dire warnings: all climbers, as far as I could see, had an ingrained habit of understatement.

Will was silent now, as we walked through the streets of the town, our clothes drying on us in the afternoon heat. His frown came and went; he was fretting about minor things: where he could get a shower for me, and what should he buy to cook, and in what order should he do all these things. For some reason I couldn't bear this retreat into responsibility, this guilt about what he couldn't provide. I told him that I would cook, I'd see to it, no problem. As for a shower, the stream was fine by me. He looked tired and ragged and I could see that he didn't believe me. I've never been able to bear the feeling of being a burden to anyone, no matter how devoted they might be, and I took his arm, bossing him and smiling. But first, I said, I was buying him a beer.

In the Bar Nationale a group of climbers hailed Will good-humouredly. They had a map spread across their table and white goggle marks in pleased sunburned faces. 'Better go say hello,' Will muttered.

Coming down on the mountain railway we'd sat opposite an acquaintance of Will's, a keen-eyed youth who had glanced at my unscarred hands and remarked: not a rock-climber, then? It had amused me at the time, this casual probe aimed at finding out where I stood in the hierarchy. As soon as he had satisfied himself that I was no competition, conversation had lapsed, he had simply nothing else to talk about. 'You go. I'll order.' I chose a table by the window and sat down. I'd had enough of being appraised and then ignored, at least for one day. 'I'll be fine,' I said, taking out my notebook to prove it. But when I picked up my pen I kept thinking of the climbers at the table – the way they tilted their chairs back and exchanged the bright jousting grins of men at their business – and I couldn't write a word, my head was quite empty. The windows of the bar overlooked a narrow cobbled street of shops – a patisserie, a ski-hire shop, a bijouterie with displays of paired gold wedding rings. One of the windows, however, was a door, and you could tell the regulars by the way they strode along the pavement and unhesitatingly pushed it open, whereas tourists and other strangers either collided with the wrong panel and

recoiled with smiles of embarrassment, or hung back, uncertain, looking for a door handle, finding – if they were lucky – a
small Rothman's sticker on the door frame which said *Tirez*.
Outside the sun was high (hot, foreign, romantic), and I was
young enough yet and far from ugly. And so I sat there,
pushing coins around on the table, and told myself everything
was fine. You know how it is. (Do you?) These moods. When
everything hollows out under you and you can tell yourself
you're loved, but inside your mirrors are broken and you just
can't see it. And you can do what you like, you can polish your
shoes or tidy your cupboards, you can fight it or you can ride it,
but either way you can't win. This is how it was then, as I sat
there trying to memorise where the door was, and I felt as
much fear sitting at that table with nothing to say and no way
back to myself as I'd felt on any ice ridge or rock face or
dangling télécabine. Although Will was only yards away, as far
as I was concerned it might have been light-years, for I loved
him and I felt shrunken, and powerless, and without redress.

  – *The girl with no arms.*

  – The dream of the girl with no arms.

  – *As opposed to the little hero.*

  – Men's chess, men's laughter, photographs of men and
mountains on the walls. The brass-topped bar, the solid tables,
the plain tiled floor – all very grave and masculine and
celebrating it. You couldn't imagine women's voices raised in
that bar . . .

  – *Does it remind you of anywhere?*

  – A bit, but the feelings are different. Sometimes my father
took me with him to the Republican club, a special treat my
mother didn't approve of. I don't remember any other girls
there, although sometimes there must have been, it wasn't as if
kids weren't allowed in. But I remember mostly men, friends of

my dad's, laughing, as my father took me on his knee and made his stomach muscles hard as a board and said, Punch away, lass. It was a game so I made small fists and punched and he went red holding his breath, and the smoke came out of his nostrils instead of his mouth, and they all laughed and said I was a fair wee fighter and I'd be a credit to him.

– *So you felt special?*

– I was as proud as anything, I suppose. Because you could see the way they looked up to him.

– *And Will?*

– Yes, I had the same feeling about Will – the way they teased him. 'Hey Will, been bagging a few directs on the sly, eh?' You could tell where he was in the hierarchy.

– *And you?*

– Well, everything female was out of place there, you just couldn't hold your own.

– *Literally?*

– Oh!

– Later on something happened when I was cooking. I was glad to be doing something domestic for a change, making a contribution. I had a pot of pasta boiling on the stove and balanced on top a pan of ratatouille simmered, smelling garlicky and good. Will was unpacking the rucksacks and stowing gear under the flysheet of the tent. Once or twice he glanced at the cooking arrangements and I could see he was dying to interfere. Eventually he came over and stood shaking his head. 'You just do things on impulse, don't you? And too bad if they don't work out, right?'

'What's wrong?' I said. 'It's fine. Energy saving.' I couldn't believe that he was serious.

Will pressed his lips together. He looked so housewifely and cross that I had to laugh. 'Well, I'm just telling you you're rash.'

'Are we fighting?' I said, putting up my fists.

'Not unless you try to compete with my camping.' He was grinning now but I could see that he meant it. 'Because you can't, OK?'

'Daddy knows best, eh?' I taunted. Just at that moment the ratatouille pan tipped sideways. I made a grab for the handle and saved it, but not before it had unbalanced the pot below. Hot water and pasta shells spilled over Will's jeans and ran into his shoes. And for the second time that day he stood looking down at his dripping wet legs and cursing . . . and I think now, well, perhaps I really wanted to mess on him, soak him, mess him up . . .

– I get the feeling we're talking about puberty here, and that other flow that bursts out and won't be stopped.

– There was blood on the man in the dream, it was trickling down his legs. The man with the shield he didn't use, the Dionysus.

– The shield he didn't use to ward you off?

– Anyway I put my hand over my mouth and waited for him to be angry or say I told you so. To his credit he didn't. He just stood there scarecrow-like and comical, looking at his legs and at me and letting the message sink in. And so I beat my breast and we ate what could be salvaged and declared it better than good and the incident passed over. The night closed in around us, the rowanberries turned from red to black in the moonlight . . .

– A hand enters my sleep: a delicate roaming over my thighs. When I mumble and brush him away he sits up, hot and complaining. Soaking a flannel from his water bottle, he wipes his forehead and chest, but nothing seems to relieve him. And then out of the blue the interrogation starts. His head-torch is full on, blinding me. 'But how do I *know* you love me?' he demands. 'How do I know I'm not just another in your string of lovers?' He gives a little laugh, flat. 'Just a toyboy.'

Sleepy, exasperated – of course he knows, how can he not know – I tried to reason with him. I came running out here, didn't I? Couldn't bear to be apart, how often do I have to tell you?

'Huh,' he says. 'But but but. How do I know it's really me . . . What if I just slot into the Lover category?'

I held him, tried mothering. Thumb touched the pulse in the hollow of his throat. If he didn't know I loved him he'd never dare to act like such a baby. 'Christ, put the light out.' I couldn't see his face, his face was a void under the dazzle of light.

'I just don't get it. What have I got to offer, compared to what you've achieved?' The head-torch clicked off, I could hear him breathing in the dark.

'Achieved?' I said, 'achieved?'

Will sat up and did something bad-tempered with the pillows. Then he lay down again with an angry sigh. 'That's what I said.'

'God, I give up!' Turning my back on his grumbles I pulled the sleeping bag up to my neck. 'If you're looking for something to sulk about, go ahead. I'll just get some sleep, OK?' I shut my eyes and my ears and left him to fume. Later I dreamt that I was clinging to a steep slope, only this slope was a breast, huge, in three-quarter profile, and the nipple was as big as it would appear to a hungry child who, sucking already at one breast, looks across in envy at the other.

When I woke I felt the tickle of Will's hair. His head was tucked in at my breast and his face was rosy and puckered, as if he had suckled well in the night. One eye opened and looked up at me, and he grinned. 'Last night. Shit. What was all that about?' He hid his face and groaned, remembering. 'You know what I was going to say? I was dying for you to ask what I was thinking, so I could say I'm thinking of just going up the mountain and I'm thinking of just chucking myself off! No kidding. But you didn't ask so I never got to say it. So I was mad.'

I laughed. 'I bet you really had your mother tied in knots.'

'I thought it was supposed to be the other way around.'

'Well, it takes two to tango.'

'OK,' he groaned. 'I *am* happy. So when am I going to admit it?'

– *Is it the notion of the hero dying for love here? Or the spoilt boy blackmailing?*

– But how do you know when to take someone seriously? So maybe I'm gullible, but was I to believe he wasn't capable of it simply because he was also capable of laughing at himself?

– *I wonder whose power we're talking about here. . . .*

– I can only see it as a film, I can construct the images but I can't climb inside. It has its own momentum, necessity – it has to happen this way. Will, swaddled, they're brushing snow off his eyelashes, they're winching him up in the helicopter . . .

In the notebook I wrote: 'Whatever happens.' Then I couldn't find myself, and I stopped. Oblongs of sugar dissolved in my *café crême*. In front of me the spine of the Chamonix Aiguilles reared up: a fine clear view. Left to itself, my pen doodled across the page – lines wrapping over and over, encasing something. Something tied up in knots. At first it looked like a foetus inside, captured or held there, but as the pen moved on, the thing was unwrapping itself, the scribble which had tied the child in knots was stretching out, attenuating, growing the muscles of a man. I watched the pen celebrate the complex insertion of tendons on kneecap, sweep of calf muscle to ankle, the flexed thigh. The knees extended to the side; a plié, bending and ready to leap. I felt the sweetness pour from me, my hand moving independently in sweetness, delineating the loved body which flings itself at the snow and rock and goes up and up, out into air and blue. Delineating memories and extremes, the days spread out behind me in all their wind-torn ridges, and as you climb through the first snowdrifts there are blue fields of gentians you don't want to crush, and the smell of goat shit on the air, and the sun sets at the apex of the world in a boiling line of gold.

On the wooden balcony of the Albert Premier hut we had squinted up at the Aiguille du Tour, watching for the Breton party. Robert, the *gardien*, looked young and worried. It was their first climb after a training week: an easy route, but they were late, very late. The fanged *seracs* of the Le Tour glacier shimmered below us; higher up, on the smooth snow-fields below the Aiguille du Tour small dots moved slowly. Robert passed the binoculars to Will and shook his head. Army conscripts, he said, taking soundings. The girl with the limp who had come up to the hut with the Bretons dipped bread into a bowl of black coffee and tried not to cry. '*Ne t'inquiètes pas,*' said Robert dourly. At eleven he would go out himself and meet them, without fail, bring them back across the glacier.

Will had been grumbling. He ought to have gone out at 3am when the others did; so what if there was new snow on the Chardonnet, you should never make up your mind in the hut, you should always go out and try a pitch first.

I was the one, of course, who'd stopped him. You can't go, I'd said, tickling him in the dark itchy bed and laughing. Through a small open hatch we could hear the sounds of the Bretons in the next dormitory, snores and creaks which would soon give way to whispers and curses and dropped crampons, the sleepy activity of an Alpine party getting itself together. You can't go out and die because I'm not pregnant yet. Will started to say that he didn't see why I concentrated on the dangers of climbing when there were also the highs, and then

161

he tugged his thumbs across my cheeks and looked at me with his mouth drooping, wanting and not wanting. He was tense, holding back the sounds of love. I can't help it, he said. I feel kind of guilty, when they're girding their loins to go up there.

On the balcony Robert smoked my English cigarettes and argued with him. The Aiguille du Tour, he shrugged – no problem. But the Chardonnet is different, more bad than she looks. How many *gens* had he not dragged off it already, on his own back? Once he had even carried an *étudiant Irlandais* down in his rucksack, cutting holes for his legs. And that was when the snow was in condition . . . but now, with the danger of avalanche, no, *absolument* no . . .

The two men leaned on the balcony rail, bodies curved, the braces of their salopettes loose and dangling over space. They were talking about *ski-extrème* and ice cascades. Robert's hands were graceful in the air, describing a line of descent, a swoop, a turn, another acute downward angle. Their two heads made little stabbing movements at each other, their feet shifted restlessly in the ugly rubber sabots. On the bench beside me the Breton girl was winding her watch. *D'accord*, she said shortly when I tried to comfort her, for I had only bad French and no expertise to offer. Those who could judge whether or not the situation was grave were the men, and the men were giving nothing away. It was as if they held the key to life and death and danger, and it was a code I could never break. And so I stared, dizzied, at the glare of sun on snow, while my mind's eye saw Will launch himself at frozen waterfalls, at the vertical and magical and impossible, on his face a cryptic half-smile of desire.

Scrape of a chair on the concrete *terrasse* and Will sat down beside me, twisting his head to see what I was writing. I closed the book and smiled at him. Faded shorts, hot shoulders, oh God. We sat side by side, staring like tourists at the Massif. Will pointed up at the summit dome. 'OK, let's see how much you've learned.' He moved his finger to the left: the Aiguille du Midi, that was easy, that was a dark spike with a whipped cream cornice of snow spiralling down from its shoulder. Next to it, a straggle of pinkish pinnacles began, beautiful but indistinguishable. I shook my head: no good, I couldn't remember. I watched his hand, the finger outlining the peaks like a lover. The sun winked on his gold ring.

'The Aiguille du Plan, the Peigne in front. The Blaitière with the crocodile tooth at the end. The Grepon, then the Charmoz, we went round the shoulder of it, remember?' Will's face had crimped into the over-jovial expression of a headmaster who can hardly restrain his impatience. 'And now the glaciers. Come on.' I spread my hands and laughed, the idiot pupil again. 'The Blaitière, the Nantillons . . . so what's the next one along?'

'Beats me,' I said. I was beginning to feel rebellious. Wasn't I supposed to love him, not the mountains? And then I realised. 'Oh, well, the Mer de Glace, of course.'

Will stood up, tutting. 'I should think so too.' He put the shopping bag on his chair and shouldered his small rucksack. Then he said: 'I arranged to phone Joanna at six.'

A huge plane tree leaf circled down and landed curled and dry on the café table. He was looking at me accusingly. 'It's a regular arrangement,' he said. Then with a dead smile he turned on his heel and walked quickly towards the metal bridge which spanned the river.

I examined the leaf. Beside the *terrasse* the flags of many nations drooped towards the river. Inside I had shrunk myself very small, for protection, but my adult shell felt strong and appalled and capable. Yes I want respect, I thought. The shock of the truth. I never wanted secrets. After all, he had never pretended to be unattached. Through my sunglasses even the moving clouds looked brittle. I watched the téléférique ply its way up to the Aiguille du Midi station: small red cabin packed with tourists, a nightmare. I sat perfectly alert, feeling the crisis move towards me.

From the snow cornice of the Midi a wisp of spindrift trailed like a prayer scarf. Automatically I opened my notebook. Everything was out of my hands now, this everything that was happening somewhere else, becoming definite; in the meantime what I needed was work, to keep busy, nose to the grindstone. Mapping the teeth of the Aiguilles, crowning them with names like a cave dweller stippling bison or mammoth in oxide and tallow – draw the teeth and they might not bite, tame the strange lands and animals by naming, so that when Will returned having said whatever husbands say he'd find me not lost and halfway but solid in my substance, my red hand signed on the limestone, clear imprint of my artist's name.

– *I'm thinking of the disjunction between the hero who climbed mountains and the man who clung to his wife. . . .*

– I can only see it as a film, no one would believe it. A man vaults a garden hedge in East Belfast, perilous in the searchlight. A man in shirtsleeves and braces. Face down in a privet hedge while the night's milk bottles shatter on the doorstep and the mother breathes roughly over the girl, flattening her to the carpet. Mam, you're crushing me. Stiff bones of the mother's brassière, dimpled glass buttons on her cardigan digging in. Her hand over the girl's mouth dermatitis-dry, flaking. Mam, where's my da, though?

You stand at the mouth of the grave and Mother throws roses, a red thud on the flag-covered coffin and somewhere out of sight ringing the cemetery are the soldiers with oiled rifles keyed and young anxious eyes and you boil up, bitter, pointless, biting at your lips: your body refuses.

– *In any triangle someone has to die?*

– Magic thinking, rage, the other side of love, the real me.

– *This is what the film contains, allows?*

– The film allows the rage to act, allows Joanna to board a

coach at Victoria, the family closing ranks. Allows Ann-Marie to put Joanna's bag in the hold of the Chamonix bus, and hand her boarding card to the driver, and kiss her goodbye on the step – Go on, off with you, off. And then you don't see much of her, except perhaps the odd narrative shot: customs, the ferry, that sort of thing. Just enough to keep you wondering when she'll arrive, how, what will happen.

I smiled up – feigned surprise – as Will set a demi and a kir on the table. He sat down, he took out his small red notebook, he was writing something. After a few moments I said: 'You've written a poem.'

And now there's the memory which says that Will closed the notebook, snap, like a door. I see the way his thumb lingered for a second in the gap between the pages, and then the notebook was flat and secret, and his thumb smoothed the red cover, and he put it away in his rucksack. And there's the echo of the memory – humiliation staining the moment, the screen turning red – even now, thinking about it, my body gathers itself into a knot, refuses: I shouldn't have leaned close and craned playfully like some would-be coquette.

And it gets worse, for now Will takes out a book – it's the diary of Nijinsky – and settles down to read. And again I wait, struggling with myself, until I can wait no longer and in a small cramped voice announce: 'I'm here.'

Will looked at me once. His fingers turned the pages. 'I'm reading,' he said. At last, relenting, he picked up my notebook. Again that forced smile. 'I'm glad I'm not a poet,' he said. 'I sure don't fancy competing with you.' And although my pride might have preferred silence to these glib compliments, my heart was desperate to believe them.

– Night. The tent. The bed is made – sleeping bags have been unzipped and spread out as quilts, towels folded to make pillows. At opposite ends of the tent they wriggle out of their clothes, silently. From outside it looks like shadow-boxing, a fight, for the head-torch casts huge shadows: moving elbows, arms, legs.

Night birds call out somewhere.

But didn't you imagine how I'd feel?

For a moment Will is very still, bent over, hands grasping his ankles. Look. I just can't talk about Joanna. And the trouble is – his voice cracking her emptiness open – I've never really been able to talk about you, either.

Outside there's a noise – Jean-Yves clumps by, late and drunken, singing opera, an intervention of the absurd which hovers behind her fright, strings out her nerves. Does Joanna know I'm here? Wondering why she avoided asking this before. Wondering why Will hasn't wondered why she hasn't asked. And so on. But mainly she's frightened of the answer he may give, of any answer he gives, and there's no moon, the moon is behind cloud and without a moon somehow there's no consent and she has to hold herself back or else everything will be a melodrama she can't believe in.

No, Will says, and she's not looking at his face. There have been other times, too, when I've lied about climbing and come to you.

And now she looks at him: he's bitter, smiling. Not that Joanna wouldn't do the same to me, of course.

Flatly, he says it, because this is awful and his mind is a barracks door through which two platoons of soldiers are barging at once, one lot going in and the other lot going out so that they all jam up in the middle and there's no space for feelings or anything except a numb calm and a clear instinct for survival.

She keeps quiet. She doesn't know what to say, or what is enough for her, or what should be enough. She wraps the sleeping bag quilt around her; it's soft and silky on her face, minimal safety. She feels raw and young but doesn't trust it, can't speak from that young part although nothing older would be true. I want you to know I can't help it. It just feels awful to me. Once said, it sounds calculating; everything, it seems, sounds calculating.

It makes you reject me, I can feel that.

And now she starts to cry, because it does, and she does, and she doesn't want to. Her nose runs. Her body twitches with small sobs. Her eyes shut tight, making her invisible. And then Will is under the quilt with her, his fingers fumbling over her face, her closed lids. His voice is an anguished mutter. There's nothing I don't want to give you. I'll do anything in my power to give you whatever it is you need. And they're pressing their bodies together, mouths, and they love each other, and she clings, frantic with tenderness, hoping against hope that this power isn't contingent, is his to give back to her, now that she's obliterated.

Tell her, she thinks, wanting awful honesty and hysteria, moving violently and jealously on him until she remembers her cap and gropes.

Oh, forget it, Will cries, and she's right there with him, hoping against hope. Forget it, he cries, and she comes, hope fear pleasure coursing through her body's mechanical arc as pure wars with impure, devotion with seduction; truth, lies, scheming – all this is allowed until suddenly he draws back, withdraws, somehow he's in control and remembers and here's the proof that there *is* no promise or permit or permission, only the punishment of the seductress, the maiden one should not marry, the place of unconscious weeping where her self bubbles up from anaesthetic darkness, where hands and dreams are bound or buried.

– *Maybe there was a box your father sometimes took you out of to play with, but put you back if you played too like a girl, too lovingly, too excitedly . . . the little seductress?*

–

– *Maybe it's safer to opt for the half share, and the fantasy of the woman distant somewhere but ruling, in control?*

167

– There was another time, earlier, before the phone call. Making love. At the noisy tender moment when he came and I should have, something trusting fell away and I broke into sobs instead. And what I said then, the reason I gave was: you don't belong to me. The light in the tent was orange, exposing. I was crying uncontrollably.

With his penis still in me, he argued. His mouth turned stubborn and he argued passionately. You don't belong to me. He chipped away, refuting it. 'You cried because you felt me loving you with my whole body and soul, that's why.' I slipped out from under him and lay on my belly, listening. He might have been a barrister, bullish, eloquent. 'You're the one I'm with,' he insisted. 'You're the one I need love from.' A watertight case, I thought. Oh yes. Except that Joanna's name hadn't been mentioned.

Outside, the dew was heavy; patterns of wet grass spears clung to the flysheet. The slight shadow of a wasp crawled over the fruit box which served us as a larder. I thought of the thief who had passed by on our first day up the hill. He hadn't taken a lot – a tin of beans, some chocolate. Yesterday I'd left him a note: *Monsieur le Voleur,* we're up the hill and not rich. Please leave us the vegetables for dinner. I'd trusted him and it had worked. Yet here was Will who wasn't a stranger and wanted me to trust him and I was frozen and tearstained and failing.

And what I said, the reason I gave, was that he didn't belong to me. But what if the real reason was elsewhere? What if the real reason had nothing to do with possibly being left or possibly being let down. What if the real reason was more of a recoil from my own jealous fantasies – my wish to force a way in. Maybe, instead of accepting the present happiness he offered, I preferred to trace a path back to some original envy – of the marriage bed, the parental embrace you mustn't intrude upon. Simply that. The thing or place I envied? I can't help imagining it as a whole sort of Eden barred to me. An entire landscape of birds rocks blossom, apricots scattered ripe across the grass, pomegranates fat in their shining skins. Hot colours among green, red and more red, and rowanberries reflected in water, the broom bushes coming out yellow and early . . . a whole mad gold land lurking and forgotten. But no, of course I don't think for a minute that this place actually lived in my parents, that joy, no, they never had that between them, it wasn't something they possessed in reality. And if they didn't have it in the first place, they couldn't very well keep me out of it, could they . . .

But the way I must have imagined it . . . was that they were owners and caretakers of this paradise place, and they kept me out, they wouldn't allow it to me, and I was angry, and the only initiative left to me was spite. Cut off your nose to spite your face.

– Cut off your arms . . .

– Active spite which expressed both the rage and the expected punishment for it . . . I cut myself off, barred myself in advance from a world which was seen to be theirs, always someone else's, never mine.

Will lies over her, slicked with sweat, expiring. She's lost count of how many times they've made love. And now he shakes his head. Passion's one thing, he mutters, but this isn't *normal*.

Is that a complaint? He's joking, of course. (Is he?)

Will lights a cigarette and sucks smoke in, feeding himself. Well, if you came more often you'd refuse me more, wouldn't you? Because you'd have got what you needed.

Maybe he's trying to soften this with a smile, but what comes across to her is a blurred rebellious stare. She gives a weak laugh. Well I don't know about this projection of yours . . . Hearing her voice shake, knowing that a shaky part of her already decided to take the blame: she's the bad mother, indulgent, can't put a stop to him. Do you see what I'm saying, she asks, determined; it sounds like a lecture but he won't get away with it. Will frowns hard but he listens, he hears her out. He nods a sweet obedient nod which makes her feel foolish. Then his face stretches and stretches, and he's laughing at her. You've got to be kidding. Don't you know when I'm pulling your leg?

Well maybe I don't, I thought later, and maybe he wasn't. At the stream I battered wet clothes against a rock. Through a gap in the raspberry bushes I could see him moving about the clearing, hanging sleeping bags out to air, waxing boots, oiling ice-axes. All afternoon we'd been wary, skirting each other. A squabble had broken out, childishly, about *Wuthering Heights*. Of course I was bound to take Heathcliff's side and Will knew it. (The maverick, outcast, etc.) 'Cathy's a bourgeois,' I said, 'she sells him out for a stake in the Linton's respectability.' My voice was brash and rising. 'Set it nowadays and she'd be a yuppy.'

'Oh well, if you're determined to be a romantic,' said Will. I knew we were fighting about something but I wasn't sure what. All the same, I was angry, energised, enjoying it.

'And Heathcliff's sadism? Hanging puppies from hooks? Charming.'

'At least Heathcliff didn't betray anyone. Cathy. Himself. And who could give a damn about the Lintons anyway?'

Will laid the open book flat on his chest and scowled at me: I could see that he was enjoying the manoeuvres. 'So intensity justifies everything?' He knew that I would have to say yes, overstate, say yes, absolutely. His mouth was prim and pleased, his eyes bright. 'Well, I guess that's a touch too elitist for me.' He leaned back on his elbows, head stiffly upright, knees bent uncomfortably. I looked at him and shrugged. He had done his duty by insisting on difference, so let him put me in that corner if it satisfied him (mad, greedy, disruptive), let him cling to *le mariage moderne* and hide in the arms of Joanna whose name was never mentioned.

'Hey, don't beat my pants to death.' Bracken brushed apart and now Will stood over me, 'Open wide,' he said, holding out raspberries. He rained the berries into my mouth until I shook my head, enough, too many. Then he held his hands in the stream to wash off the stains. He gave a short, grudging laugh. 'Of course, if I resist Heathcliff so strongly, it's probably because I'm dead scared I'm like him.' His eyes were dark smiling shadows but his hands in the running water looked as if they were bleeding. With my mouth full of raspberries I nodded, feeling him come back to me, and as the pain lifted away – taken, transferred – it struck me that what he wanted was just this pain; his, mine, mortality, admitting it. What he wanted, whether he knew it or not, was to escape from the cool delusions of his own invulnerability.

– There's no easier place to fall apart in than a supermarket. Too many chrome surfaces reflect you already in bits or at odd distorting angles. You see a partial eyebrow, or an unwelcome view of the inside of your nostrils; a sudden familiar foot shocks you, or as you turn the corner at the end of an aisle a middle-aged looking woman faces you with a startled accusing frown and your stomach jolts in recognition.

Also there are far too many commodities to choose from, and Will never was any good at choosing, particularly when – as now – his mind is full of téléférique times and logistics and the responsibility of planning a feasible expedition from the Aiguille du Midi across the snow-covered glacier of the Vallée Blanche.

So, in the Chamonix *Codec* – inoffensive enough as supermarkets go – we wandered the aisles with a wire trolley which contained only our two rucksacks. Both of us were scattered, and fragile, and saying little. A man called Walt appeared, another American. His thighs bulged under salopettes, his unbuttoned shirt revealed brisk blond hairs on his chest. He looked me over and gave Will a sardonic smile. His hand rested on the shopping trolley, keeping us captive. 'So what's on today, Will? More walks with women?'

I stared at tins of *cassoulet*. I couldn't look at either of them. So that's what they called the Petite Verte, the Mer de Glace. Once upon a time the Matterhorn was considered to be serious business. Until a woman climbed it. Ever since then it had been a pleasant day out for a lady. I turned as cold a shoulder as I could manage and marched off to buy bread and chocolate for the mountain.

'I told you it was chronic,' Will said, as I threw my packages into the trolley. He nudged me and said softly, 'That's Eva Kostolowicz.'

Turning, I saw a woman some ten years older than myself, ordinary and impressive, greyish short hair, a shopping bag full of oranges.

'Everest. K2. Top Polish climber.' The hush in Will's voice told me that Eva K was ranked higher than he, Eva K whose eyes were blue and distant as the snows, who was ethereal among the matrons queueing for *jambon du pays* and the strong girls in skin-shorts choosing shampoo.

Envy is as invisible as it is violent. I can't see it, can't position it on the screen. Except perhaps by representing subjective size, which changes like the weather in the Alps, from hour to hour, if only we admitted it. So that the image of Eva K inflates, becomes huge, while Kathleen, placed beside her, is the size of a doll. Or else Eva K is an enormous doll and Kathleen a small girl whose arms can't possibly encompass her. Or to be realist: perhaps the partial reflections in the chrome display stands show a disembodied eye, or a mouth puckered up in self-reproach as, transfixed by the unlovable feelings, she makes herself pay for them.

At the door Will divided the packages unevenly between the two rucksacks: heavy for him, light for me. Outside in the street the sun was high and the Météo unequivocally promised *beau temps sur la montagne*. Madly I wanted to get away, dive into a café, avoid Will. Sit over a solitary *café crème* until I felt whole and hardy again. Then, perhaps, I'd be able to face the Aiguille du Midi.

What the fear looks like.

The téléférique station had been prinked out as a *châlet*, with fretted wooden balconies and painted shutters, but it was a thin disguise, like make-up on a terrified face, for behind it lay a concrete blockhouse in which machinery banged and clanked and cogs engaged and the red *cabines* began their long haul upwards.

> '*A few advice to follow: the Aiguille du Midi stands at an altitude of 3842 metres. Which means weather changes and rapid température variations. Conséquently take warm cloth (especially for the children).*'

At the café table where we waited for the next embarcation, I tried to laugh, I tried to smile, I wanted to smile gratefully in the sunshine so that Will would believe that what I wanted was exactly what he was giving – this dream, this mountain, this inspiration. There were children waiting too, playing around the tables, and none of them looked terrified. Meanwhile Will was staring at me and he was disappointed.

'I can't put the two things together. You're so brave in your writing, but then . . . this timidity.' He was irritated, my fears irritated him. I cupped my hands around the cool dimpled glass of the Orangina bottle and made excuses. Writing's about control, I said, vertigo about the loss of it. Etcetera etcetera. Existential insecurity which begins in childhood and goes on and on, like those endless jargony phrases. I could see that Will was no more convinced than I was. Fear, after all, is what climbers play with, play on like an instrument. That thin line between panic and elation is what they seek out, a self-mastery on the flip side of which lie fantasies of omnipotence – a boundary which they push against, push back, for in the end who's to say what is and is not possible, where courage ends and delirium begins? There was no way of telling Will that my fear was like looking down the wrong end of a telescope, looking for a memory – Did it happen? – a vision of arms around you, of rolling over in them, but it's a pinpoint, too small to see although you're sure it must be there. I said: 'So I have to be a hero in everything?'

'All I'm saying is, it's confusing.'

No tears allowed then. No fears. All he wanted was to make a man of me. 'You *could* try accepting it.' The Orangina bottle slipped from my grasp and rolled to the edge of the table. Will grabbed, but too late; the bottle had smashed on the pavement and the children stopped short in their play and were looking to see if it was their fault – no – giggling.

Will eyed me. He was hurt. I'd put him in the wrong and he always hated that. Behind the téléférique station a cabin was slithering downwards, ready to dock. 'Come on,' he said, 'or we'll miss this one too.'

I pushed my way through the crush of bodies in the *cabine* and found a spot at the far windows, the windows which faced into the slope of the mountain. As the hauling gear engaged and the first swing of the cabin brought the first shrieks from the passengers, I gripped the hand-rail and stared into the trees. There was an atmosphere of high holiday, horseplay, men teasing their wives. Here and there, a pallid face, a muttered *Mon Dieu*. A small dog began to yap wildly, and I felt Will's hand on my shoulder. 'We'll get out half way. Take a breather.' I leaned against him, watching the skyline with its ragged towers: the Aiguille du Plan, the Peigne, the Grepon; my mind recited them numbly.

When the cabin berthed at the *Midi-Plan* station Will led me out on to a grassy shoulder overlooking the valley. I took deep breaths, I started to shake. Will threw his rucksack down in the grass. 'God,' he exploded, 'I hate the French! Packing them in for all that profit.' Angrily, he calculated. 'Sixty people at fifty francs each, at least twenty-five times a day, and double that for returns.' He put his arms round me and we stood, rocking.

His hair was smoky, his earlobes pink and cold. 'If we wait for the next one it'll cost us time. But at least we'll avoid the bloody dog!'

The connecting cabin was smaller, and yellow, and advertised things: ski shops, a disco, The Restaurant 3852 Metres, which promised A Good Table and Cordial Welcome in a Refined Décoration. The floor of the cabin was tinny and riveted, and far below it the trees fell away as the first full blue startle of snow hit us. High altitude sun glared into the cabin, intensifying the colours of parkas and ski-pants, turning the skins of the passengers deep bronze, glamorous as a Martini ad. Will flashed me a gold ironic smile; only his eyes were dismayed.

Cold shadow. We shuddered to a halt among girders. The rock of the *Piton Centrale* stood frozen above the platform. Shivering, we hurried up dank flights of steps until we came out into the sunshine of a wide *terrasse* where tourists milled and video cameras gaped across at the smooth blue summit of Mont Blanc.

From the high point of the Aiguille du Midi the Vallée Blanche dipped gently west and rose again to the Pointe Heilbrunner like a white hammock strung between rock pegs: soft, easy, welcoming. To the north the frilled *seracs* of the Géant Glacier marked the head of the Mer de Glace, and above them the three tiny linked *cabines* of the Heilbrunner téléférique moved and stopped, moved and stopped. 'An easy day out for a lady?' I said.

Will grinned. 'The crevasses are snowed over. We'd better rope up.'

We descended past maps of ski-runs and came to the mouth of a tunnel, a mouth no longer concrete but solid ice which the sun gleamed on but didn't melt: our point of departure. The snow was trodden to a narrow path bulwarked on one side by a high snowdrift; on the Vallée Blanche side a hawser draped between iron posts served as protection. This time I put on my own waist-sling and crampons. I felt glad and sensible, waiting for Will to clip me into the rope, watching the ill-clad tourists who, ignoring the warning notices, shuffled out into the sunshine to inspect the view. The Italian woman had her hair in a chic bob and her hands in the pockets of a padded Armani jacket. I watched her slip and slide in her fashion boots to the end of the fence. A few yards further on, where the path began to curve behind the snowdrift, she turned abruptly, lost her footing on the trodden ice, and let out a sharp cry. A man in a parka grabbed for her, held her, and she bent over, white-faced, as Will shook his head at the craziness of tourists. 'It's a bit exposed,' he said in a neutral voice. 'Better go take a look.'

At the end of the fence I held on tight. A group of army trainees came round the corner, roped together. Their eyes were blanked out by goggles and they looked neither to left nor right, just kept coming at a rhythmic plod, their breath steaming, their faces unsmiling and exhausted. I picked my way back to the tunnel. 'I can't see a thing for tourists,' I said, with that strange insouciance which lives in the lull between one danger and the next. It was as if I'd grown tired of my fears, or perhaps somewhere in me I'd decided that up there, where failure could be terminal, dwelling on the fear of it was a luxury I couldn't afford. Up here in the snow I was in Will's hands, and if his climber's judgement decreed that the traverse wasn't objectively dangerous – I clung to the word 'objective' – then I could do it, it wasn't beyond me.

'OK,' said Will, clipping me into the rope, 'I'm the anchor man, I'll be right behind you.'

What the fear looks like.

A series of shots variously clichéd, taken from a camera mounted on a helicopter which hovers fifty metres out from the corniced ridge, high above the Plan de l'Aiguille. She is poised on a ragged rim of snow, silhouetted against the sun. Below her, blue shadows indicate the overhang, the serious-ness of the exposure. The next shot, which would have to be taken over her shoulder or from a few feet farther down the ridge by a cameraman with perfect balance and even better nerves, is of her left foot, the one adjacent to the drop, booted, criss-crossed by the leather straps of the crampon. Six inches to the left of it, and 8,000 feet below, lie the matchbox hotels of Chamonix.

'Bend your knees,' said Will, as we passed the end of the fence and kept going. On the right the snow sloped away to the Vallée Blanche, 1,000 feet below. On the left the comforting snowdrift tailed to a low wall of snow, two feet high at the most, beyond which I glimpsed the drop for the first time. Sticking my axe-shaft into the snow wall – some small security – I crept down the ridge. And then the wall fell away too, and ahead of me the ridge narrowed to a foot's width and swung out to hang, utterly exposed, over the Plan de L'Aiguille.

'Don't look down,' Will shouted, and I looked, the space drawing my gaze as inevitably as fireworks or lightning: the blue swaying sky, the snow which dappled into a latticework of deep ultramarine shadow and brilliant pale yellow-blue where the sun struck it. The glitter spread away and away, a pure frost-fear in that blue drop, the animal glimpse of the going away of the self. I saw my shadow thrown out and hanging over the edge and my bent knees shuddered uncontrollably. 'Oh Will, I can't.' The shriek was thin and terrible but I was far beyond shame.

'Don't turn!'

From behind me the order came on a voice broken by the wind. In the burning sun, a terror beyond weeping. Above all I wanted a rescue but the rescue was forbidden, for Will's rough instructions forbade me to turn, look, see the source of the power.

'Kathy, you MUST MOVE!'

The impossibility of effort, of knowing that I must move the right foot forward, swing my weight sideways on to that left hip which might treacherously and literally let me down, for nothing could be depended on. If I could have spoken I would have said, Oh, I wanted to walk, wanted to please him but he was asking the impossible, impossible to hold steady, to set in motion the known and necessary mechanics of it.

'You can't fall. I'm belaying you. Now listen to me. Look straight ahead. Yes you can, Kathy. Now just walk.' A hypnotist's voice, filling in the gaps. When it counted to ten I would wake up somewhere else and refreshed.

Imagine the ridge as an alleyway with high walls and lilacs, or as a broad mall bordered by shops. Imagine it as a life without doubt or pause, a life whose clear imperatives pull you towards the future. This is the rout of the childish, the discipline of the intelligence which wills, which says I can, which shifts the weight on to the left hip, which drags the booted foot out of the snow and plants it six inches farther on, which breathes deep into the stomach and tells the other foot to move. Which says that only by trusting the body and all that is my self would I truly trust him. Only by trusting the knees that bend and the thighs that brace, the belly that breathes, the hand's strong grip on the axe . . .

– And the womb that bleeds?

–

Later Will said that there behind her, with his eyes boring into her back, he saw her faltering first step and heard a series of short cries, feral, and he talked to her; he didn't remember the words, God knows he didn't, just talked and talked while the fear glittered from her. He braced his legs and got ready to throw himself to the right, over the other side of the ridge; his axe poised to stab in deep and be his body's claw if his body's weight alone was not enough to stop her fall. He said that the message of fear ran electric along the rope and his voice cracked, for she was not separate, but in him, he *was* her, crying abandoned in the curve of the cliff while his brother raced cruelly out of sight and the wind fanned the tears out across his face.

Later I saw that this was the moment when the fear lifted and left me, and my joints lost their rust and moved fluidly again, and I knew that I must take control. Keep my eyes focussed on the near and not the far, on the narrow trodden ribbon of snow under my feet, on the deep blue prints of others who had passed this way before us. Focus my mind, too, on safety, on this dance of pure artifice, on that safer place fifty metres ahead where the ridge swung back towards the Vallée Blanche and softened into the folded dunes of the snow-field.

Sharp spears of frost patterned the surface of the snow, like iron filings pulled this way and that by the opposing poles of a magnet. I came to the wands which marked the head of the ski-run. Somewhere out of sight over my shoulder the valley gaped, but my legs were swinging now, my breath coming looser. My boots fitted snugly into the line of prints that led down beside the markers. When the crest of the ridge was a horizon behind me, safe as a blanket, I turned and watched Will run down the slope towards me. His splayed feet threw up sprays of snow, his rucksack bounced on his back. I dropped my pack and threw myself into his arms, crazy, babbling. I did it, didn't I do it? Above us the tiny orange *cabines* paused, spied, moved on. Gusts of laughter came out of my chest, the stopped energy released. Will stroked the hair back from my face, soothing me. Yeah, you did too. His mouth moved against my cheek and he whispered to me that we should make love there in the burning frost, wet, harnessed, standing up like animals. Death was unmentionable on our minds but it was sex that shuddered in us. I felt his tongue, the roughness of his jaw, his insistent hands. His body spoke in little cries, he needed, I knew we could annihilate each other, I knew we were done for.

– *I'm trying to understand this equation, sex-death.*

— But listen. This is the wish at the heart of terror. For hasn't she sought out someone who'll take her to the limits and beyond, to the place where other times and possibilities intersect? The transforming terror which folds her back on herself and sends her spiralling down through the impossible to the place where the gate is unbarred and she slips through, leaving her flat shadow empty on the ridge, and she's gone entirely, leapt out of her swaddling skin and her being lives in its light strong triumph and she *is* Will, she has travelled a continuous curving plane and emerged in a different body, time, sex, in that parallel truth which she always knew was truer.

— *The omnipotence of the will? I suppose the question that comes to mind is — Who has the power now? Who contains whom?*

—

They are out in the centre of the glacier when the helicopter comes, suddenly a red helicopter high up in the palisade of Aiguilles which guards the summit, whirring crablike among the needles, dangerously near, casing out the narrow gulfs between them. Eyes and heart rise to the unseen emergency, her eyes scanning the ledges, all of her leaning towards the summit in a yearning for the connection to be made between injured and rescuer, a yearning for the gap to be closed. They stand still, the two of them, saying nothing, for what is there to be said? Shadow of a cloud settling over them. Cold pours off the snow. Her eyes sting, secretly ecstatic with tears as she stares up at the bright granite buttresses, so stark and sunburned and lovely, at the vicious edges, at the blue sky ripped with noise.

— *The meaning of the helicopter is . . . that there must always be an interruption, a reminder . . . ?*

— The meaning of the helicopter is desire, the catch in the

throat when you see something so beautiful and beyond you, something precise and brave, something so purely good, like the good mother in whose belly you might be saved, nurtured, bandaged, soothed. Fed with sweet air and milk. Hands on your brow, the wink of a digital watch on the wrist of the man who crouches by your stretcher, tending to you. The meaning of the helicopter is the end of all effort, it's when you've done the impossible and there's no more to be done . . .

   – The impossible thing is to transform yourself into . . . ?

   – You've done all you can and the helicopter swings you up into whiteness and the blanket on the stretcher is blood red and the whirring blades sing as they work and it's enough, love without interruption or end as the helicopter flows down into the valley like a bird carrying you. This lasts a long time, this holding, this flow which lasts just as long as you need.

   – Like a pregnancy, full-term? It won't throw you out?

   –

Walk normally, says Will, as she tiptoes over the snow-bridges. Acts of faith. If she goes through he will hold her on the rope, he will haul her up. From time to time the snow gives way to reveal ominous boot-shaped holes, holes which lead to crevasses. Walk normally, says Will, who knows depth hoar and windslab and which snow is firm *nevée* and which snow is rotten, while above the Aiguilles the helicopter hovers, circles, returns, sways like washing in the wind, and finally lifts up and away, without anyone. She's taking off her rucksack, rubbing snow on her cheeks. Her feet have scuffed up the frozen snow, she kicks thick rafts of it from her crampons. Ahead the trail of other prints winds between crevasses, along the lips of chasms. To the north-east cloud flows across the *seracs* at the head of the glacier, and the Mer de Glace fills up like a bowl. And now Will stops and asks for a photograph, him, blue vest and salopettes, red rope coil on his shoulder, one leg braced and one bent, the thrust hip ironic, the ice-axe triumphal: this is how she'll remember him, a half-smile under goggles in front of the Peuterey Ridge, the rope which hangs from his waist brushing the surface of the snow delicately as the tail of a fox, the rope leading out of the frame to where she invisibly is . . .

Then it will be night and raining, and Will and Kathleen walk through the lit streets of the town. They've hitched back through the Tunnel, he pulls her into a shop doorway among postcard stands shrouded in wet polythene. She's going to buy him dinner, they're so happy, it's her last night, he pushes kisses at her, they're laughing. The boys in the Bar Nash nod greetings. Walt is there with his cronies, there are even one or two women in the company. Someone has been drawing cartoons on paper napkins: a climber falls backwards, his rope severed by a woman with exaggerated breasts. 'Next time, shithead, remember the Milk Tray.' And this prefigures the farce to come, this is where the farce begins, Joanna's trajectory intersecting with theirs, Joanna standing on the pavement outside the steamed-up window, Joanna's eye and hand deciding which one of the glass panels is definitely the door, and will open.

Two women with hair wet from the rain. Kathleen's is light red and frizzes into ringlets; Joanna's dark and straight and straggling. But now Kathleen has gone, vanished downstairs to the *toilettes* to dry hers and be beautiful, leaving Will alone at the table, and right on cue Joanna is framed in the open door behind him, unseen, entering, slipping into Kathleen's empty seat, tense, forcing a smile. Babble of the bar drowning what they say, but you can imagine the shock, all the chickens come home to roost and Will's face as he jumps up and puts an arm around Joanna's shoulders and bundles her out of the bar, out into the downpour, protesting, she can't understand. And

Walt, opening his eyes wide, popping his eyes for his friends: rough stuff, man, as Kathleen runs up the tiled stairs from the *toilettes* all smiles and sits down at the table with its oil and vinegar and cutlery and wine glasses and lights a cigarette all unaware and waits.

In the square where the statue of the mountain guide points up at the summit of Mont Blanc, where the Arve torrents yellow under the bridge and the flags of all nations hang limp in the rain, Will pulls Joanna into a telephone kiosk, a kiosk with folding doors which trap her holdall until he wrenches it inside and then it's hard to see them through the glass which streams with rain, and impossible to hear what Will is saying – indeed, what excuses could he give? When we can see from Joanna's face her absolute unknowingness, incredible blind spot in a woman so strong, self-aware, even cynical. Betrayal beyond words, a contract now out in the open, exposed, a contract broken. I thought we were supposed to . . . We always said we'd . . . His power, his power to lie, Kathleen's power to force him, to forbid confessions. I can't talk about her. A language indecipherable as Finnish, a language breaking down into separate syllables. And Will, incredulous. Don't give me that, Joanna. You must have known. You must. And her hand goes up and she hits him once, and again; unlike Will she doesn't wear a wedding ring.

From the image of Will blurred by rain, shielding himself, we cut to Kathleen and the wine arriving, *Merci*, and she's pouring two glasses, sipping, cupping the glass in her hands, lacing her fingers round the rim, while in the telephone kiosk Joanna is struggling, incoherent, vulnerability refused. Let me go, I'll sort her out. Will's arms are wrapped around her, restraining. They have to talk, but where can they go? To the tent? Joanna delivers another punch. Where you've been with *her*? The telephone receiver, dislodged in the scuffle, hangs from its cord, burring. They'll go to a hotel room, and damn the cost. In the hotel lobby Joanna slaps down her Access card and looks at Will challengingly. They follow the receptionist upstairs; they're silent, the receptionist has a cold and sniffs badly; the bedroom is neutral: divans with striped duvets, bedside lamps shaped like teardrops, a Ricard ashtray. Joanna tilts a bottle of duty-free whisky to her mouth. Do you know what Ann-Marie said? She said maybe he's lonely out there. She said maybe he needs you. Go out and surprise him, she said. Joanna's hunched on the edge of a divan, face white and sick, waiting. So. Drink? Laughing bitterly. Will tinkers with the ashtray, he wants a cigarette, he has to telephone at least. Well, cheers anyway. The room key dangles from Joanna's finger, she watches it circle like a gold ring on a hair, clockwise for a girl, anticlockwise for a boy, this is unlike her but she's lost, she's waiting, she can't tell how much territory has been taken, her nipples are cold with fear, her laugh cracks like ice. She wants to shower, to comb the tangles out of her hair; as she imagines the comb stroking through, separating the strands, she shivers, thinking of some point before all of this, a place of relative certainty, she wants to turn the clock back to a place where Will couldn't stand in front of her peeling her life like an onion, and she lifts the bottle and drinks again because that way her centre will be stinging and terribly clear and rage will take over, a rant with justice at its heart, a meting out of punishment, sentence, hangings, excisions, rage of the despot undermined, the righteous despot, the female despot who believes in the divine right of wives, the despot with roots in the working masses, the self-made despot, the paranoid despot, the theoretical despot, the born-again despot, the zealot, the fundamentalist, the dogmatist, the sectarian . . .

And Will, wondering how to reason, argue. Suddenly shouting when Joanna the despot crumples. Well I can't just let her sit there, can I? And Kathleen with a fallen face, split and in love and tugging at her hair while the phone on the far wall rings faintly and the waitress balances her tray on one hand to answer it, irritated beyond measure, *Quoi? Quoi?*

Turning her head to scan the room of blonds, *Americains*, the cheap *Anglais*, the *Boches* who should know better than to come here. Fetched at last from the table, Kathleen leans against the wall in the hubbub. Covering one ear with her hand. I can't hear you. Will's face in the mirror above the telephone in the lobby, a face not looking at itself but elsewhere, fingers plucking at one eyebrow, lips pressed into a pout. Don't ask me to, Kathy. Please. I have to. But the receiver is slammed back on the hook and Kathleen is standing in the noise of the jukebox, someone pumps money into a fruit machine and she's cut him off and she sits down and counts out notes at the table with its *pichet* of wine and two glasses and when she goes out it's stopped raining and the clouds are clearing on a moonless night. Crossing the railway track there's the flash of a shooting star from the Pleiades, a streak, a split second's gap of darkness and then the explosion of light in Orion's belt, lovely like all things that were never meant for her, and she's lost everything, possessions scattered behind her, a nomad of pain in the wet streets, but it feels right to be this artist in the garret with the roof open to the sky, it feels savage and pure, like wading thigh deep in freezing water. Her limbs tremble; Will draws near and far, but if she cries – tears floating down her face like stars – it's for his loss more than hers, because only by losing him can she have him for as long as she needs, and because it's too beautiful with the station clock round as a moon and even if we don't know what she wishes when she looks up we can be sure that nomads, like all those who have no part in the ugly power of the temporal (which winning requires and which she has renounced), feel uniquely entitled to wishes, illuminations, the protection of the gods. It couldn't happen any other way.

– *I'm wondering what you were forced to renounce as a child.*

– Listen, she loves him too much to fight for him, it's beyond her, she feels her hands are tied.

Only Joanna can say no, refuse, pummel, get drunk, be in an ugly mood which she can't be cajoled out of. This is how Joanna will be ugly. Fear making her crude. She'll be sitting on the carpet, legs splayed out, face flushed from alcohol and the central heating. The whisky bottle is between her knees. Well, has *she* got her marching orders? She doesn't want Will's pain now, if he's withheld it she doesn't want to know; from now on all pain about Kathleen (which she sees rearing up like a great black horse on the horizon) will be his burden to carry, not to share, she won't have it, won't listen, won't take it from him. Anyway it's not really about Kathleen, is it. It's about us. The balloon of love threatening to burst when Will shrugs and won't say yes. She drinks hard under the teardrop light. Prove it to me. Prove that I don't count for nothing. The words refused, pride won't say them. It's that old business again, isn't it, you're getting back at me. He's shaking his head, no, he might cry. He takes Joanna's hands and folds her arms around him. His knees are wooden, phlegm in his throat and nowhere to spit it. Hold me. Blank-faced, unbuttoning her blouse. Silence of his wounds. This is how men are, dumb, their penises asking for solace, offering it, it isn't what you think, it isn't always a question of strategy. Please don't freeze on me, Will says. Not now. She's warm, her breasts fall from the unbuttoned shirt. Nagging sex-wish he tugs up from her, she doesn't want to belong to that particular perversity of pain wrought by the presence of the other, the triangle, the other pubic triangle which liquifies, sucks, surrenders itself to the crashes and cries of orgasm. Will draws back the duvet; his eyes plead. Full of hope and hate, she stiffens, love stiffens her for husband and home and garden and gate, the enclosure broken into, violated; her vagina is dry, its gate is closed, she can't take him, he holds her, lights of cars speed out of the mouth of the *Tunnel Mont Blanc* and zigzag down the shoulder of the mountain, cars speed to Geneva and Grenoble and the Frontière Suisse and he holds her, she turns her back, she raises a hand to turn off the teardrop light. Tell me you don't love her. He holds her, she recoils, they're exhausted. Tell me you don't love me then. He holds her, he can't say sorry, his love lies stiff against her reproachful thigh, speechless. Outside, the first pre-dawn birds are singing. Dim light creeps into the room, they sleep, they're exhausted, there's no more for us to see.

Morning comes, and Kathleen has bags under her eyes from the night's punishment, Joanna reaching into the tent with ragged fingers while she waited for sleep, frightened of the dark and evictions, the transgressor whose hands have already been cut off. Across the clearing Jean-Yves picks raspberries for his morning yoghurt while the rose withers in its box and the girl who meant it as goodbye marries a car dealer in München. Dew falls on Kathleen's hair, dew rusts the zip of the tent as she packs her rucksack and flees from Joanna, while high above her the glacier moves slower than anything you can imagine and Will draws near and far, ice on his eyelashes and they're kissing on that impossible edge, sunburned faces which lick each other, the lips of the crevasse open to kiss them, they're together, laughter falls from the air.

The image floats like a moored boat in the head which concentrates on dodging the whizzing traffic on the main road, holiday cars which toot and wave good-humouredly. She's gone, there won't be another image, no replacement and Will won't find her, for the oxygen has cut herself off. Already he's dying without her; fluids puff up his tissues, lungs, he's spitting up blood, small oedemas clog his brain, this is the decay of altitude, the starved cells withering, their dying accelerated and she's transfixed by pity as she steps into the coach and walks up the aisle to the back seat, head held high, face calm as Garbo's on the prow of that Spanish galleon, a *tabula rasa*, this is the only way she won't die without him.

– I'm thinking of rage clamped behind the teeth, rage eating into the jaw.

–

– I think that your Father could either make you feel very very good or very very bad . . .

– A plate chipped, bitten into: microbes proliferate unseen, eventually spreading a grey stain under the pure white glaze. Once, high up in the mountains, Will took a shit in the snow and all I could imagine was that it would be cylindrical and glossy as his penis, it would be perfect like the rest of him, preserved in the slow ice of the glacier.

But now he's waking, looking at his watch in the dimness. Joanna is asleep, one unconsciously fond hand thrown across Will's belly. He's overslept, he slithers out of bed, he's running through the streets, it's late and his blood is pumping and he's mad with love, flickers of marigolds in window-boxes and the white curtain of the Massif high, still, enclosing: the mountain which has its own laws, the mountain which can either accelerate the process of ageing or give you a young death and freeze you unblemished in its glaciers.

– I'm remembering the beginning, I'm remembering that you were the one who feared decay, dissolution. As if it were a contagion that might spread.

– On a woman the upper thighs go first, stretching and pocking. Often the back remains smooth and taut but the bagging of the flesh on the thighs is the giveaway. At my age my mother never bled again; in the hospital everything had been taken away. After this blood sacrifice she said she felt nothing but relief, she was finished with all that mess, maybe at last she thought she could be pure as the driven snow. But then it was my turn to stuff sanitary towels wrapped in brown paper into the grate. Once my father caught me red-handed and I saw the grimace he couldn't hide. He turns away, he's embarrassed,

188

he raises his newspaper, erases the fact of the brown paper glowing and peeling back to reveal the white cotton with the red stain catching fire and crumbling to a black ash which flutters up the chimney and out into the smoky skies of Belfast, burnt blood in the wind.

– *The fantasy is that your rage is the disease, contagious, that's what he died of?*

– My blood. He's under the ground, worms. Time passes, the fluids bubble up, a viscosity of decay.

–

– Our blood. Mine and Joanna's, splashing and flowing. Our blood written on the skin of Dionysus who makes no war, lets no blood. In the glade Jean-Yves sits cross-legged with a spoon, pointing. Dappled shade, the bowl of raspberries glint red in the green wood. She's gone, and it's madness to go after her. Jean-Yves disagrees, his face lecturing. The raspberries are good, you want to try some? *L'amour, une folie,* yes, but it's *une belle folie, n'est-ce pas?* Slumped by the ring of stones that marks the camp-fire, toe of one trainer stirring the embers, Will looks at the raspberries in his palm, eats one, two, crams the rest into his mouth, crushed mess on his hands and now there's a mark on his forehead, a red accident, you'd think he was going to war but it's an inscription, red, he doesn't know it but he's inscribed her on his skin and he's on his feet again, dashing for the square and his *belle folie.* There's the coach, blue and cream, drawing away, and Kathleen with her hands pressed against the window, trying to open it. It's jammed, it's stupid, she's on her feet, laughter jerks out of her, she's crying out for help, help comes, it's open now but Will has inexplicably stopped running, he stands pigeon-toed in the road in his blue anorak, Petrouchka with hands dangling, his body won't move, everything saying he's helpless as the coach makes a slow circuit of the roundabout, accelerates over the railway bridge, is gone.

Pastel chalks lie strewn across the table-top, broken, they powder the floor of the cell. Nijinsky draws red-eyed masks of soldiers, drawings composed of intersecting circles, infantile and terrifying. Nijinsky who's going mad, the beginning of disintegration, Nijinsky the perfectionist, God of the Dance. Romola must get him out of there, they must take a train to a place far from the contagion of war, to neutral Switzerland, peace, the white sweep of mountains. He will fly down the slopes with Kyra on a painted sledge, the faun will feather the snow with his light prints, barely touching, he will drink pure water and eat only vegetables, no blood, he will cleanse himself, eat no decaying meats from the filthy war, the war which tears him apart, he can't have enough of the mountains, the white purity of snow.

– *I'm thinking of the gun in the chamois leather. I'm thinking of the conflict of loyalties you must have felt in relation to your father.*

– Listen, it's he who can't bear the conflict, he's never felt anything like this, the terrible choice. He's in shock; back in the hotel where Joanna sleeps he leans over the washbasin, retching, sick. He lies down; passive, he lets Joanna hold a glass of water to his mouth, it's cold, a relief. He's home, empty and peaceful as Joanna floats in and out of his vision, miraculous cool hands fastening her slightly frayed white bra in the centre of her back, zipping up her jeans. She throws him the hint of a smile, ordinary and wry – Well, you asked for it – her old trenchcoat hangs in the wall cupboard and her hairbrush lies on the dressing table and she's hungry if he isn't. He's ill, inside he crows to himself that he loves her and that she won't leave him, outside the bedroom is the future but it's very still here with her pink toenail varnish winking at him.

Memories of ice hockey breaks, winning: the athlete spins, hands behind his back, grins; electric music grinds out from loudspeakers sat high in the vaulted ceiling of the rink. He's graceful, supple, his skates strike out left, right, left as Joanna holds the rail, balancing unsteadily. Her smile is spunky and familiar and angry. So. So. Are they going to have a good time then? Will takes her hand, Will places her arm in his, and, stately as the church wedding they never had, they start out across the ice. Left, right, left, crisp bite of the skates like a whisper, if you love, you move ... But now Joanna feels steadier, she shoos him away, she wants to try alone. Leave me, she says, as Will hovers, for when he comes near she wants to lean on him and her balance goes up the spout. She wards him off. Don't touch. Will spins off expertly, he's dancing backwards, he's holding out his arms. Hey lady. Grinning. He circles, memories of ice hockey breaks, winning, if only Kyra would stop clinging to his hand, if only she'd stop crying.

– *Perhaps we need to look here at the idea of loss, mourning?*

– But Will won't mourn, he won't lose, he can't go on like this. They're in the hotel room, they're making love wildly, he's bursting with love. Afterwards Joanna lies quietly, exhausted, but Will gets out of bed and pulls the curtains back to reveal the white sweep of mountains. All tears are past, his eyes are bright, feverish, the rush of adrenalin returning. If Joanna had found in some other man or woman what he found in Kathleen, such a love, how could he have asked her to renounce it? The mountains are blue and gold and white, he's filling up with light, he's complete, knowing his destination: boundless love, boundless. But you can love two people, of course you can, of course. What else do the mountains prove if not this. Running to the bed, landing on it with a bounce. So excited. He tucks her hand under his arm, holds it tight. Such revelations to confide. You can, Joanna. Joanna is angry. She's frightened, she snatches her hand away, she hugs herself defensively under the duvet, eyes dark pinpoints blinking in the sudden glare of light which the white peaks shed across the room. The mountains illuminate the room, assaulting her with strangeness, this strident note of alarm. Under the duvet the heat is stifling but she won't come out, she's weightless, she has no body; a moment ago he made love to her and now he's turned her into Mother, trapped her by pleading. She can either be punitive or permissive, there's no other choice. What is he asking of her? She sees them together and she can't bear the sight of it. Ditched. She covers her eyes, the word empties into her throat. But what blazes out is rage. So now he's God, is that it?

His face pales, you'd think he'd been slapped. His insistent heart still certain that she'll understand, for this is Joanna who loves him, who has travelled with him, his friend till death. What does she want from him if not this honesty, this destination which illuminates his very self, bones, roots of the hair, this honourable endeavour. His eyes are on her, entreating, he's forgotten how to lie. Think about it, Joanna. He has more to give than you ever wanted to take. That terrible reserve of yours made you back away, twitchy, sceptical. And now she's killing him with her jeers or trying to: this is how he sees it. He looks at her under beetling brows, brows like precipices in a nineteenth-century painting. This is how Nijinsky might have looked at his interlocutors when he in his delusion became the very son of God: severe, martyred, even a little scornful. So what's required is that he dissimulate? Oh well, OK, so he'll be patient, cunning even; whatever it takes to persuade her. He's thirty, he's slipped through some boundary of possibility and if he looks back at the world it's refracted and distasteful: the ice mirror in the eye. He's thirty, he's scowling, he's not known limits, he won't have them. Lost in Kathleen's arms he might long for a boundary to be set but now that Joanna is here, the palpable barrier that is Joanna, his mind dodges aside, leaps, flies high, finds a kind of irridescence. He's thirty, age when the baleful Saturn returns, planet of limitation, he's cracking up, this is how I see it.

*

It's dark, it's the dark ballroom of the house that Will remembers, the house on the road to Vallorcines. The shutters are being prised open, Will's shoulder enters, his leg; he's walking jerkily across the room, soles of his trainers making patterned prints in the thick layer of dust on the floor. Earlier we've seen him inside a car, expressionless behind sunglasses, a French driver making hopeful conversation. *Vous êtes étudiant? Grimpeur?* The driver takes his hands off the wheel and mimes a climber scrabbling for holds. *Grimpiste?* A tour bus passes, a double-decker, its roof brushed by hanging larch branches. *Anglais?* the driver persists, *Americain? Americain,* says Will. *Oui, Americain.*

There's a staircase, a half-circle wending up into a gallery. Brass doorhandles which he touches one by one. He's going into a room where furniture sits shrouded in greyish cloths. He's crouching down with his back against the wall, it's dark, it's the dark of dreams but he doesn't open the shutters because he wants his eyes to become accustomed to it, he knows it's necessary. He's got to think, punishing though it is. He's crouching, finger drawing little pictures in the dust between his feet. Baby Christmas trees with serrated branches, a house with chimney smoke. He's waiting for something to arrive out of the dark, time's passing and he doesn't know why he's here except that he's waiting for something. And for that he has to shut himself in, become opaque. The walls are richly papered, a tapestry effect like the faded print of old dresses. He imagines walking to the peak of the mountain, small cracks in the rocks, trickles of pebbles rushing down. Transparent fluted ice-falls like whole sentences frozen in the uttering, whole poems. But no, that's for later, it's too soon; first he has to shut himself in, be narrow, small, wait.

And now the chink appears. As if a switch had been thrown, a line of light glints under a door. Glimpsed from the corner of his eye at first, so that he starts, turns his head, stares. Gets up shaking his head, he's smiling, he can't help it, he's on a rock at the river's edge and Kathleen's head leans against his knees.

193

His hand plays in her hair; it's sundown, a bluish bloom like grapes hanging above the distant foothills of the Larzac. He's pushing the door open, his eyes slit in the dazzle of sunlight, he's standing there shielding them. It's a broken room, roofless: snow shrouding the mantelpiece, the clock, snow quilting the double bed. Gilded by sun. There's a small boy sitting up, tousled, rubbing his eyes. Grinning. You can see the energy crackling in him, the rosy health of it; in a moment, you know, he will hurl on his clothes and snatch up his fishing rod and race downstairs to bellow for his breakfast.

Will. Will in profile, eyes shut, head leaning against the window of the téléférique cabin. Cigarette in his mouth. All the snowy tops of trees flowing down behind him. We're going up and up, as far as the Aiguille du Midi station. Clear mountain air thinning, leaking into him. The clarity far above the piggy-bank houses and the damp fields of mud, clarity of ice and throwing himself up and on, clarity of surfaces where shadows are precise. He is crossing the concrete bridge, he's at the blue mouth of the ice tunnel, high, blank, no gear. They're shouting after him, warnings in French. Hands in his pockets, he's smiling back blankly: *Americain. Oui, Americain.* Sun startling on the Dent du Géant. Up in the deep blue sky there are hang-gliders, microlites, and he's home now, the little horse who's very tired, and everyone's here, everyone, and it's so very blue and dazzling.

You take a train to Geneva, and a narrow gauge to Chamonix, and then you change on to the Montenvers, the mountain railway which goes up to 7,000 feet. Then you move up the Mer de Glace until you come to fixed iron ladders in the rock, climbing past snow banks pitted with marmot tracks, and behind you is the Charmoz and before you is the Grandes Jorasses, and then there's the solid stone refuge, perched high above the glacier, a helicopter pad, and there's no one.

Can I tell you why I'm happy? Because nothing on the mountain is lost, no, never, and the Gods are wise and know this when they sidle their fingers through your hair and tug you and your heart says you have to go. Because the mountain can't be spoiled by you or anyone, it's undamageable, a harmony. Everyone is there and in their proper places, imprinted on the air waves, contained there. All heavy burdens of blood fall away in the clear air. Life, death – the difference is only a matter of velocity, you can reach out and talk to anyone you like: spirit to spirit, with love and luck, synchronising.

Part Four

Si quelqu'un m'a laissé une lettre

On a day in Chamonix when banked cloud hid the Aiguilles and the rain fell through streamers of mist, Kathleen and Will took shelter in the Musée Alpin. The galleries smelt of mould and old leather. There were hobnailed boots and black iron crampons and worm-eaten sledges. In a glass-topped display table Kathleen saw a photograph of a crushed torso, arm wasted as a dead branch with broken fingers curled back. Rendu par le glacier.

Fragment of a rope lost in a catastrophe in 1832, recovered on the 21st of September 1878. Rendu par le glacier.

Fragment of a ladder recovered in 1938 from Walker's first ascent of the Dru in 1878. Rendu par le glacier.

It was grisly. Awe-struck, Kathleen hovered over the glass cases. Fragments of ice-axes, a knife with several blades. When she rejoined Will in the doorway he was frowning out at the weather. 'I guess I just don't share your veneration for relics,' he said to her impatiently.

Sept 20, 198-
My head-torch failing in the darkness of the tent, barely the light of a candle as I read your poems and burn another hole in the nylon inner with one of the cigarettes I smoke so much since feeding my love on you, as I struggle to get out my notebook to write this down before the light goes out. Hand over hand into your bed where your breasts can fill my mouth like plums and I can't get enough of you, wondering where the ice that fuelled my engines has melted to and gone. My Mer de Glace must live in my hands, for now my stomach demands more precious fuel and

warm-blooded dreams, a softness like squirrels in the snow, and stars, not tombs, in my eye.

(Dear Kathy, hope this reaches you before I get back. Wish I was there, the weather has been disastrous since you left . . . Love, Will.)

Monday, Nov 19, 198-
Dear Kathy,
I can't think about the present with you, about what I'm feeling, about loving you. It seems so wrong and hard and even that hardness doesn't convince me of its truth*. Maybe you're right in saying that I shouldn't have had an open relationship if I'm so entwined, so inextricably dependent for my past and future on Joanna, but I can't put it away in a drawer, what you are to me and how much I love you. So instead of the present I think about the past, the recent past and you and you. I don't let it close in on the narrowness of a few months. I re-read, somewhat hopelessly, what I have that you've written to me. In your letter to Chamonix you say how much junketing across France we've done for each other and that's what I think about. About how much of everything we've done for each other. About you reading Proust to me on the first real holiday I've ever had, about you coming sleepily, warm and naked except for your open blue shirt, down the stairs to hug me after my tiresome dark hours in the residential fields of greater Paulhan.

There's no accounting for how I grew to love you and could ask so much from you because there's no mystery about it. I can't and comfortingly don't need to explain the obvious.

It's afternoon and I'm back from the college having done my work, ie attended my lecture and seminar. I'm trying

---

*Oftentimes hardness in itself as both solidity and difficulty has seemed important or worthwhile to me.

to be diligent. I'm hoping it will help me get over the loneliness of being without you. It doesn't and I still think and masturbate about you.

I entered over the weekend the first of what looks to be a short but serious round of disarmament talks with Joanna. I'm glad for what's still possible there and I cover up my ambivalence more or less. It's hard, and I hate not giving you my love.

Went on my own to a hockey game at the rink on Sat night (Glasgow Dynamos v Lea Valley Lions) and felt strongly that I want to try and play this winter. I had lovely thoughts about flying along the ice in the chaos of the game as I lay down to sleep on Sat night and last night. And it has something to do with you. Like my feelings for you insisting on somewhere to go, refusing to lay low between me and Joanna.

Joanna can't make it go away and it would be wrong to expect that.

I wrote this I think just because I had to say that I hurt, and to admit that I keep thinking you love me . . .
Love, Will.

PS. I'll come by later in the week on Thurs or Fri morning.

Thurs 22 Nov, 198-
Dear Kathy,
So there's no question that you're definitely hiding from me, there's only the question of whether you're hiding in South Wales or in the closet in your flat. I at first didn't believe Louise at all and was angry and immediately started thinking about what I know of your movements and where would be the best place to find you. On the North London line on the way to therapy? At college after your class? Or I considered just standing in the rain in the Square and waiting. Ultimately the vision of hours beneath

the nearly-bare plane trees in wet trainers and a steaming face deterred me. I also had to admit if you don't want to see me there's not much I can do about it in terms of changing your mind, but I will act on what I want, just as you will act on what you want. However, I do recognise that I owe more than just respect for your desires at this time. Having done or tried to do what I want I now have to do what other people say, so there's not much good my entering your flat and looking in the cupboards for you. God, Kathy, where are you? How are you? I both do and don't want to know what you're feeling. I washed the blue shirt last night but couldn't be bothered to bring anything but myself when I came by this morning, that's the only reason I was coming, the only reason I wanted to come. Pathetic, perhaps. Maybe you think, like the college counsellor, that I should just accept there's unhappiness and not bother you. Maybe I should, but it's just not on offer from me: not to write this letter, not to want to see you again. You've loved me so well that you know what I mean and I know how you hurt.

Since the beginning of the class last year I've always wanted to give you something, and I believe I have, but you're a person of such scope and depth, as well as being, like me, an inveterate risk taker, that you'll always end up getting more than you want – the pain as well as the love. Maybe more pain than love. I hope not. Did you call me Monday afternoon? The phone rang three times then cut off. It was next to my hand but I was writing to you at the time so I waited to answer it. God, Kathy, you're so beautiful, important to me.
Love, Will.

Dec 10, 198-
Since I left you last week, with you so nervously final and me too dumb to protest, I've noticed how far into winter

we've come. I wake at seven and notice the black dawns, waking in my single bed in Les's comfortable flat, and I feel heavy, like I'm on a mountain face. Even looking at the safety of his polished pine floors dressing feels like a struggle, and there's none of the mountain's cold to make it happen regardless. I lay, all mattress and bent spine, remembering that early yesterday morning I rode the bus round your Square. The pale green blinds were still down on your bedroom-workroom-lovingroom-readingroom windows. I brought my key and thought, stop, find you underneath the duvet, sleeping and struggling to be self-contained. But no, I'd disturb your sleep. And what would I bring you? Sugared tea, anxious need and requests, demands no doubt. Lying here it's winter, dawn and black. The house lights visible outside my window are yellow and on. It appears dark and settled, you and I, a full moon over a New England lake, but I feel sunk below water and gurgling; my eyelids won't lift and let me look around. I can't complain or cry about this black winter dawn. Only small thick tears come out, drops of painful cement – grey, dull, hardening. I laugh in hope that they might chip the polished floor. Hard solid tears. So different from the soft weight of your thigh and my liquid lust. I stop looking at the yellow lights of houses, I hold on to you, one hand beneath your hips, and I push through your melting centre, lifting and delighted. I see your eyes closed, breasts swollen, tender, and me certain that you know I love you . . . Then I remember how you cried, afraid of my love, my demands to fill you up, and I lay here black and dawning.

– The debris is rendered up scrap by scrap, to be reclaimed, made use of. It's there under your eyes, history, banal as are all possessions fallen out of the layers of time: a furry toy, a Republican beret, a book of fairy tales. This is the story you wanted to hear: loss, attachment, change, mourning. This part takes years.

– *I'm wondering which one of you it was that was frozen, held in suspension.*

– What Thomas Mann says in *The Magic Mountain* is that death is a great power, and reason stands simple before him, for reason is only virtue, while death is release, immensity, abandon, desire.

– *Rather a dead hero than . . . ?*

–

–

– I can still see him falling, it's cleaner by far.

Jan 1,198-
Dear Kathy,
It's New Year's Day and the wind is blowing a freezing cold draught down the chimney into the kitchen so that my knees and ankles are starting to go numb. I do my bit as far as I can but have not felt in the festive mood.

Kathy, I'm just torn apart and distracted all the time because I'm thinking about you and pretending I'm not. It's driving me crazy. I'm not there for you or Joanna or myself any more. I walk around during the day flushed and prickly, hiding my madness under dark-coloured jumpers and heavy coats.

I admit you're right that my wanting us to be clandestine lovers after all we've asked of each other is small and bitter, and doesn't fit in with your or my ideals. We have to talk, though, about what's between us. We can't ignore such loving and dreaming we've done together. I still need to see you and for you to call me. I can imagine how you hurt. I've been disoriented and pained to the point of obsession since we met on Wednesday.

I woke up the other morning thinking about things for you and me to do and about how we dreamed, and I grew damp and hot having to face that I was losing all that by going back to Joanna. I admit I'm ambivalent, even schizophrenic. However at this point it's a *fait accompli* that I can't leave Joanna and I can't see a way that we can have anything that's satisfactory in terms of my being there for you. Joanna won't have it and it's destroying me to be so patently dishonest. Despite all there is between us that's vital and real, and what more there could or should be, it's clear that I've made my bed and I have to lie in it. You're right that I'm not as rash as you, but then again I don't think I know anyone else who is.

Part of my distraction this past week has been my trying to reassess everything and return to you – but it's clear to me that it's insanity my dwelling on possibilities I won't act on.

And it's getting to the point now, Kathy, where it doesn't matter, because I'm just making myself a wreck. I'm pretty good at appearances, but inside I'm collapsing and I admit I'm now worried about myself. I've been out running and down to the climbing wall, but I find I'm constantly on the verge of tears stripped of my dark jumpers and thick coats. Part of the reason I love climbing is because I have to concentrate – and I do have to do that, concentrate on it. So many bits of me keep falling out of place and my course work is a mess, for loving you and not being there or strong enough to do so is making life marginal at best. I know how you feel about me and you know that I love you. You can rage against it and with cause, but you can't deny it.

Being realistic I know I've got to stop trying to keep you there loving me while I'm pursuing my desires and commitments to Joanna. I know that it's tearing you apart as well. I want us to still be willing to see each other. I don't know if I can stop coming to you with my needs which is why I'm so afraid of your having to cut me off. I know that's more easily said from my side with someone meeting most of my needs. But please don't be fierce to prove to me that you can be. I already know that.

You were supposed to get a rowan red fibre-pile vest for a present, but unfortunately the manufacturer has discontinued them. The shop came up with an olive green one but it just wouldn't do. I'll be in Glencoe from the 5th to the 11th, I'll call you when I get back.

The picture is of me (of course I realise it could be anyone) setting up the second bivvy about three quarters of the way up the Eiger. The sun only hits the North Face for an hour or two each day just before it sets and it's remarkable how it lights up the rock all red and warm. I've got to go now and I'll see you when I get back from Scotland. I love you, Kathy, and I don't think either of us can benefit by ignoring each other. We need to talk.

Love, Will.

She stood at the mirror, sending magic messages. Flooded with the knowledge of what he gave, she was beautiful, and the answer in her eyes said clearly that he would come. A vision. The air waves crackled to infinity. He was on his way now, buttoning up his jacket, drawing on his arsenal of excuses. But he didn't come, at least not then, for synchronicity wouldn't be bullied by her or anyone, and when he did come it shocked her, the splintered rage which rose behind her eyes, and her heart was muffled and battering and unsafe, unable to act or protect her. Passive, she let his desire draw the circumference. Since nothing she could do was good enough, she let herself be used. Only afterwards when he'd gone did she quake with the knowledge of what he had taken away, and curse at the dumb telephone, and plan her reprisals.

Wed 16 Jan, 198-

Dear Kathy,

The poem is very beautiful, and hurts. I guess the truth does. While I was in Glencoe Joanna found and read some diary pages I'd written back in October and was shocked and pained to see how much I loved you still. She had seen it all as more of a problem between her and me. She told me on Sunday as we were walking back from a party at four in the morning that she'd read it and she gave vent to a drunken pained rage as we walked along the snowy Hackney streets. We shouted at each other, surely disturbing people asleep in houses, and ignored passers-by as if they were lamp-posts. She doesn't mind my being with other people but she can't comprehend or accept that I can love and want someone as well as her.

And I can't explain to her. Maybe that's my problem, that I could never really talk to you about her and I can't now tell her what you mean to me.

While I was in Scotland I thought maybe it was wrong for me to pressurise you by insisting how much I need you – sexually, emotionally, intellectually – when I was offering so little in return. But I thought, No, you were used to my asking and would tell me when it was unfair. And now you have. And I have to accept the awfulness I feel. Joanna and I have been too self-contained as the 'independent but loving couple' and I don't know if I'll be able to tell her all I need – but I love her and will try. Still, when I look depressed or act agitated I say it's not having a handle on Hegel or the pompousness of Wordsworth. I couldn't tell her over the holidays and don't see any way now to admit it's the hollowness and resentment of not openly loving you. How I feel about you has happened and it's there. But it's my pain to deal with because Joanna has made it clear that it's not hers and she doesn't feel any obligation to deal with it. What can you expect me to do? I can't see how I can

object to that. In the end I went so far with you and wanted
so much more that it can't be explained away – so it's not
explained. And I'm left, not alone, but with you telling me I
must leave you alone. I'm writing, I guess, to tell you that I
will – and that it's not just altruistic; for me there's also pain
to go on talking when there's no future and there's always
the immediate danger of your not believing that I love you.
Love, Will.

*Bread. He cut the bread. He cut it with a Swiss army knife. He
smeared it with Camembert, no butter. He wrapped up the
sandwiches and filled his aluminium water bottle from the stream
and hung it on Kathleen's belt. 'You haven't even said you'll miss
me,' she burst out at last. She threw her cigarette into the damp
ashes of the camp fire. Perhaps he didn't believe in speaking of his
pain; perhaps he loved it even more than her.*

*Will's face quivered. He took a sharp step towards her and her
body shrank from some memory of slaps, but there was nothing,
only his arms locking around her and his breath brushing her face.
'You can't say that.' It was raining lightly. He took her wet hand and
clasped it tight between his thighs. 'You know how ill I get missing
you.'*

Jan 19
Dear Kathy,
Pain that *I'm* not trying to find a way for us to be together?
You wrote me the studied, lyrical letter to say 'enough' –
what happened to all those sentiments? Or was that really
nothing more than a challenge, a test, that I was supposed
to rise to and not to take literally?

Fine. I love you. You know that or you wouldn't dare
write a letter threatening your denial of it. It would be
meaningless to do so. It's equally pointless my protesting
about something we both know is true. Such talk is not

about that truth, it's about getting what we want and not wanting to let it go.

Love or no, God knows that I want you: that I ache from my cock to my heart to my brain over not having you. But it's no good fantasising that I'm something I'm not. I patently am 'real, powerful and fruitful' – in *part*; but as you know I'm also transparent, infantile and degenerate. If that's not the man that you love then you're loving a ghost. Your parts are also in evidence as you first write that you have put me behind you, and then hate me for not being selfish and refusing you that right. I can be selfish, and I admit that my 'mess' doesn't have the beauty and artistry of yours, but it's no less strongly felt. I'll come over on Monday morning because I need to have you and hold you and the parts will just have to look after themselves. Will.

Tues, Jan 22
Dear Kathy,
Here's the photocopy. I didn't make it into college yesterday. It didn't seem very important by the time I'd gotten out into the rain thinking of you still lying there warm and so full of love.

I turned in the essay today and told my tutor that it was my birthday yesterday so I'd taken the day off. I didn't tell them that I was now stabilised, compartmentalised and consequently demoralised. No point. They'll all be happier now because I'll spend hours in the library and evening after evening writing my opinions and giving these opinions the pretence of credibility, authority, etc by observing the techniques of undergraduate cleverness and mock erudition. I *can* be without you but I can't forget about us. Maybe you'll have to do better than that. Think of me in the summer when it's warm and blue or in the winter when you're exercising. My counsellor said today that I should

know that I'm not Superman. I said being inferior means
not having dreams. She quoted Kipling's 'If' which says
we should recognise triumph and disaster for what they are:
'both great impostors'. I said the mass of men lead lives of
quiet desperation. And the beat goes on. I think I like my
mother more than she does. She believes in animal instincts
and the law of natural selection and pooh-poohs any too
human desire. Unlike me, she'll never know you. What's
more, also unlike me, she'll never care. Sometimes I think
idiots assault me in squads.
Love, Will.

(PS. Other times I think I'm a member of those idiot
squads. You were right to ask for your keys back. God, how
stupid and weak I can be.)

*It was late September when Will came back from Chamonix; she
saw him from her bedroom window, riding head down and fast
round the Square. He told her that he had moved out and that he
loved her; for days Joanna had struggled with this fact, she had
tried but she couldn't bear it, and so Will had to go, she'd told him to
go. 'Well, will you have me?' he said, and she knew that he meant
for good. The shock of the future made her clumsy and inhibited,
she couldn't move to embrace him.*

*'Have you?' she cried. 'I'd marry you tomorrow.' Neither of them
weeping or singing but neither of them shamefaced either. This is
the story you wanted to hear, how the colour of the room changed,
it's size too, so that it no longer constricted her as it had in these
wretched days of waiting, waiting to hear, waiting for Will's
decision.*

*That night Joanna rang in a red rage, and Kathleen said meekly,
'Yes, Will's here,' but it was Kathleen she wanted. 'How could you?'
she cried. Saying bitch, traitor, taking her to task. 'How could you
let yourselves?'*

Like a broken clock-hand a picture on the wall swung loose as

Kathleen listened and wondered how on earth she thought they might have stopped themselves. At last the phone slammed down and Kathleen went back through to Will. It was late. Joanna had sounded drunk. She lit a cigarette, shaking. 'It was awful,' she said. 'She was screaming at me.'

Will looked down at his hands. It struck her that he might be smiling. 'That sounds like Joanna, all right.' She listened for pity or remorse but heard only an echo of triumph. In the face of Joanna's pain – tumultuous – she had for one mad moment almost been ready to relinquish him, but he sat there heavily, showing no inclination to move.

'It was me she wanted,' she said, and he nodded. His face was charged and luminous. She had seen that expression before, in the Bar Nationale: he and Walt and the others, psyching themselves up for some mountain. In the silence the conviction grew: one hell of a climb, one hell of a woman. Will leaned his head back and shut his eyes, and she listened to his ragged sigh and knew that he was paying tribute.

June 3, 198-
Dear Kathy,
Just a note to show you that I've made a note to remember your birthday. So, Happy Birthday!!! I'm also enclosing what I wrote the morning after our Bank Holiday Monday encounter on the M1. My first impulse was to send it to you immediately I got your accusatory note with the book, but I stopped myself, deciding that I didn't have to justify myself like that – especially since I was sure you knew enough to expect me to do so, but here it is.
Love, Will.

Hitching back from climbing in the Peak District with Neil, I'd gotten dropped at Watford Gap. I stood there at the run-out from the car-park watching cars full of families head south after the holiday and stuck my thumb out somewhat hopelessly when all of a sudden I saw what looked like the Hackney mini-bus. Comrades, I thought to myself, and went over with the vague thought of a chat or maybe they had some room in the van. Hell, Kathy, what were the odds against it? My rational parts say OK, so you *knew* she was joining. And yes, every climbing club in the South-East is heading back down the M1 on Bank Holiday Monday. But none of that accounts for the shock and desire when I saw you coming across the car-park, with Jess of all people. You must have had tea and you were laughing, hurrying a bit. Curly hair in your eyes, your jeans fitting your hips snug but comfortably as always. When you saw me it was as if you didn't have time to remember and draw back or even be surprised, you came straight into my arms and we kissed but it was I who had to remember all the inquisitive faces inside the van. The bus was packed so there was no room for me, and then you were waving and gone. Only by interrogating Jess unmercifully did I finally elicit the news that you'd been crying and upset. Myself, I felt like I'd gotten plugged into some high-tension cable and when I eventually got a lift I was so confused I thought they were the ones who were meant to be thanking *me*. An hour and a half later on the platform of some Northern Line station I never heard of I smoked a couple of cigarettes having come back to normal but not wanting to let the distance, already fast growing, between now and our recent meeting, take over and obliterate these confused feelings. I remembered how I'd smoked cigarettes to think of you before and accidentally burned two holes in the fragile nylon inner of my tent. There just is no way to sort out all these feelings. I love you and I'm not denying that. And I also love and am living with Joanna, which makes the former cold comfort or worse. I don't know.

– People and nations freeze, are held in suspension, but

under the surface the past moves on, and then when the thaw comes . . .

– *When the thaw comes?*

– Recently Italian police began a search for the bodies of 111 victims who died in 1966 when an Air India 707 crashed into the south side of Mont Blanc in a snowstorm. Late this summer articles connected with the crash – scarves, sandals – appeared in moraine debris at the tongue of the Mirage Glacier. Now the police think that bodies may also start appearing, possibly even preserved intact in the ice.

Fri, June 7
College
Dear Kathy,
I don't know. I don't know about what you say. I love you and miss you and think you're right, I guess, in what you say. Except for what's at the centre of your letter: the accusation that I come round and make love to you and then reject you. On the other hand, maybe you're right there as well. On one level, at the surface of the narrative perhaps, there is no other way to see it. But you don't see the other times when I'm in the country or with a group of people, or at the theatre or a film and I suddenly remember you like I remember that I'm tanned or fit and then I see that I'm not. It's awful, for some long moments it's like dropping down a great well and I cry inside for the white of snow and shake involuntarily with fear, the rip and rags of separation. How can I not think about wanting to soak these wounds in the wetness of your thighs caused by my fingers sliding into you and not want to thrust my prick into your hands?

I'm glad that we fucked. It was so important to me to love you like that after all the shit concrete silence. Important because I've loved loving you and because I

213

remember with fear all the times like in the tent in Chamonix when I had you pressed naked in my arms and you stopped, couldn't let me love you. I didn't want to feel that was all that was left. But since we've seen that it's not, you're right in saying that lovers is what we still are.

And given that fact, you are being very sensible. And it's really hard, but it's true. So we'll write or call. Write to me here at the college and they'll put it in my box. I know that may seem like paranoia, but while I do have my own correspondence, if Joanna collects the mail I do normally acknowledge who it's from and what news. I come into college every day now if for no other reason than to use the swimming pool for my knee or read periodicals. I'm seeing some dance-therapist massage-healer at Pineapple Studios tomorrow about my knee – do you remember how I twisted it a bit slipping into that wet pothole on the Mer de Glace? I guess that could have been the start because the same knee went so badly in the descent off the Droites last month that I had to come down the last 1,000 metres backwards.

God, Kathy, this is really tough. You wouldn't believe it if you saw me here in this always-empty classroom where I work, holding back tears. But I do want to work this out and not just be sensibly hypocritical because I don't want to hurt you or me. Maybe I can arrange to give you a one hour/hour and a half tennis lesson and just meet on the court and part again at the end of the time – of course it will be up to you to see that we don't go together searching for lost balls behind the tennis shack! No, seriously, I understand what you say about temptations of this sort and I will accept my responsibility in sorting it out. Yes, considering how dangerous everything is, like loving, nothing is really very frightening. Writing is natural to you, but I think I'll phone when I need to talk to you. I probably never said that you broke down some of my inhibitions about the telephone because I actually enjoyed it with you. Do call Neil if you

want to speak to me, he's more taciturn and uptight on the telephone than me, but he's the only one I can talk to openly about you and as a result we've become quite close (for two macho-type guys trying to repress it). I have to go now as they're closing the building and I want to get this in the post. Enough.
Love, Will.

Wed, 12 June
Dear Kathy,
I'm feeling a bit uptight and unsure, sort of anxious and nervous, which is why I've come up here. This room has a bit of a view and as the sun is shining through the clouds every now and then I thought it might help to cheer and stabilise me. I hate this sort of feeling. It makes me inert and I can't seem to get on with things. Not that I'm particularly ambitious about doing things, it's just that in this state I can't even get on with being aimless or indulging myself. I just mope about incessantly indecisive with an irritating electrical buzzing just beneath my brow and behind my eyeballs. And I'm constantly tripping over bits of normally useful plastic persona. The sort of things I normally deftly dodge if they drop out of my pocket, and which I normally find amusing to play with and display like a good hand of cards in a bridge game: the perceptive student, the committed climber, the concerned socialist, the hedonist, the sensitive male, the controlled individual, the lover, the dependable, the dependant, the healthy, the invalid, the hero, the king and the coward. Sometimes it seems so hard to like things, and I wonder why, because at other times it seems so easy and the possibilities so multiple and infinite and amusing. It's always some sort of insecurity prompted by self-consciousness: just the minute shift from being conscious of how people see me to being concerned about how they see me. It seems so awful, negative and

soul-destroying and when I realise this I remember with a combination of relief and desperation that I can always throw myself against a piece of rock or ice, or preferably rock and ice, to get myself back together. Sometimes just the memory of having done so in the past is a useful salve, but mostly it's the thinking about it, anticipating it or actually doing it that helps.

Wednesdays, huh? Despite nearly jumping out of my seat with excitement in the common room at the thought of putting some energy into you and having you twisting on the train seat next to me *en route* to the sun of the Mediterranean, I just can't see it. You wouldn't be happy because I'd still be leaving each time with commitments to Joanna, verbalised or not, as the fact constraining us, and I guess it's just not a boundary that it's fair to ask you to recognise. I tried living without it and couldn't, but it naturally doesn't have any such meaning for you. And we couldn't keep it all together before when we had an open friendship and sexual relationship. It was because I knew you were unhappy and I thought you were going to call it quits that I left Joanna in the first place. I think at the time I thought she'd understand and let me do what I felt like and although there was obviously going to be pain on both sides I didn't think she'd completely push and lock me out. I guess you can't get more pathetically egotistical than that, but it just seemed inconceivable and certainly proved impracticable.

You said that it seems hard to get that into your head, and I was afraid to admit when we met that things were OK with me and Joanna and that I wasn't regretting six months later a decision made in a moment of weakness, because I was afraid you'd not recognise or enjoy me at all if it wasn't a prelude to us loving completely. And I know how you can cut me off, and not just sexually. This limpness physically is only the most obvious manifestation of being blocked out at all levels of interest, emotion, amusement etc. I just do have parts and I do love you and that's just what I have to deal with.

Yeah, I've just been thinking, maybe every other Wednesday would be all right? And 'strict dear friends at the end of summer'? But I guess it's not the frequency of the sin, but just the systematic nature of it that makes my hypocrisy meter blow. God, it doesn't seem very fair all this, to you and me, and I guess it isn't.

OK, I won't phone for the time being. Neil's number is 021 622 0956.

I got my pictures back from the North Face of the Droites and will have to show them to you as some look nearly as dramatic as it was.

I've got to get down to work. I'm still feeling indecisive. I think it's because I'm not getting any exercise. No climbing for weeks and can't run with my knee and swimming has seemed like too much trouble.

Write to me. It's odd thinking about you and not knowing what you're doing.

Love, Will.

When the thaw comes it's painful. Pins and needles. The blood rushing back.

Imagining now how Joanna felt when Will came back from Chamonix, how she begged him to tell her what was wrong, how her voice went on and on into the night. How in the early hours of the morning she sat on the chest at the end of the bed and Will said, Yes, well, there is something I wanted to say. The light from the street lamp shone through the curtains on to the ceiling, and she sat on the Chinese chest at the foot of the bed, the black lacquered chest which Will's mother had given them. Her back was turned to him; perhaps she had her feet tucked up on the chest, his voice came from behind her. For she'd known for weeks that he'd been holding something back from her, but she hadn't consciously thought – she didn't know what her fucking unconscious was doing – but she hadn't consciously thought that Kathleen was in Chamonix with him. But then, thinking about it, why had she almost gone? At one point she had actually started to pack her bag, for she'd wanted to go, yes, but she'd been frightened somehow, perhaps of this truth which rendered itself up at last in the early hours of the morning as she sat on the chest at the end of the bed and Will said that he loved her and didn't want to leave her, all the things you'd imagine someone might say, either then or later, adding damningly the words, Well you can always stop me. The room was dark except for the wedge of light the street lamp cast on the ceiling, and her whole body changed and withdrew into itself and she was very very cold on the outside.

This is how our bodies are, our senses squirm and say no as Will moves between them. This is where briefly we bleed together, equals, I've cut her down to my size. Pity and remorse, yes: the desire to make reparations, but the feeling, the intoxication, doesn't last long, it's too unstable, for Kathleen was never given time to get accustomed to winning.

Remembering how her body was pinned to the sofa, her thighs full as two cushions, apart. How Will's eyes narrowed, how his eyes turned stilted and flat as rulers as he drove his feelings out. He had decided that they needed boundaries, reason would circumscribe energy: this is what she understood from that look of his, and she was a balloon, a bag of bad goods and discards, blood, cast-offs of the family she couldn't tip out; at the same time her mind swearing that once under the sky there was a horned moon, squirrels ran, in one stride her leg might have taken the Aiguilles. All this was present and veiled, that time when the hair on his body was moss and multitudes. Perhaps it had all been imaginary: the smoke slithering up their nostrils. Figures. A landscape: star or rowanberry, equidistant, you, me, I didn't then and don't now care to put my finger on any difference. Orange peel damp and unburnt in the ashes of the morning fire, flakes of sunburnt skin which they brushed from their shoulders, sleeping bags encaked with urgent smells. Animals know no perversions; his arse, sweat-damp, encased her finger like the pierced rind of a tangerine.

He separates to see and saw her. In half. Joanna's eyes look through his, Joanna who had gone through to the living room in the early hours of the morning and picked up a book with random craziness and read an article on Psychoanalysis and Feminism and why didn't feminists draw on Klein instead of Lacan because Klein stressed the primacy of the mother; Joanna to whom Will said, helplessly and disconnected: Why don't you come back to bed, what are you doing? And Joanna looked back at him, at this person she'd been completely fixed with, familiar with, and who had suddenly become a person she didn't know any more, talking to her, and touching her, and the touching was like burning flesh. Day by day these are the eyes that look through Will's, and Kathleen's thighs spread like two cushions – on a woman the upper thighs go first, pocking – as he measures her against that proper alliance: time, the real, crushing her.

5th Feb, 198-
Dear Kathy,
Thanks for the birthday card. You needn't worry that it compromised your letting-go policy. That was made pretty clear. Your earlier card said you couldn't end the year on such a 'destructive note'. Well from this side of Mare Street it was more like the 1812 Overture. I felt awful for weeks and still feel a bit queasy. I knew there was pain – that much, albeit by my choice, I had to experience as well – but the hate took me by surprise and the desire (not to mention the proven ability!) to hurt me also came as a shock. I guess it shouldn't have, huh?

I'm naturally envious of your trip to Australia. My world seems a bit grey at the moment. I'm a bit sick of academia for the first time in an otherwise fairly enjoyable stint as a student. Also my knee is continuing to give me trouble, so this is the first winter in five years I won't be going to Scotland or Chamonix – hence the opportunity to celebrate the thirty-second birthday I said I'd never see! I miss the climbing like mad, I've collected a few names of doctors/ therapists to see but have done nothing, and get almost no exercise. I find it hard to motivate myself with just the activity of rock climbing. It doesn't affect my knee, but seems hollow as an end in itself. I'm used to dramatic changes and if a climb doesn't last for at least two or three days, I don't feel like I'm really involved. I wish I could meet you in Katmandu on your way back from Australia. You should stop off. It's a cheap flight from Delhi and Nepal is more peaceful than India, so easier to enjoy if you are on your own.

I wish I could see you. I feel very estranged since our telephone call, but I appreciate you have to insist on what you feel is right for you. You were wrong to say I found you fascinating or exciting because you were the Other Woman or the Enviable Writer or whatever, that was a cheap shot and we both know it. I wrote tomes to you after that call, all angry and hurt, but since I effectively chose the game I decided I couldn't complain how you moved the pieces. And I don't want to be plaintive. Let me hear from you when you can.

Love, Will.

March 31, 198-

Dear Kathy,

If I remember rightly, it's early fall weather in Sydney and can be a bit fickle, but even if you aren't toasting your limbs daily you've escaped miserable English weather these last three weeks. After that mild week at the end of February it has turned bitterly cold again. I went away climbing with Neil this Easter weekend – we were around Tenby and St Govan's Head which I find very attractive: miles of climbable rock. It's calmer and less touristy on the whole than Cornwall but unfortunately packed out with climbers this holiday weekend – school trips, Loughborough University etc, with 25/50 people per group so you're talking about maybe 200 climbers on the top, at the bottom and in the middle of the mile or so of crag where we were. The cliff top is very flat, so they were all highly visible trundling along with their coiled ropes, skirts of nylon cord and hardware and fibre-pile jackets, marching, standing or peering over the edge like small flocks of newly imported sheep. We managed to climb on each of the three days, in between showers, snowfalls and hailstorms (bet you miss it, don't you?) but personally I was happiest sitting in the car listening to 'Dream of Blue Turtles' and reading Marge Piercy and Beckett.

I was seriously struck in Piercy's books, as in yours, with how awful and emotionally one-dimensional the male characters are. Even though it's still strange to recognise this side of herosexual males I can see the truth of it, and see that it is changing, if only slowly – the ten years' difference between you and me, as between the hero and heroine in *Vida*, is just enough for some, even if only a bit, of what the Women's Movement fought for to have sunk in, or snuck in, to the latter half of the same generation. Only a small but I believe growing percentage of men my age can really accept intelligent and justly autonomous women, and given the unacknowledged central importance of gender relations for social subjectivity perhaps it isn't surprising to find your and Marge Piercy's male contemporaries so lacking despite (often adamant) insistence that they are 'trying'.

Of course progress is only partial, as you point out to me, but I do try self-examination and I know the difference between rationalising and genuine self-questioning, only I don't have the same access to feelings – my own, no less

221

yours, that you as a poet and a woman have. If you must 'mistrust' me because of this inadequacy then you must. I recognised from the first few times I saw you how warily open and vulnerable you were, and within my limitations feel I respected that with my soul and my will and my own vulnerability. That is why hurting you hurts me, even if I know so only after the fact. In fantasising Katmandu I didn't mean to just exotically and ephemerally posit you for me, but also the openness of the world for *you*. I can see with an exercise of transposition that I would sneer if our positions were reversed and you made such a comment. In fact it wasn't just to point out that I missed you, but also that with empathy and even envy I was interested in your trip. And it's ironic now and when we met that you were attracted to the outreaches and novelty of experience whereas I have been going progressively local and inward. I believe now less in metaphors of depth and more in the intricacy and intimacy of surfaces and it has always been the excoriating (sp?) overlap of lives between you and me that I've found so vital.

There's such a lot I would say to you – about books and politics and things I've worked out on my course this last year – but I'm self-conscious about being selfish and maybe you find long letters boring. Also I must get this in the mail as I believe your tour of duty is fairly short and the post to Australia sometimes seems to go by camel. Write and let me know if this is the right address and what date you return. Write soon.
Love, Will.

– *The failure hook goes in deep?*

– You value the ones who jerk it, and so you wriggle, trying to prove you aren't. You try and try, for deep down it's the only hook you know.

– *You can't allow that there might be more benign reasons for endings?*

– Magic thinking. People don't go just because you're bad, do they? They don't just because of that.

–

May 27, 198-
Dear Kathy,
I hope this reaches you in time for your birthday, which it will only do if you are still in Sydney and in touch with the Institute. I assume you are and that you received my last letter, although I've received nothing to date to confirm it? I hope this isn't a signal and that this letter doesn't arrive unwelcome. It was hard answering your last letter. I was so pleased to hear from you, but in conjunction with saying that the loving, believing part of you wanted me to account for myself you also chastised me for being self-concerned and defensive. Obviously the loving, believing part of you is the one I would touch, but, maybe because I'm too coldly self-protective, any explanation seems like an excuse and any expression of missing you seems to hurt or make you angry with me. I do try to see the effect on you of my feelings and indulgences, but I am not the poet, so I have no choice, if I'm going to walk at all, but to *try* not to be clumsy. And I do try.

I hope you've enjoyed Sydney and not found it too parochial for the European sensibility? As I remember it the city is a strange blend and can be too urban to be relaxed and too relaxed to be properly metropolitan. Of course, sometimes all I seem to care about is the weather which seems to me typically miserable this spring. Have had one or two sunny and/or warm weeks since you left, but the last four weeks have been cold, 45 to 55, and heavy interminable wind which makes the London streets feel like draughty stations in the underground, complete with concrete-grey sky. I went up to the Peak District again this Bank Holiday and drove back yesterday evening in the first sustained sunshine of the weekend. It didn't actually rain much, but it was hard to believe that the summer solstice is only four weeks away. You should come back for the summer, though, because the winter in Australia is nothing great and you would end up back in London for the onset of winter. And if we could untangle the worst knots, maybe there could be tennis lessons on the summer days when it forgets to rain?

I understand what you've said about boundaries and my position of being able to retreat behind the limits of my relationship with Joanna, which I can't deny, except to say, as I think you know, that I would never use this as a game. Obviously it's up to you to decide what the value of such suggestions are. For me, my relationship with Joanna is not a retreat any more than my relationship with you was an escape. Both were what I wanted for positive reasons, even though they were painfully exclusive. Even though my love for Joanna is not a retreat, that doesn't mean that I don't regret, still, what it has meant to my love for you. At Christmas when I was miserable with the short, cold days, my college work and the state of the world and very much in the midst of missing you – and then we had that futile, awful and bitter telephone call – I did think about what you said, about not bothering you until I had something better to offer you. I thought that since I did feel the missing of you so much, that Joanna would have to understand and accept my being with you, if you were willing to accept my feeling for her, but in the end concluded that it wouldn't work. We had permission before and it wasn't enough. Boundaries are always drawn, but always artificially, and each recognition is a matter of choice, a renewed decision – and that's the responsibility that comes with the freedom we can't avoid for our feelings. Of course I know the making of boundaries is different for you and difficult. Although I spotted you for me immediately, in the first couple of classes I came to, in a way that you couldn't possibly have done with me, I admit that it was only your lack of boundaries that allowed me to be so bold in loving you. It defines both your power and your vulnerability.

Perhaps I'm getting too abstract now and should cease. I just finished my exams on Thursday and it's a bit difficult getting back down to earth. On the other hand, the exams themselves were very down to earth in that they were very hard work. Five three-question, three-hour papers – Socrates to Sartre, Shakespeare to Brecht in twelve days! I actually tried and didn't give in through excuses of nonchalance or existential *ennui* as has been the case in my previous academic history. I found it harder work than I thought and I would have done better if I'd spent the two and a half month revision period actually revising. Instead I worked on this project I'm writing now on 'Post-Saussurian' critical theory (don't ask me what's critical about it, it's all about power and politics as far as I can see). One of my primary sources is Vladimir Voloshinov, who was in the same group as Shyvlovsky, Osip Brik etc, which included a number of artists encompassing of course your friend Mayakovsky. Anyway the reason I'm pleased about the exams is that once I started I really stuck with it. I started revising a week and a half before the first one, confident that as I'd left my mind ticking over and well-oiled, all the material would come back to me quite naturally. Bad plan. I spent one whole weekend revising Aristotle and Plato and my sole achievement was at the end of two days I could actually read and partially understand one of my own essays. Not the sort of confident and flexible grasp of material I was planning on having when it came to answering the exam questions.

I don't think I told you, but the project I did on Emily

Brontë – 'The Narrative Structure of Wuthering Heights: History, Closure and Elements of Form' – went well despite the lack of encouragement from my non-Marxist advisors and I was told off the record that it was First Class material, which both surprised and encouraged me and gave me more confidence than I needed. Unfortunately my exams and my second project, 'Marx and Materialism: Determining Elements in Social Formations' (!) didn't go as well. I'm sure this third project will be good, as it represents what I personally have been doing with the course for the last three years, but I don't think it will be enough to raise my grade overall.

If I did get a First it means I could probably get a grant from the British Academy to do an MA before doing a PGCE which, although I know it's spinning my wheels, I don't think I could turn down. The self-indulgence of reading the *Guardian* every day, long holidays, and a day or two with a novel whenever you want it is just too much for me to deny myself, even with only grant or dole money to live on.

Of course, I've not been making much of my holidays as my knee, although OK for most things, still isn't good enough for the Alps, and this makes me badly miserable from time to time. I keep resolving to see some of the knee specialists who've been recommended to me, but so far I haven't. Maybe I'm afraid of what they'll say. Either that it's unalterable or that it's not serious enough for them to bother with. In fact probably what I'm most afraid of is that they'll say it will take a long time, months or a year, and a lot of hard work, so that my inveterate indolence just won't be able to cope.

Well, I didn't mean to write such a long letter, and I have to get back to my project or at least get the paper read. I hope this finds you for your birthday and that your birthday finds you well.
Much love, Will.

Sept 23,

Dear Kathy,

You're right about the process of separation – that it is something that happens over time and in stages. I guess I thought that having acted as an adult, ie having fought through the contradictions, and the horrors, of being in between two loves and made my decision, that I'd done what was necessary; that the pain of separation was behind me, done – for the most part, if not completely, accomplished.

It's all too apparent that we are still lovers and not friends. I was very hurt back in January when you said friendship with me seemed 'meagre'. I see now that being close friends is not so much unworthwhile as impossible – certainly, at least, in the foreseeable future.

I was shocked by my passion and desire for you. I so wanted to take off your clothes from early on, and tried to put it down to the red shirt you were wearing – too vivid, too intense, too Rhône-valley a colour for my sensitive state. I didn't write before now because all I could suggest was an afternoon together to finish off what we had started so suddenly and broke off so quickly. It's still the only suggestion I have. It's too hard not to say that I want to hold you intimately and completely. I'll never be able to just evaporate like a dream. We both must live with what we are to each other.

I am happy in my life even though there's still much I want to understand and to feel – obviously there always will be, but I understand and feel more at thirty-two than twenty-two and I must count on that continuing. My only dread is missing you, and sometimes thinking Joanna may choose independence over my love. I, as you know, am the dependent one. I thought friendship would solve my missing you, but talking to you so formally and properly as we did in the first hour of meeting was almost like being

227

interviewed by Mother! You said you wanted to know where I was at. This sounded like a reasonable request, but made me talk about what I'm doing, academia, like it was serious and important to me, and that now seems a bit unfair. You know where I'm at, in the sense that you know who I am so what I do is not so important. I think academic knowledge and formal understanding is important and serious, but I hope never to think it's what I am. (That failure to think it's what I am is an ironic function of my bourgeois male identity – it makes me apathetic where a good liberal capitalist should be ambitious!) But as I talked beyond that it was obvious why I still experience the shock of missing you. I don't want to deny my responsibility for that, but I don't want to deny my feelings either. I miss you. Love, Will.

– The quality of the object recedes, leaving behind the spectre of addiction. Without erotic attachment to the object-world unadulterated destructive elements rise to the surface. These then become the means of holding on to objects.

– As far as I recall you were the one who complained about technical language.

– You never say it but I can hear you thinking it. Narcissism, and so on.

– Am I to take it that you want me to call you names?

– Like Dirty Pape or Proddy Dog, you mean? Look, I'm fighting for my life here. Will's language dried up like a dead thing, to Kathleen each word was a flat refusal of love, a withholding.

– I can see that you're angry with me.

–

228

– I'm wondering what it is that you withhold. . . .

–

– I'm aware that you've expressed fears that I wouldn't be strong enough to withstand your rage.

– Listen, at this moment he could be holding her in his arms.

May 30, 198-
Dear Kathy,
I've been thinking for months about writing to you for your birthday – always comfortably, nicely, easily as it was always something off in the future. It's more difficult now, of course, than in my projections, but I really need to, to stop my writing fantasies being pure self-indulgence. I'm sorry I didn't answer your response to my letter written after we met last fall, but your letter ended rather abruptly and I realised that while keeping in contact with you completed things for me in a way, it offered little or nothing to you. And sexually we were too full, too irresistible for me to have something just emotionally and intellectually, which was all I could afford. My confidence and optimism engendered positive fantasies of keeping all the balls in the air, all the plates spinning on the ends of their sticks, but I could see this was more a recipe for a nervous breakdown than personal fulfilment.

I kept expecting it wouldn't be so impossible to reconcile knowing each other – but it does seem difficult. I think of you a lot, often nervously if I'm down by your college or around the Square, which I must admit I usually avoid and occasionally deliberately seek out. There are no easy answers, I know.

I've been doing this MA in Romanticism and Modernism at University College in the English Department and have really enjoyed it. The students have been a bit of a disappointment, mostly young and ambitious, but the

229

tutors have been great. I've become friends with one who turns out to be the brother of someone I know through the climbing club. His name is Richard Watkins, he is working on a novel that's something similar – from a male perspective – to your last book, at least in the period it focusses on, the political issues, etc, and he seems the first male in a long time that I feel I still want to have conversations with six months after meeting him.

My work on the MA has been well received and at the awards ceremony for my BA I was awarded the Humanities Prize for 'outstanding academic performance', which was the top award amongst the thousand social science and humanities graduates in my year. However, despite this gratifying encouragement I've decided not to carry on. These last four years have been great, but the prospect of another three years in some English dept doesn't really excite me. And besides in these days of cuts and closures who wants to employ a just-qualified 36-year-old Phd – they're half the price if they're ten years younger, not to mention easier to manipulate.

I've got a place to do a PGCE at the Institute, but the thought of another year to do that, also the depressed state of educational resources and pay, has led me to think about something in local government or trades union work – if there's anything left of either by the time I get in there! I've also been thinking about going to the States to do this high-powered, slightly dubious course in public administration. I'm not so keen on the course itself, but the idea of going back to the States for a specific purpose and limited time does attract me. I was really keen on this idea a few months ago – a full-blown fantasy about combining my formal education in cultural production with some practical skills for working in the public sector and coming back to England as an organisational knight-in-shining armour to work for the Loony Left council of my choice. It seems desperately important to me to do some sort of work that I can consider progressive and politically coherent. For the past six years I've nurtured a sense of the world and myself in terms of the Left social, intellectual and cultural tradition of Britain and Europe, and within this what has been of particular importance to me is that while the Left has been mainly critical and oppositional it has not been marginal. I feel now, as not only the Right but the Labour Party leadership itself attacks the so-called Loony Left and socialism disappears from the vocabulary only to reappear as a swear word, that Thatcher will get her way and Britain will become like America. Politically this means the Left becomes ineffectual even if more 'radical' and the only forms of conjunctural struggle are those of single issue groups which are usually depressingly apolitical.

But I didn't mean to give you an analysis of things I'm sure you know better than I do. It's just that I've only recently realised what things like the marginalisation of the Labour Party Left mean to me personally. While I have considerable respect for extra-parliamentary groups as part of the spectrum of socialist political practice I find vanguardist politics in particular arrogant and elitist – in America it's as often as not solipsistic self-indulgence. In the local Party branch I've not been particularly involved in the power politics of my peers but over the last five years have shown up at meetings, distributed leaflets, etc, and I've been encouraged to see the back of the Freemasons and family dynasties that formerly ran the council, and that this year there has been political agreement for the first time – and fairly uniquely in Labour local government through-out the country – between the three main policy-making groups, the GC, the LGC and Labour Group. And this coherence has meant that the Direct Labour Organisation has been turned around from a builders' con to a model of workplace democracy, blacks and ethnic minorities make

231

up 33% of the workforce compared to 10% in 1979, nursery schools and council houses have been built, etc. This may not be revolutionary, but it's important to me and the fact that the Right has been so successful in setting the agenda in the press so that none of this can be defended in public makes me start to feel like maybe I really don't exist after all. It's like, just as I'm growing up I find out I'm shrinking in relation to the rest of the world. I like my socialist friends, but once it becomes just a social thing, I don't think I could bear it.

Anyway, I wanted to write just a short (!) letter to say hello and obviously didn't mean to bore you with my complaints about British politics. I'd like to hear from you, and would actually like to see you, but I feel I know too well the contradictions and difficulties between us, so please don't feel you have to answer if you don't want to. I just did want to write, however inadequately.

Happy birthday, and love, Will.

– What you don't see is the Turk in the wide-brimmed hat like Gauguin's, grave faced, his palette on the pavement at his feet, painting ladies and lagoons on the window of the travel agent, or how the bread comes roasted from the ovens and the smell of sesame seeps up through the floors of Kathleen's flat.

What you don't see is Greece, the spray from the jetty splashing over them as the *meltemi* batters the burned beach, the young German under the tamarisk tree who reads Goethe with his cock unself-consciously big and bare, and Kathleen, dusted by salt, her sarong tide-marked with it. Coming out of the sea her body wears a salt skirt of wind.

What you don't see is the blue, here everything is blue: the oil cans filled with geraniums, doors, the interiors of pure white boats. Perhaps there's a law, Terry suggests: on some statute book in Athens. Let houses be cubist and white and let doors and windows always be blue. Every postcard stand flickers in

the corner of Kathleen's eye, images of hot hills piled white
with houses, but she has hallucinated glaciers, their white-
cubed *seracs* stark in the blue of altitude.

What you don't see is the temple of Dionysus, the stubborn
way her hand lies reverently on the eroded pale flutes of the
columns, for somehow there always has to be a son, arrogant
and encouraged to it, who flies too high or believes he's god or
offers his soul to become so.

– *Whose fall are we talking about here?*

– I'm talking about the good things. Her friends have been
worried about her. This terrible intoxication.

– *All the good things you have to hide?*

5 Fitzallan St
New Haven
Connecticut

Monday, Nov 9,

Dear Kathy,

Yes, I write – I miss you – but please don't think too much
about what I write because I cannot afford to indulge my
commonsense or self-conscious censorship as I feel so busy
and so weird over here, particularly at the moment as I'll
try to explain.

It is so bizarre that it isn't even surprising to come home
a few minutes ago and find a letter from you on the floor as I
opened the door – I had been talking about you only a half
hour before, in passing, to Ray Lucas, Shoreditch Labour
Party, who I met about 12.00 on one of the streets in the
middle of the University. How's that for synchronicity? I
walked right by him at first but something kept nagging at
me and I thought I must be imagining things so I walked
back, overtook him and then stopped and asked him what
his name was, he said 'Ray Lucas' and I smiled and said,
Well you're a long way from home aren't you? He smiled
and looked at me like I was a brother from another planet

233

until I explained where we'd met, etc. Anyway there are no licensing laws here and we've spent the last five/six hours in the bar discussing Thatcher, Kinnock's Labour Party, etc. In addition to this we discussed the American Trades Union movement, the Russian Revolution (Lenin, the Bolsheviks, and Trotsky as a ruthless but visionary idealist) and socialism in Britain. He is working-class, from a single parent family from before there were single parent families and now works for the post office where he has worked for the last ten, fifteen years since the LSE – he is not an entryist, just somebody who wanted a job without too much pressure where he wouldn't be screwing anybody. Anyway he was talking about the Atlee government, the state school system, and how he would never have gotten an opportunity or an education or maybe even have survived if it hadn't been for the Welfare State. He may not be *au fait* with women writers and politicos but is nonetheless certainly reconstructed and it was very worthwhile for me, with my heavy primary-social-relations-of-class-race-gender focus, to have someone to talk knowledgeably and directly about the impact of class and economics. It was so strange and so great to have this sort of conversation in the middle of this bastion of bourgeois society and amorphous liberalism; this liberalism is so soul destroying some of these people don't even understand you are arguing with them!

I'm writing on and on without getting to the point, which is that I'm coming back to London on the 19th or 20th of November and want to see you. Joanna is still in London and not coming over till Dec. I have to go back and sort out the flat and give her a hand for a week as she is trying to complete her thesis before she comes over here. I hope you'll be around the week of the 23rd to the 27th as it feels really important for me to see you, partly but not only because I'm so damned lonely over here. I've got some good friends at the graduate school and in the Labour

Support Group (the contracts for the 3,500 clerical, technical and plant workers expire in Jan and the college has a disastrously patronising and incompetent labour relations history – see enclosed flyer I wrote for a meeting I organised at the school) but I don't like being on my own and I miss the social and political niche I'd grown into in London.

I'll call you on Monday and hope we can meet during the day as I'd prefer not to tell Joanna. She is less vehement but still focusses all of her anger and pain on you, and I have always felt I could only be honest in acknowledging how much you mean to me, both then and now. Joanna knows I love and am committed to her more now than I have ever been, but I have not been able to tell her that I don't love you, and because I haven't she prefers for me not to see you.

God, I wish you were here now – which I know is selfish and unfair, but I seem to be at my wits' end for reasons I'm not sure of, I guess because there are so many reasons. Ever since I came here I find I'm always on the edge of tears and the last couple of weeks I keep busting down and crying, always around political things: a news broadcast from South Africa; one of the women at the meeting I organised talking about how much she liked the Union, how she was forty-five years old and had never spoken to more than two people at once and now she could organise, win arguments and address a room full of people; something I read in Jane Rule or Adrienne Rich, or at times just the effort of keeping all my arguments on culture, politics, literature and economics together to be able to counter all the naïve liberalism around here.

I'm worried I may be cracking up and don't know it. I seem to be functioning quite well in terms of the relentless school work, but with that and the Unions and the time I need to read for sustenance, I guess I'm exhausted. I've stopped drinking and smoking out of necessity and eat

235

really well nutritionally, if a bit boringly: fresh steamed vegetables, lots of fruit, raw vegetables and salads. I think a lot of it is the culture shock of being in the States: both familiar and alien, comfortable and repulsive. The first few weeks were so strange it was like being on acid – I would look at things like the stainless steel counter in a coffee shop or a spacious wooden porch in front of a house on a tree-lined street and the image would flash on and off in my mind and I couldn't believe I was here and I couldn't think of what to say to people. Now I feel I've adjusted too much and am unhappy and why at thirty-three am I still in school trying to acquire yet another piece of theoretical armour in order to defend myself against a system I don't even respect? It was good talking to Ray this afternoon because he reconfirmed my belief that left-wing technocrats and socialist financiers are needed, I just hope that the left and the need will still be there in two years' time. But I feel like I'm fighting so hard right now and it's going to go on like this forever and I just want to cry and cry. So far I've kept from breaking down in public or even with friends but I either have to stop myself talking about things that are so important to me or if I do I have to stop because my voice starts to crack and I get angry and sad and weepy. It's completely against my jolly veneer of competence and I'm starting to feel schizophrenic, like it's happening to someone else when this kid bursts into tears as I'm walking along the neighbourhood streets back to my apartment. I am trying to let it cry if there's no one about but my censor is very strong and the worst thing is that it's stopping me talking about the things I most want to talk about. I've got to stop now and go to sleep, I could not afford to spend this day in the bar and at least ought to get some sleep as I live mostly on six hours when I've been used to eight or nine for the last four years. I don't want to be depressing and I'm sure I'll cope, but I love you and need to tell you since I

have this opportunity. I'm sure I will feel better back in London and will call you on Nov 23, Monday.
Much love, Will.

That night she dreamt that her mother was bleeding. Publicly. Blood poured down her legs like pee. Her mother couldn't hide it, giggled about having had an accident. Opted for the prerogative of the old lady – messes, clowning – while Kathleen, full of shame, tried to cover her, cover her up.

All morning the thought of their meeting made her beat the bed with her fists but Will's voice on the telephone changed everything. Power flowed into her, her love surrounded him.

'Let me look at you,' she cried, pulling him into the flat. He was angular, hugging her to him awkwardly. Remembering his jet-lag, she asked what she could give him. 'I suppose you don't drink coffee?' While he looked at her, shaking his head, frowning a little at the sight of the red sweater which used to be his favourite.

She broke away first, holding him at arms' length. She was wearing high-heeled lace-up boots which drew a wan smile from him. 'I love the shoes,' he said. She looked down at the pointed toes, two neat black beaks, phallic; she had never been able to walk in them but perhaps he'd forgotten that. Light-headed she sways into the kitchen, takes cups from the cupboard. Through the screen of plants she sees him roving the room, circling, like a cat flattening the grass for its bed. The moments race like always and she's conscious of hurrying, of the joy running in her wrists and the winter sunlight imprinting shadows on the familiar room, yet at the same time she's watching a gap widen between this taut-strung self and a slower inner one which, leisurely and satisfied, prepares to look after the man who has come home. Will sits on the edge of the armchair drinking herb tea and she starts to laugh, energy rushing across the space towards him, for the trick is lovely and painful but it's far too late to be embarrassed by something which is such a part of her, by this reckless gratitude which she's tried and tried to lock

237

out. *'Well,'* she says, and she can't hide her gaiety, *'I need wine myself!'*

Will looks back with eyes that don't recognise her, or else suspect her of something. *'I've got a whole lot to tell you,'* he says impatiently. He can't wait for her to return with the bottle, but follows her into the kitchen and starts talking very fast, about Yale, corporate power, American liberalism, everything that has to be conquered or combatted. Let him get it off his chest, she thinks, waiting for him to settle.

After a while she holds up her hand to stem the flow. *'Yes, you said that in your letter.'* But still the voice runs on, dislocated. She watches him, concentrating. His mouth talking politics as if to a mirror, some frantic rehearsal in which the words gape at themselves. Under the T-shirt her armpits grow damp with sweat. She folds her arms and listens, steeling herself, remembering how after the flight to Australia her mind had blanked: for a week she'd existed without dreams or feelings, a work-horse, bleak and wooden as a puppet. Then one night her lagged dreams caught up with her, slamming into her like a piece of elastic which had been stretched as far as it could go and now snapped back, stinging. Her mind ticks on, neutral, like an analyst's, as one by one Will piles his causes in her lap, weighs her down with his impossible labours. She sees the grey specks in his hair. His shoulders are hunched under the burdens of being good. Coolly her mind tells her that she's invisible, that it's someone else, not her, that he can never please; some imperious and demanding other for whom all his best efforts are insufficient. Will's voice battles on, fanatical, and for a moment she isn't sure that she doesn't love him simply as a friend, so firmly has he exiled the flesh and all the rhythms of feeling that flow from it. At last, exhausted, she interrupts him. *'Why is it your responsibility to put everything to rights?'* She's alert, straining to be gentle, as if he were a child in a darkened room and the disembodied voice might frighten him.

Will stares at her. For a moment his face is in pieces, and the analyst flees out of her, leaving her motherly, all clasped hands and *painful concern. 'Sorry,' he says wildly. 'People ask me a question and get six lectures instead of an answer.'*

She hears the disinterested voice urging him to rest, take care, make space for pleasures; she even hears it say that he'll feel better when Joanna comes out to join him. But then the voice trails to nothing and she turns her face away, on the astonishing point of persuading herself that she could and did love him like that: with tenderness and scruple and without thought of return.

Will is silent, listening. His suede jacket is still zipped up tight to the neck. 'It's like when you all cried when Sartre died. I guess I don't see the point of crying, I've got to do something instead.' His voice is low and non-committal, but his hands are clenched into fists, and it strikes her then that it's hopeless, when he looks at her he sees nothing but chaos, sees himself all awash, like some drunk helpless with beer in the midday Square, and there's nothing she can do, nothing. Will gets up stiffly, the sun catching him, and she shrugs, accused of nostalgia, accepting it. So now he's going, she thinks, with his principles intact and his face pure criticism.

'Well you know where to find me,' she says, ironically, recognising this as the bluff voice of an earlier self, of the comrade who meets each hardship with renewed pledges of loyalty. Smiling up at this fearsome new face which he has made for himself, because it's true, of course: if he ever really needed her she would never be able to refuse him.

Will nodded, frowning. He put his hands in his pockets and took a few steps towards the door. Then he came back and only when he knelt down beside her and touched her breasts did his eyes warm, sex flickering in him like a memory of wickedness.

Ah, she sighed, for that was better. She leaned back against him, passive and disbelieving. Soon he'd be gone and she knew she mustn't wonder what was going to happen. Across the courtyard a Turkish love song started up, flinging an insistent plea at some hard and hidden heart. 'It feels just the same,' she said, exhilarated, wanting it to. Whatever happens, she had written in her notebook;

and so it had, the worst that could have happened, and still they were together, the selfsame current catching them.

'You don't know what it's been like,' Will muttered, kissing her. She could feel the rage in him. His heel had knocked her glass over, spilling wine on the rug. A dark stain marked the knee of his pants. She couldn't look him in the face. Maybe in his eyes she was already naked and caressed, maybe he hadn't been listening. She heard bread tins slam onto the metal shelves of the oven in the bakery below. She held him hard to her and in her mind she was rocking him.

'It doesn't matter,' she said, 'it doesn't matter.'

In the bedroom she draws down the blinds on the darkening afternoon. Naked, she wants to cry. His body is thin and Jesuitical, his skin has seen no sun. She doesn't want this looking, just touching, diffuse and timeless. She lies back in a rush and he pushes into her immediately; she kisses and is kissed, she's wet, she scoops her hair out of her eyes and wants to sleep, die, call back that vast absent-mindedness, a feeling beyond compare. Even the dim light that borders the blinds is too bright and lies between them. He hadn't been fully erect, he'd had to use his hand. She fights the thought, closes her eyes, crosses over for just a moment. 'I love you,' he says hopelessly, and she feels him remembering, full, dark, he's using the words to remember. She might have believed him, answered, but she doesn't, she's silent, disgraced. The failed seductress. In his soft convalescent skin she has found her definition and he can try but he won't dissolve it. She feels him struggling. He rears up on one arm and looks down at her belly, hairs, his cock sliding in and out. His mouth pouts, watching her. She sees a shadow of wanting cross his face like greed, guilty. He reaches for her, grasps, rubs his chest against hers. She touches his grey hairs, her jaw clenched, smiling into space. Somewhere in her there's panic pushed down and held there, while her mind summons up someone better than she, heroic, someone she might have been but isn't, and she thinks about seagulls and everything high, horses with wings and how she could fly out of herself and she wants to cry out, No, I can't do it, skirting her body, the body which couldn't but wanted to, which had failed, was afraid, shrank from exposure. She takes his fingers in her mouth and sucks at them, lean fingers which didn't know how to hold her. Sorry, she mutters, sucking, and she's there on the dim bed with him, but hot, absent, a fierce omnipotent generosity swelling up in her, her mouth saying no, giving without taking, her mouth making absolute reparation, until Will shut his eyes and pushed and pushed and when he came she cried out on that fine point of emptiness, knowing that she loved him.

And now he's leaving, and it's not yet terrible, intolerable. He stands at the door, he looks around, he pats his pockets to check that he hasn't forgotten anything. Under the hall light in the blur of her white moment she feels herself clearly and unaltered. Alone, high on the catwalk, complete. Phallic and glittering, she stretches out in gratitude to cover all spaces, and on the other end of the rope are all the things she might have done but didn't: pleading, rage, lies, supplication. She's already said, strongly, You don't have to be a martyr. Hands on her thighs. She said: Remember. He said: I'll try to. See you later, he said, and she closed the door and leaned her head against it, later being American, later meaning any time under the sun, one year or ten. Still living she stretched out her calmness into him, teetering, indispensible. Near and far were both real in that image but now his eyes are pockets and fading as he goes on his way, zipping himself into his jacket and intact. She fights it, this thinning of the image, disintegration, his forgetting the ending as she writes and rewrites, trying to make it better. One by one birds dive from the eaves and fall to the ends of the earth as if seized by some wild self-immolating urge, and she grasps the arms of the chair, clenching herself. Thinks of some final sacrifice, grave and dangerous, which hasn't yet been performed. Some way to prove the glittering. Her hands lie desperate as thinking parades for her, all her parts prinked out and falsely foregrounded: the mother, the orphan, the comrade, the competitor, the poet, the

241

seductress, one by one they try to hold the audience of his heart and one by one they are catcalled and rejected. He is pure warrior with his parts in place and she knows she should be glued to him but instead she's bleeding, platformed and obvious while her father tap-dances and the poetry book shudders in her hands, and Will's voice speaks in her ear, the old voice, plural and beguiling, telling her about climbing, about trying to take this idea, this maybe outrageous idea, and convert it into an emotional and spiritual and physical reality, and on the end of the rope where she is is the hook of failure and it's familiar, it draws her knees up to her chin and places her hands flat against her cheeks as the voice becomes manic, boasting. When I get frightened, it says, then I get this rush of adrenalin and when I get the adrenalin my mind takes absolute control of my body and I know I can't make a mistake. And she thinks of her dream, of the night intelligence of the body, and feels her tears concentrating, knows that she's weak, wants slippers, is bleeding, but still the voice goes on, although it's more distant now, disjointed, and it's saying that you have to be intimate with the rock, manipulate, not dominate, it's saying that if you took away the possibility of death it wouldn't be the same, it's saying that this is the most complete experience of any, and she's hooked and blanked out, believing it, and she goes to the bathroom and turns the bath on, sees herself with the razor, turns it off again. Then she's on the floor and it's dark and she's ill with his illness and her own, there's no particular length of time to this, there's no structure; the moon rises and the moon dies, food moulders in the fridge, and birds look in from the windowsill; sometimes, for instance, a magpie with his arrow-tail holding the hard edge of light and in the tick of his paranoid head is the moment's vanishing point.

–

– So yes. So I can't really remember the days, only . . .

–

– . . . only that he was trying to kill off all the good things in him.

–

–

– *Perhaps you can go back over it? Rewrite it so that it comes out as you'd wish?*

– Well, he's fallen out of place. He knows he's mad and his life is off-balance because he hasn't followed the way of his heart and it's killing him. He knows this. So he's not going back to the States, and he's leaving Joanna, he's making some pledge which is full of emotion and which makes her feel safe and loved even despite the age difference and all that's happened.

– *And the pledge would be?*

–

–

– No, it's impossible, it won't work. She can't feel safe enough.

– *So what's missing?*

– A stability. I have to imagine a helper, to strengthen them both. Then I'm soothed and can feel safe. He's taking the responsibility off her shoulders, she doesn't have to try so hard to hold herself together, she doesn't have to save the son. Probably he's Saturn, the principle of integrated structures. The one who's been missing. He might be a monk or a magician or a law-maker; he's everything, surprisingly, that's wise and fair.

– *I'm remembering that you've seen Joanna as the structurer, the law-maker, as it were . . .*

243

– OK, so it's surprising, it's everything I've consciously rebelled against. But on the other hand this magician isn't rigid or constricting, he's nothing to do with monotheism or patriarchy or any of that perverted authority which mistakes symbol for sign and myth for history and spends its time slaughtering its own shadow . . .

–

– No, he isn't frozen like that, or singular: he's benign, an archetype, one among many. He's waving no banners and you know you can trust him.

– I think you wish that your father could have had these qualities.

–

–

– He's just grizzled and smiling, as if he's been waiting a long time to be summoned, and when you look at him you can't help but welcome him, because you know he's a rescuer, and he's part of you, and all manner of things will soon be well.

New Haven

May 10, 198-

Dear Kathy,

Afraid I can't write much now. I am in the middle of exams and moving to NY for the summer to work as a financial analyst for a risk arbitrageur – sort of a glorified stock-broker – pretty awful but it pays and it could be interesting to see how the excess millions are skimmed off the billions traded on Wall Street, couldn't it? This semester has been unbearably (nearly) busy. The Union-University negotiations looked to strike in January so I spent the first two weeks of classes working full-time on preparations for that – thought I might have to drop out of school, but an eleventh-hour settlement saw the administration cave in and all seemed worthwhile except I'd put my studies here in jeopardy and also had to get an extension for my MA dissertation.

I am all right, no better, but I guess stable. Since the negotiations I'm too busy to reflect on anything I care about which keeps me from crying in the streets, but I'm so tense it's exhausting just being alive. Sometimes I like the busy pace and feel like a taut vibrating platinum wire gleaming in the sun and at other times, like during my week in London, I recognise how my physical fitness has deteriorated and I feel flaccid and emaciated like I'm on an involuntary fast and crossing a long barren desert. I spent an afternoon that same week with my ex-tutor Richard Watkins, and it was great to have an older male friend I could say this stuff to. Like you, he thinks I need professional help, and I'm sure this is all part of what you were saying about how I need to give time to other parts of myself, to acknowledge that those parts just want to be and don't feel the need to control, master and kill everything in sight. I just wish I were on the second day of some serious but not desperate Alpine face with my life in both my hands, laughing at how unimportant and transient such milestones and measurements as exams really are. I am promising myself that things will be different next year and I will concentrate more on myself. I just wish the world wasn't so fucked up because I just can't rationalise not being responsible, through a simple lack of protest if nothing else. However, I'm sure there's more going on than this and I guess at some point I'll have to give myself the chance to find out. Being in Manhattan will be fun but I miss London, and you, and wish that even my tense and manic self was there to hold and tell you, but of course I

can't be there and it is selfish – but sweet – to miss you so.
(Fancy paper, huh? This is for writing letters to people
begging them to give us hyped jobs which pay obscene
amount of money.) Gotta go.
Much love, Will.

Figures without a landscape. This is ordinary, a Tuesday, the first day after New Year. Dull streets of Hackney. She turned her face away in the last split second in which she could still pretend not to have seen him. If she'd gone out when she intended to, earlier, she would have missed him. Earlier the sun had sparkled, spring-like, after weeks of grey, and she'd gone to the mirror and her face or the sun said plainly she would meet him. She'd run out of paper, her typewriter ribbon was fading to grey, but she couldn't step outside the door.

She procrastinated. Hours passed in this way. The end of the book was in sight, tantalising: a structure on the point of being achieved. Later a voice masquerading as reason said this was stupid: she hadn't seen him since Thanksgiving two years before, had heard nothing for a year, if she sat there any longer she'd only make tangles and messes, her brain was burnt out, etc etc.

By this time it was afternoon and the sky was lowering for rain. She threw on her jacket and pulled a brush through her hair, and at the last minute, hand on the door, she turned back to the mirror and slapped her cheeks lightly, as if preparing for an assignation – which in fact she was, which in fact she both believed and didn't and laughed at herself for it – went down the stairs and across the Square and past the council estate where a fire had blackened the third-floor balconies and skeletons of push chairs lay abandoned in the muddy forecourt. She was alert and shifty, red scarf muffled high up to her ears so that she could retract her head at the first sign of danger.

The main road was wet and empty and glistening. She felt safe then, and ridiculous beyond belief, pushing open the door of the

247

stationers with the familiar pleasure reflex, legitimately going about her business. The shop was crowded, a sudden outburst of commerce after the long holiday. She squeezed down the aisle towards the shelves beyond the cash desk where the typing paper was stacked. On her right were racks of notebooks, envelopes, bulldog clips: everything she didn't need but wanted all the same. On the left was the photocopier, doing brisk trade and there was someone's back, a woman assistant with black frizzed hair.

The voice was drawling, high-ish, nervous for no reason. She looked but she couldn't mistake it. She saw his hands, improbably familiar, splayed on the black glass of the lid. A scrap of typescript which could have been a CV. But all this was later, fragments after the impact: the worn curve of his cheek, and the way he'd been holding himself, chest tensed and drawn in somehow. At that moment her heart took him whole, primitive, kept the shocking integrity of the image, understood nothing, understood that time had compressed to an entity which was love and rage, impotence and omnipotence, all sealed up so as not to shatter him, understood that she'd been duped most magnificently, and that by running away she had only ensured the collision. And her mind said that he had made his choice, her mind in an instant preserved her, turned her back on him and forced her past the assistant hoping against hope to be invisible despite the preposterous whiplash of her head and the wound scarf red as a beacon.

She hid herself behind the shelves, trembling. The paper was in boxes of different colours for different grades, she couldn't read, remember, tears in her throat, his presence interrupted everything. Later she couldn't describe it to anyone, that lovely quaking which made fun and fraud of all the meanings she'd constructed, quietly or noisily, alone or in company and with honest effort, ending after ending: hope, normalcy, integration, acceptance, or how she might have hailed him but didn't, should have faced, perhaps, the shock of being denied, banal, of fantasy shattered, how maybe she hid from that and nothing else, peering through the slats of the shelves and seeing his dark jacket gone and the lid *of the photocopier closed and white. And then she was lost and wanted to look everywhere, under the counter, behind the display cases, outside the door. Each second spent at the cash desk was a second wasted, she'd forgotten what she wanted, what kind of ribbon, scrambled for her cheque card in a rage, for perhaps like her he had seen and he had fled, or perhaps he hadn't and she had missed the one chance that still remained to her, and that feeling was a feeling like death, limb-wrenching and intolerable, regret beyond compare.*

– And so it happens that after days and nights and weeks and years you still move to the peak of the mountain, drawn by that same inscrutable order, and the shoulder of the Chardonnet is already below you and red; it's summer down in the valley with flowers whisking about and the seeds of pale grasses fly everywhere on the wind, but up here you pierce the joy of all seasons and the sky so wide as only the presence of death allows into your life, into your house, and you swear you'll no longer love pain as pain loves you, and you think you're off the hook and you laugh in your delusion. . . .

–

– And then you're dancing, dancing.